Lake
Effect

Also by Cynthia D'Aprix Sweeney

Good Company
The Nest

Lake Effect
Cynthia D'Aprix Sweeney

b
THE BOROUGH PRESS

The Borough Press
An imprint of HarperCollins*Publishers* Ltd
1 London Bridge Street
London SE1 9GF

www.harpercollins.co.uk

HarperCollins*Publishers*
Macken House, 39/40 Mayor Street Upper
Dublin 1, D01 C9W8, Ireland

First published by HarperCollins*Publishers* 2026

1

Copyright © Cynthia D'Aprix Sweeney 2026

Cynthia D'Aprix Sweeney asserts the moral right to
be identified as the author of this work

A catalogue record for this book is available from the British Library

Hardback ISBN: 978-0-00-879943-4
Trade Paperback ISBN: 978-0-00-879944-1

This novel is entirely a work of fiction. The names, characters
and incidents portrayed in it are the work of the author's imagination.
Any resemblance to actual persons, living or dead, events or
localities is entirely coincidental.

Printed and bound in the UK using 100% Renewable
Electricity at CPI Group (UK) Ltd

All rights reserved. No part of this publication may be reproduced,
stored in a retrieval system, or transmitted, in any form or by any
means, electronic, mechanical, photocopying, recording or otherwise,
without the prior written permission of the publishers.

Without limiting the author's and publisher's exclusive rights,
any unauthorised use of this publication to train generative artificial
intelligence (AI) technologies is expressly prohibited. HarperCollins
also exercise their rights under Article 4(3) of the Digital Single
Market Directive 2019/790 and expressly reserve this publication
from the text and data mining exception.

*For Matthew and Luke,
world's best lads.*

*"So it happens that when I write of hunger,
I am really writing about love—"*
—M.F.K. Fisher

*Have you found a seat in your room
For every one of your wayward selves.*
—Charles Simic

Part One
1977-78

Prologue

Bess Pfeiffer didn't mean to start anything when she walked into Honey Finnegan's house with seven copies of *The Joy of Sex*. She thought it would be fun. Their group had been meeting for years and even though it started as something that kind of sort of resembled the consciousness raising groups they'd been reading about, it had, predictably, become a watered-down suburban version of consciousness raising. The wives and mothers of Cambridge Road weren't talking politics or sex or activism or civil rights or even a light, sugarcoated feminism, but mostly trying to help each other as their children climbed the slippery shoals of adolescence to the sebum-soaked years of puberty. They discussed teachers and curfews and their concerns about cigarettes and liquor and peer pressure. That their kids—some of them only yards away from where they met—were already smoking pot and bringing Welch's grape jelly jars refilled with Smirnoff to the massive tree house in the Tannenbaums' backyard would not have occurred to any of the mothers in the room. Except Bess, a high school nurse and trusted confidante of some of the older teens, especially the girls, who couldn't talk to their parents about sex or, God forbid in this neighborhood of Catholics, birth control.

The women chatted about husbands and cooking and which families were not obeying the local leash laws, and should their bowling league move from Wednesdays to Tuesdays, and why were Father John's sermons so excruciatingly boring, and did they still need to abstain from meat on Fridays?

So when Bess saw the book on display while browsing at Sibley's she thought, *Why not?* Why not have a little fun, stir things up. Her status on the block was already dicey as the first divorcée, the first victim of a burgeoning national trend if the media was to be believed, when her husband walked out because he fell in love with his office manager, who was the spitting image of twenty-three-year-old Bess. She brought the stack of seven books to the checkout and enjoyed the look on the face of the young girl behind the counter when she asked if they could be gift wrapped.

"I guess?" the girl had said. "I'll have to check." She returned quickly and said she could only wrap three books for free.

"Pity," Bess said. "Well, then I'll take them unwrapped." She made cheerful small talk as Dana, according to her name tag, rang up each copy and quickly slipped it into one of two large shopping bags while trying to hide her mortification.

"Have you read it?" Bess asked, tapping the cover with her fingernail. She couldn't help herself. She'd lost all inhibitions since Doug left. Who cared about manners? Maintaining pretenses? Life was absurd.

"Me?" Dana's voice rose two octaves. "No!"

"How come?"

"Because it's basically pornography."

Bess sighed. "Who told you that? Let me guess. Your mother?"

"No. I mean, yes. But no, I looked at the pictures. They're disgusting."

"Honey," Bess said as Dana finished ringing up the books and slipped the last one into a shopping bag, visibly relieved, "let me give you some advice: don't marry anyone who isn't as concerned with your orgasm as they are with theirs."

"Oh my god." Dana put her face in her hands.

"Someday you're going to thank me, Dana. In some glorious postcoital moment in a room somewhere in a town other than this one"—Bess paused while Dana groaned and then warily looked back at Bess—another room in another town? *Interesting*—"you're going to wonder who that fairy godmother was who gave you the best piece of life advice in the Sibley's book department in 1977. You're going to wish you could find me and thank me, so I'll tell you now: you are *very* welcome." Bess reached into one of the shopping bags, plucked out a book, and said, "Here. This one's for you. From me."

"I can't."

"You can."

"I can't. My mother will have a conniption."

"Ah, it *is* the mother. Do you know who I'm buying all these books for?"

Dana's expression went back to confused. "Your—children?"

"No. These are for my friends. For all the *mothers* on the block who are horrified that I'm divorced and have thoughts about sex. So here." She put the purchased book on the counter in front of Dana. "Don't put it under the mattress if your mother still changes your bed. Hide it in a closet somewhere and educate yourself."

"Okay." Dana took the book, slightly less reluctant. "Thank you?"

Bess started to leave, got as far as the shelf of nonfiction bestsellers and turned back. "Dana? One more thing. I'm a nurse. Get on the pill. Do what you want to do, but be smart."

Dana leafed through the book. She didn't look up and she didn't look disgusted. Bess walked closer. "Did you hear me?"

"Uh-huh."

Bess peeked over the counter and read the subtitle on the page. "Ah. *Mouth music.* That's a good section." Dana slammed the book shut. She smiled a little.

"Keep reading, Dana! Keep reading."

One

Nearly midnight. Nearly November.

The evening was winding down but not quickly enough. Somebody needed to make a move to bring Sam's birthday dinner to an end, but it couldn't be Nina because he would pout the entire next day if she stood and started clearing plates, the universal signal that the party was over. In her life, Nina had never known anyone who could string out a birthday longer than her husband, and tonight's gathering had already disappointed.

The calls began late in the morning, just as Nina finished baking the pound cake she would use for the bottom layer of baked Alaska, a dessert she found too fussy and common, but the one Sam requested. His cousins who lived down near Canandaigua cancelled first. Peter had a nasty cold and Grace didn't drive, so they couldn't make it. Nina had barely put the receiver down when the Tannenbaums from down the street phoned. Such a terrible cough. The whole family. And it wasn't even winter yet! Nina offered to send Sam over with some soup she had in the freezer. "No real loss," he said as he loaded two mason jars of chicken noodle into a grocery bag. Sam liked to say that Ned Tannenbaum's personality was 98 percent *I've worked at Kodak since I was eighteen* and 2 percent golf. Only thirty minutes later, the phone rang again. "Let me guess," Nina said as she answered. Sam's boss at Xerox and his wife were laid low. "I don't even want to think about the dinner we're missing," James said, his voice hoarse and raspy through the phone line. "Please give us a rain check."

So. Only five around the table tonight. Sam and Nina. Honey and Finn Finnegan, who lived directly across the street in a house that was the mirror image of Nina and Sam's colonial revival. Next to Nina sat Bess Pfeiffer, who, in her typical, drunken, combative fashion, seemed determined to pick an argument with Sam or Finn, equally disinterested parties. In twenty-two minutes, the digital clock in the kitchen would gently flip to Sunday morning and this dinner would spill into the start of a new day, the kind of shift Nina used to think signaled a wildly successful evening.

The remains of the meal littered the surface of the long, gleaming mahogany table. Empty wine bottles. A cheese plate with crumbs of Stilton and half-eaten crackers. Splashes of port on the ivory linen runner next to a hardening baguette heel. After dessert, Sam resumed pouring the elegant French Bordeaux he'd chosen to accompany the beef Wellington, the potatoes lyonnaise, the mushrooms with brandy and cream, the roasted carrots with fresh thyme. For the last hour, the same Dionne Warwick album had played on repeat until the songs seemed to come from Nina's own head (*One less bell to answer, One less egg to fry*). She swallowed a yawn.

Every year, Nina tried to make this dinner a little more interesting, but tonight's version felt warmed over. How many ways could a person prepare a slab of beef? And Sam always wanted beef. "You're a victim of your own success," he said yesterday as she rolled and folded and chilled pastry for the Wellington, aiming for the proper distribution of butter and fat so the pastry would puff. She supposed he was right, but that didn't explain why she no longer felt the old urgency to dazzle her guests the way they still expected from someone who wrote a monthly food column in a local rag. Back when their two daughters were in middle school and Nina suddenly had too much time on her hands, she'd volunteered to do something—*anything*—at the local city paper run by her old friend Thomas. He somewhat reluctantly gave her proofreading and light editing jobs that she could do at home. Nina was so fast and reliable that Thomas asked her to write up some short items on local arts and dining. Within a year, she'd inherited one of the paper's columns, "Simply Put." The previous author, who retired with her husband to Fort Lauderdale, had exclusively featured her suburban Junior League friends and their most trusted recipes, which led to a surfeit of casseroles and jellied salads and various roast beasts. Every column ended with the same sentence construction: "*Simply put*, Marilyn Field is the reigning lemon meringue queen of Brighton!" "*Simply put*, Bernice Dorman's Lipton soup brisket is the one to beat!" "*Simply put*, Carol Hendrickson is on to something when she says coconut adds a kick to both sweet and savory dishes!"

Thomas wanted her to take the column in a more lively, sophisticated direction. "Find some interesting people around town who like to cook," he told her. "Or like to eat. I don't care which." He wanted to rename the column "The Gracious Gourmet" or "The Gallant Gourmet" or something equally anodyne, a nod to the Galloping Gourmet's popularity. Nina lobbied for "The Wolfish Gourmet" or "Cravings" or just "Famished!"

"Why are these all so *hungry*?" Thomas complained.

"Because hunger is the root of all cooking."

"No, hunger is at the root of appetite. Ego is at the root of the kind of cooking we want to write about. And 'Cravings' sounds like a dirty movie."

She finally capitulated to "The Ravenous Gourmet," after extracting a promise that she could pick her own subjects and not only feature suburban women and their unappetizing canapés. Eventually, "The Ravenous Gourmet" morphed into Nina interviewing chefs around town and featuring one of their popular entrées adapted for the home cook. And then she started to offer cooking classes based on the column in her kitchen. She loved doing both, but not the pressure it applied to every meal she presented.

For so many years, the revolving dinner parties on the block were a lifesaver, a gentle valve release, a chance to forget the gray landscape of winter in Rochester or celebrate its beautiful summers. The women would dress up and drink too much and the men would talk about work and drink too much and everyone would stay up too late. They'd wearily wave at each other the next morning at church, miming head pain and lack of sleep while corralling their children down the aisle, all of them quietly thrilled by the previous night's misbehavior.

Maybe the modest size of tonight's group wearied Nina. They'd all known each other forever and had had the same conversations dozens of times. They knew each other's cocktail orders and food quirks and who was a mean drunk and who was a weepy drunk and which of their teenagers were "testing boundaries" and which were barreling toward delinquent. And now Bess had started her favorite worn rant about how Nixon shouldn't have been pardoned. She blinked back angry, drunken tears while claiming she'd landed on Nixon's enemy list due to her activism around *Roe v. Wade*. They'd heard it all before. "Nothing in my life," she said, pointing a bony finger at a slightly amused Finn, "has made me prouder." Like everyone else, Nina'd had too much to drink and was trying to follow Bess's diatribe while looking for a place to break in and divert.

"Free speech!" Bess finally blurted out, gesticulating and knocking over her glass of wine just as Sam opened a new bottle. Shit. How much of that beautiful red had they gone through? Judging from the way Sam slopped wine into the glasses, at least five or six bottles. She tried to catch his eye. "Whoops!" he said, after spattering Honey Finnegan's untouched dessert. Her wedge of baked Alaska slouched on the plate like a children's book illustration meant to convey sadness.

"Slide that over here," Finn said to his wife. "I'm not afraid of a little booze on my meringue."

Honey pushed the plate across the table with the tip of one finger. "A lot of sugar."

"I think that's the point of dessert," Finn said to the plate.

"Sam," Bess said, raising her empty glass. "I'll have another splash."

Nina saw her chance. She stood and picked up a few dirty dishes. "Can I get anyone anything else? Coffee? Tea?"

"I'd kill for a Sanka," Honey said. Of course Honey would kill for a Sanka.

Two

Upstairs, Clara had stopped trying to eavesdrop on her parents' boring dinner party. Instead, she resumed her recent favorite game, where she pretended she was under surveillance from hidden cameras installed behind the bathroom mirror, at the dinner table, in the school hallways. This state of constant watchfulness by people she imagined as faceless judges, a committee of elders evaluating her life skills, and sometimes as peers (okay, boys) gave her a self-consciousness she leaned into. Helped hone her awareness of awareness. Nothing made her sadder than the girls in her school who seemed completely oblivious to how they looked to others, as if they didn't deserve attention. The game made Clara mindful of her posture and her gait and her smile. She would never mindlessly pick her nose like Ruth Ambrose or pluck her underwear out of her ass while walking down the school hallway like Pauline Sanders or worry a pimple in public. Private vigilance would prevent public slovenliness and insulate her from accidentally doing something embarrassing. When she got ready for school in the morning, she went through her closet miming exasperation, like an actor on a sitcom, never mind that she wore a uniform to school and only got to choose which navy sweater to bring that day. In the bathroom, she'd brush out her long hair and apply makeup, pretending to give a tutorial to the readers of *Seventeen*. She'd make breakfast as if she'd be graded on her efficiency. And if the game got exhausting, she'd turn the cameras off. Poof! Back to plain old Clara.

Now, for example, alone in her bedroom she had to mentally disable the cameras because she'd been idly, almost unconsciously, playing with her breasts, reassuring herself that she hadn't dreamed up their recent existence. To have this gift long after she believed it could happen—at seventeen!—still felt miraculous.

"You bloomed late, but you bloomed hard," her mother said in the dressing room of the little clothing boutique they frequented. Clara had burst out of her training bra, and when the saleswoman fitted her for a new one, she landed at 32C. 32C! A miracle!

She stood and lifted her nightgown and looked at herself in the mirror above her dresser. Yes, her breasts were perfect. She lowered the nightgown and went to her window and for the millionth time in the past weeks, wished that Dune Finnegan's bedroom faced the street so they could signal each other like they were in a Nancy Drew book. Clara had never read a Nancy Drew book, but one on the shelf downstairs had an illustration of Nancy on the cover looking out of a window with binoculars. Spying on a crush seemed the kind of thing Nancy would do. From downstairs, raucous laughter. A good time to call Dune from her parents' bedroom extension. Then maybe she could sneak into the kitchen and filch a glass of wine. She grabbed a pair of jeans off the floor and pulled them on. Changed into her 32C black bra (it had taken A+ whining to convince her mother she needed a black bra) under a sweatshirt and tiptoed down the hall to her parents' closet. She didn't want to wake her sister, Bridie, because she'd insist on joining Clara and ruin the fun.

Her parents' bedroom still felt a little bit like church, hushed and dark, the air redolent with her mother's perfume and hair spray, something mustier beneath. The dark and foreboding furniture in this room had been inherited from the grandparents Clara had never met, and her mother hated it. The rest of the house had her mother's easy sense of style and airiness. Lighter wood, lots of plants, homey and elegant. Clara picked up the phone and dialed the house across the street. Dune answered.

"Sundance?" she said.

"Hey, Butch," he replied, and she could hear his smile. Some weeks ago, they'd gone to see *Butch Cassidy and the Sundance Kid* at a revival house downtown and she'd insisted they call each other Butch and Sundance on the phone when other people might overhear. Unnecessary but fun. "How's the party going?" he asked.

"Fine, I guess. Lots of people called out sick. Your mom and dad are still here. Obviously." Clara could hear Dune's sister, Fern, in the background bugging Dune to resume their chess game. "Do you have to go?" They couldn't say anything interesting with Fern listening.

"Yeah."

"See you tomorrow. Three o'clock."

She hung up the phone and decided to shop in her parents' closet. She and Nina wore the same size shoe now, so Clara went through the meticulously stacked boxes and tried on some of Nina's high heels. They weren't her style exactly, but she enjoyed the extra height. Maybe her mother would let her borrow a pair for the New Year's formal. She carefully rewrapped the shoes in tissue paper and put them back exactly as she'd found them. She opened the bottom drawer of her mother's dresser and pulled out a plum-colored scooped-neck short-sleeve T-shirt. She went into her parent's bathroom and flipped the light. The top fit her like a dream, like a very breast-revealing dream. The color flattered her olive skin and dark hair and eyes. She posed in front of the mirror, imagining the audience of editors from *Seventeen* magazine talking about how perfect she'd be for their next cover. Her mother might even give the shirt to Clara when she saw how it flattered. She opened the medicine cabinet and took out a vial of lipstick. She applied the light pink color carefully and added a little mascara and blush. It was magic. She looked like herself, only better, a little heightened. Too good not to go downstairs.

Three

"Clara!" Bess jumped out of her seat as Clara appeared at the threshold of the dining room. "Look at you! So grown-up."

"Hi, Mrs. Pfeiffer," Clara said as Nina came back from the kitchen carrying Honey's Sanka. Nina didn't know where to look first. At Bess, whose wraparound skirt had come undone—since her divorce Bess only bought clothes at a boutique downtown that was half head shop, half gauzy clothes in batik prints—or at Clara, who was wearing—what was Clara wearing? The dining room lights were dimmed and the candles Nina had lit hours ago mostly spent, some flickering. She vaguely recognized Clara's top and its flagrantly low neckline, and were those her breasts glowing in the candlelight?

"Bess," Nina said, "retie your skirt."

"Oh my," Bess said, laughing. "I loosened it before dessert." She casually and completely unwrapped her skirt. Honey Finnegan gasped.

"Bess!" This was too much, even for Nina.

"Oh, relax. There's a whole leotard under here," she said while removing the skirt to reveal a burgundy bodysuit that still showed way too much of Bess below the waist. Nina put the Sanka on the table in front of Honey.

"Yum," Honey said, lowering her face to the bitter brew.

Nina turned to her daughter. "Clara? What can we do for you?"

"I wanted to say hello." Clara could tell her mother was annoyed, so she made her voice extra breezy. "What's everyone talking about?"

"Your dad is telling us about all the exciting developments around here," Finn said.

Clara crossed her arms in front of her chest. "Developments?"

"From the big conference in Boca Raton. Futures Day! Apparently, Xerox is going to start giving out personal computers like candy."

"I wish," Sam said, pulling out one of the empty chairs and motioning for Clara to sit. Clara hesitated and looked at her mother, who nodded.

"What do you think about these computers, Clara?" One of the things Clara liked about Mr. Finnegan was that he spoke to her like an adult, like he was interested in her thoughts, but what did she know about computers and offices and what all these men did when they hurried out of the house every morning? Her father was in charge of the marketing strategy for Xerox's new products. She had no idea what *marketing strategy* meant or what he did all day. Even Mr. Finnegan was a mystery. He ran grocery stores—his job should be pretty straightforward, but what did he *do*?

"It sounds cool," Clara said. "Mom got to try one."

"You did?" Finn asked Nina.

"I did. All the products coming out of Palo Alto were on display and all the wives got a chance to try them out. Want to guess why?"

"Manners? Ladies first?"

"We were the only people in the room who could type."

"Ah, that's not entirely true," Sam said as everyone else laughed.

"I'm not counting the engineers who invented the things," Nina said. "And you're right, it wasn't just about typing. All the executives stood around acting embarrassed and looking for a secretary to rush in and assist."

"You have a point," Sam said. "We *are* all going to have to learn how to type."

"I type," Finn said.

"You do?" said Bess. "Finn Finnegan, president of Finnegan's Grocer, *types*."

"My father insisted. Invoices, schedules, inventory. I mostly hunt and peck, but nothing's faster than a typewriter."

"Not for long," Nina said. "You are not going to believe what these machines can do or how lightning quick they are. The engineers in Palo Alto were sending documents to the computers in Florida and we could edit and send them back with the touch of a button."

"This is what terrifies me," said Honey. "Things moving too fast. One wrong command or code or whatever you call it, one wrong message sent out into the universe and that's it!" She snapped her fingers. "Nuclear mayhem."

"What?" Clara said, alarmed.

Sam put a reassuring hand on Clara's arm and said to Honey, "Last I checked, Xerox wasn't in the nuclear warhead business," but Honey continued to shake her head. She pulled her cardigan tight around her shoulders and gave a performative shudder.

"The computers have something called a universal undo," Nina said.

"Like backspace?" Clara asked.

"Sort of, but better. The word processor can reverse any action in perfect order. If you make a mistake or change your mind, you can undo it in a second. For writing and editing, well, it's going to change everything. No scissors or tape or Wite-Out or eraser ribbon. One button and—"

"Undo it," Clara said.

"Exactly." Nina smiled at her daughter.

"Wow," Bess said. "Like God."

"Bess, please don't say that." Honey crossed herself rapidly in case, Nina guessed, God was watching this dinner party slowly unravel.

"Okay, everybody," Nina said, avoiding Sam's eye. "Clara, time for you to go to bed and it's past my bedtime, too. I'm beat."

"The general has spoken," Sam said, an edge to his voice. Clara looked at her mother, worried. Nina resented when Sam called her *the general*, but she smiled and winked at Clara and started clearing the table.

"Undo," Bess said, pressing an imaginary button on the tablecloth, inordinately pleased with herself.

"Clara?" Nina motioned to her daughter. "Want to grab a few plates and help me in the kitchen?"

"Undo!" Bess said a little louder, like a kid going for a bigger laugh on the same joke.

"I'll walk you home, Bess," Sam said.

"Undo! Undo! Undo!" Bess pressed the tablecloth over and over.

Everyone else stood and pushed their chairs back. Nina and Clara walked through the wooden swinging door into the kitchen and Clara started rinsing plates.

Clara had enthusiastically helped Nina cook earlier in the day, much to Nina's delight and surprise. Like her father, Clara tended to be moody, and the teen years had sometimes been hard. But the best way to quiet Clara, even as an irritable toddler, was to engage her with a task in the kitchen. Three-year-old Clara had loved to pound dough and crack eggs into a bowl and beat them with a whisk. At four, she would hold the electric hand mixer and help Nina cream butter and sugar. At five, she could sloppily frost a dozen cookies or more, her brow knit with concentration wanting to get the edges just right. By junior high, Clara could cook simple meals—grilled cheese, omelets, pancakes—on her own and she became an able assistant for Nina in the kitchen, especially when Nina held her classes. They were a team. Until sophomore year of high school, when Clara's time and attention were co-opted by academics and all her extracurriculars, which Nina understood and didn't *quite* take personally. But here Clara was now, helping to scrape plates into the sink and looking for all the world like she was twenty-two.

"Clara?" Clara turned and looked at Nina and smiled, a faraway smile, one Nina knew wasn't meant for her. Sometimes Clara looked like Sam, but most of the time Nina saw her own face in her daughter's. She and Clara had nearly the same dark almond-shaped eyes, and it could be unnerving for Nina to gaze into them, almost as if too much knowledge was at the ready. That Clara was beautiful was no reflection on Nina; the bit of Sam she'd inherited—his angular jaw, high forehead and cheekbones—made her so lovely. And even though Nina didn't want her wearing makeup yet, whatever she'd done to her face tonight worked. "You look nice, honey," Nina said.

"Thanks." Clara screwed up her mouth, biting back a satisfied smile. Nina pointed to Clara's top. "Where did that come from?"

"This?" Clara shrugged. "I don't remember. The laundry room?" She lifted her chin, ready to argue.

Nina nodded. "It's late, don't you think?" She sensed both Clara's relief and disappointment that Nina was too tired to start an argument over the purple top. As Clara headed upstairs, Finn came into the kitchen carrying dessert plates. "You can put those on the counter." Nina gestured to her left.

"How come this kitchen is so much more appealing than mine?" he said, scraping the remnants of baked Alaska into the sink.

"Probably because my kitchen has actual food in it."

Finn laughed. "Maybe. Does it seem a little nuts to you that Honey married into a family of grocers and hates to eat?"

"One of life's little tricks. My mother was the same. Some people don't have much of an appetite."

Finn turned off the water and picked up a dry dish towel from a stack on the counter. "But not you." It wasn't a question. The door between the two rooms swung open again and Sam came in wearing his overcoat. "I'm walking Bess home."

"Over my strenuous objection!" Bess called from the other room. "My undo button needs a repair!" Walking Bess home because she was divorced was a bit of theater on the part of the good husbands of Cambridge Road, clothed in ostensible concern for Bess's safety on this very safe dead-end street. Shepherding Bess to her front door as they would a teenage babysitter was a reminder of her status as formerly coupled, currently alone.

"Finn?" Honey stood in the door now with her coat on, looking pinched. "Shall we?"

"You go," Finn said. "I'm going to help with some of these pots."

"You don't need to do that," Nina said. "Sam will be back any minute."

"Happy to help with the big pans." He waved Honey off. "Home in a few."

"Okay," Honey said, pulling her belt tighter around her waist. "Don't dawdle."

"I'll kick him out in ten," Nina said to Honey. "Promise." Finn and Nina worked side by side in silence. She washed; he dried. "So, what would yours be?" he finally said.

"My what?"

"Your universal undo?"

She handed him a large ceramic platter. "Aren't we supposed to know better than to try to *undo*? I've read 'The Monkey's Paw.'"

"I can tell you mine," he said quietly.

Nina turned off the faucet. "Don't."

"We need to talk."

"Now? The girls are upstairs. Sam will be here any second."

"I would undo a lot of things," he said, taking one of her fingers in his hand and lightly tugging her closer, "but not us."

"Finn. There is no *us*. We decided. *Us* is unsolvable." They stood for a minute, allowing themselves to occupy a space they'd been avoiding for months. They'd been avoiding one another for months. His fingers grabbed her wrist and Nina thought she would burst if he didn't take her in his arms, which he did.

"Nina Larkin," he whispered into her ear. "What are we going to undo?"

Four

Bridie loved the weekends when her parents entertained. She particularly loved the days leading up to the party, when she'd wake up to the sound of her mother in the kitchen thwacking dough with a rolling pin or to the smell of onions caramelizing, stock simmering, wine reducing. And cake! Nothing smelled more like home and love and her mother than baking layers of vanilla or lemon or chocolate cake. It seemed to Bridie that her father appreciated her mother most fully when Nina was conducting a meal in their home. The mood in the house lightened in the days leading up to the designated evening, and today there would be leftovers. Whatever wasn't finished last night would be set out for a late Sunday lunch. Cold, sliced tenderloin. Buttery potatoes. Her mother would make a fresh salad, and her father would open a bottle of wine and pour a little into juice glasses for Bridie and Clara. It was possible, during those languorous Sunday afternoons, to believe her family was the luckiest one on the block.

By midweek, the glow would recede, and it was always hard to tell where the gloom came from. Was it her mother? Her father? Bridie or Clara? Their collective unease?

Since second grade Bridie had kept a mental list of all the kids whose parents had divorced. It started when her best friend Carrie interrupted their regular argument—whom did they love most after Bobby Sherman: David Cassidy or Davy Jones?—to explain divorce because her parents were getting one.

"I don't get it," Bridie said. She and Carrie always swapped bagged lunches. Nina would never pack the kind of store-bought lunch Carrie brought to school: cold cuts, American cheese, Fritos, and an ever-revolving selection of Hostess desserts. And Carrie oohed and aahed over Bridie's lunches, which were usually leftovers and always had a piece of fruit and sometimes a homemade cookie.

The day of the divorce conversation, Bridie was carefully peeling the outside chocolate layer of a Hostess Big Wheels. Carrie was eating Bridie's leftover meat loaf on whole wheat bread. "I wish my mother would make meat loaf," Carrie said, wolfing down the sandwich. "Maybe she will when we move."

"You're moving?" Bridie panicked. Carrie had been her best friend since kindergarten, the entirety of their school lives.

"Not far. I'll still go to school here. I'll have two houses."

"Why?"

"Because my parents are splitting up."

Bridie didn't understand. She had an involuntary picture of her beloved stuffed horse Apple, the one she slept with every night until she woke one morning to find its foam innards all over the bed. The seams had somehow ripped. She'd found the denuded shell of a horse next to her pillow. She'd cried and cried. "Why?" was all Bridie could think to say.

"Because they don't love each other anymore."

Bridie vaguely understood divorce but hadn't registered its particulars. She'd never known of parents choosing separate houses. "Where will you sleep?"

"I'll have two bedrooms. My dad said I'll have all the things in both places. He said I'll barely notice." Carrie finished the meat loaf and fished two small tangerines out of the paper sack. She started peeling one slowly and carefully, trying to get it off in one single strip. Bridie didn't know what to say. Two houses did not sound amazing.

"Sometimes parents need to live apart," Carrie said in a rehearsed monotone that made Bridie understand not to ask any more questions. "It's not my fault. They still love me."

Bridie worried in fourth grade when Paul Claffey showed up looking sad and pale and when she saw him crying in the school principal's office and when he started coming to school with a duffel bag every other Friday because he was going to "his father's" house.

She couldn't sleep when her favorite sixth-grade teacher, Mr. Mitchell, started taking the bus home instead of cheerfully hopping into his wife's sky-blue Volkswagen bug with the Ecology bumper sticker on the window at the end of the day. Sometimes he let Bridie and Carrie decorate the classroom bulletin boards on Friday afternoons, and when they were running late, he'd send the girls out to the parking lot to tell his wife he'd be down soon. His wife had long, straight brown hair and wire-rimmed glasses and they thought she was beautiful even in her white dental hygienist jacket. "How come you take the bus now?" Carrie asked him one afternoon while they carefully cut out paper hearts for Valentine's Day. "Did you guys split?"

"As a matter of fact—" he said, and Bridie had to run to the lavatory so he wouldn't see her stricken face.

And then divorce came to their street, which was terrifyingly close! Bridie woke up one night to voices in the kitchen, women's voices, one in distress. She crept down the stairs and sat on the landing and listened to Mrs. Pfeiffer say some of the most remarkable things she'd ever heard. She'd caught Mr. Pfeiffer kissing his office manager and when she confronted him—"I thought, well, this is dumb. So predictably dumb! But we can get through it"—he confessed to multiple affairs. Told Bess she was frigid (Bridie'd had to look that one up in the dictionary) and insipid (ditto). He packed his bags and moved into a hotel the next day. The Pfeiffer kids were grown and all lived in other cities. Bess told Nina she was unable to sleep alone in their house. "What's going to happen to me?" she cried to Nina. "What am I going to do?"

Bridie climbed back upstairs that night and got into bed and tried to calm herself. She was not used to parents not knowing how to move forward. The thing that rattled her most about divorce was how people changed overnight. How the partner left behind was lost and scared or bitter and furious or all those things at once. Mrs. Pfeiffer was a different person now. Harder. Louder. How could a family created from love just dissolve? People could fool you in the ugliest ways. She was always on the lookout for trouble with her parents. How could Bridie spot trouble between the mysterious adults in her house who were attentive, generous, unfailingly polite, but had she ever seen them kiss? Even once?

Her fear made her a snoop. She rarely found anything illuminating, but sometimes she found something interesting. Lately, she'd noticed that her mother was buying new cosmetics. A different perfume and face cream. She also had a few fancy bras in her drawer and Bridie wondered, drawing on her years of Talmudic-like study of "Can This Marriage Be Saved?" in her mother's issues of *Ladies Home Journal*, whether her mother was trying to entice her father in a new way. Was she heeding the warnings of divorce all around them? Sometimes Bridie would liberate small souvenirs from the room and store them in a shoebox in her closet—a pearl earring minus its mate, loose change, a peppermint ChapStick. Last week, in her father's nightstand, she'd found a clipped picture of the Xerox Palo Alto Research Center (PARC). Her dad was in the middle, sitting on a beanbag chair, looking a little out of place in his suit and tie. She put the photo in her box, too. Something about the way her dad was smiling at the camera made her want it.

She decided to pop into her parents' bedroom for a quick surveillance before lunch. She went straight to the handbag shelf on her mother's side of the closet and was randomly taking purses down to see if she could find any spare change when she pulled on a black leather handbag and a book came tumbling down with it, hitting Bridie on the head.

"Ouch," she said quietly, even though no one could hear. She picked up the book. Bridie stared at the cover, mouth agape. *Shut your flapper.* She heard Clara's voice in her head even when Clara wasn't there. She closed her mouth and read the title: *The Joy of Sex: A Gourmet Guide to Love Making.* She was momentarily confused. Was this somehow related to her mother's cooking column? She opened the book, and it fell to page 141. She saw the heading "Scrotum" and started reading.

Five

"Where did you get this?" Clara asked Bridie, practically tearing the book out of Bridie's hands.

"In Mom's closet." Even amid her confusion about how to hold Clara's interest and dodge her scorn these days, Bridie knew she'd struck gold. "Why do you think she has it?"

Clara sat down on the edge of her bed and started paging through the book. Bridie gingerly sat down next to her, braced for banishment but Clara laughed and pointed to the page in front of her. "What *is* this?" The drawing was of a woman wearing what looked like an unbuttoned, sleeveless dress, arms above her head, breasts covered but pubis and underarm hair on grand display. "Why is she wearing *jewelry*?" Clara said.

Bridie leaned over to look. "It looks like she just got home from the hairdresser."

"Totally." Clara turned the page and showed a different illustration to Bridie. The same woman, now wearing white go-go boots, a push-up bra, and a G-string, being clutched from behind by a fully dressed man with long hair and a beard. "This guy is—"

"*Super* weird looking," Bridie said. She didn't even care about the book, she wanted this moment of sisterly enjoyment to last a little longer. "Do you think Mom bought this?"

"Uh. No. I do not think Mom bought this."

"Dad?"

"*Dad!* Are you mental? I mean, can you imagine?" Clara stood and squared her shoulders, squinted into the distance, looking so much like their father. She theatrically cleared her throat. "Excuse me, miss. I'm looking for a good biography of Winston Churchill.

No, no, I've read all those. Many times." Clara, still in character, tapped her chin to indicate deep thought. "Well, that's a shame," she said to the invisible salesgirl. She took a deep breath and looked up at the ceiling. Bridie could tell she was trying not to laugh. "Okay, then. How about an illustrated guide to fucking?"

"Clara!" Bridie covered her hands with her mouth and they both sat back down on the bed, laughing so hard they couldn't talk. "But seriously," Bridie finally said, "it has to be for them."

"I don't know." Clara picked up the book again and kept turning the pages, shaking her head in disbelief and amusement.

"Why else would it be in their closet unless—"

"Unless they were engaging in *mouth music*?" Clara said, pointing to one of the subtitles on the page.

"Gross."

"Okay." Clara slammed the book closed. "I have to practice my audition song for the musical." She pointed to the door. Bridie reached for the book. "No way," Clara said, clutching it to her chest. "This stays here. I don't want to pollute your brain." Bridie, only fifteen months younger than Clara, thought to object but wasn't sure she wanted to look at the book anymore. "If you want it back, you just have to ask," Clara said.

"Girls?" their mother called from downstairs. "Can you come help with lunch, please?"

Clara's eyes widened. She waved Bridie over and pointed to the page she'd been reading. "'Dinner is a traditional preface to sex,'" she read in a whisper.

"Stop!" Bridie said, meaning the opposite.

"Girls! Some help, please."

"We're *coming*," Clara yelled with a suggestive spin on the word that Bridie only sort of understood. Still, she echoed Clara's intonation: "*Coming*, Mom."

"Here we *come*!" Clara shouted again, opening the door and motioning for Bridie to follow her. As they ran down the stairs laughing, Bridie was so happy. This was the nicest Clara had been to her in months.

Six

Nina's favorite part of a dinner party was the next day, when she could involve her daughters in preparing a midday Sunday dinner. When she was a girl, that's how all the families ate on Sundays. A big meal in the early afternoon and something light in the evening. She couldn't get Sam on board with that schedule as a permanent thing—he liked to go into the office for a few hours on Sunday afternoons—but he would do it when they had an abundance of food left over from entertaining the previous night. He liked extending the evening and its charms for another day as much as she did. Today, Sam didn't wake up in his usual post-birthday jovial mood. He was sharp with her all morning. Nina and the girls were used to calibrating around his various humors. A good or a bad thing? Nina couldn't decide. Today he walked into the kitchen trailing a palpable cloud of disappointment.

"One more birthday meal, for Dad!" Bridie's forced cheerfulness was a little heartbreaking to Nina. Couldn't Sam get over himself? Even for the girls?

"Hey, Dad," Clara said, giving him a kiss. "We made fresh potatoes." Clara had carefully sliced and layered raw potatoes in a bright red casserole dish, covering them with warmed milk and sage. She'd browned the top perfectly. Nina watched Clara remove the dish from the oven and test the doneness of the dish with a fork. She was wearing the shirt from last night and had her long, dark hair piled on top of her head. She had an elegance to her movements that felt new to Nina.

"What do you think?" she said, handing a forkful of the steaming potatoes to her father. "Careful, they're hot." Nina could hear the echo of the millions of times she'd handed a fork or spoonful of something to the girls using the exact same words. Clara waited for Sam to taste, hand on hip, expectant. "Sublime," he said, cracking the first smile of the day.

Clara gave a quick nod and said, "They should sit for another ten minutes. Then we're ready."

"You're so grown," Nina said, unthinking. Clara hated being observed by her parents, but this time she smiled and said, "I guess."

Where had this remarkable human standing in her kitchen, confident and poised, come from? Where was the little girl who wouldn't even cross the street without holding her mother's hand? Who needed a step stool to reach the counter and burst into tears if Nina wasn't around to tuck her into bed at night? Nina was flooded with pride and love and—she was ashamed to admit—envy. Clara had so much ahead of her.

"Want a taste?" Clara said to Bridie, proffering another forkful. Nothing made Nina happier than kindness between her girls. If Clara was seventeen going on thirty, Bridie was fifteen going on twelve. Bridie who still slept with her stuffed horse, now on its third repair. Bridie, who cried when she lost her first tooth because it meant she was *growing up*. Because Clara was more independent and confident than Bridie, the air between them could be fraught, but Clara, no matter how she tried to toss it off, was a nurturer at heart.

"Oh my god, they're so good!" Bridie said with a mouth full of potatoes. Nina and Clara smiled at each other in acknowledgment. Teammates.

AFTER LUNCH, NINA NERVOUSLY WATCHED the clock. The girls had rushed back upstairs to do schoolwork, and Nina made a mental note to check on what they were really doing because their enthusiasm for homework on a Sunday was suspect. Sam, who usually spent a few hours in the office on Sunday afternoons, was puttering around helping her clear plates and wrap food while enumerating his concerns about recent sales numbers or order numbers coming out of Japan, where smaller and faster copying machines were demolishing Xerox's market share. "The future of the company is sitting out in Palo Alto, but nobody wants to admit it." She wasn't absorbing the specifics because any minute Finn would amble across the street and put something in the mailbox meant for her eyes only, as he'd said on the phone earlier. They'd exchanged books this way for years, so a book in the mailbox wasn't suspicious, but she had to retrieve whatever else was in the box before Sam did.

She poured the rest of the wine they'd opened for lunch into her glass. A clean, crisp Chablis. "Not sharing?" Sam said.

"Oh, do you want some more? Aren't you driving to work?"

He sighed. "I guess I am. Not really in the mood."

She forced a smile. "Don't go if you don't want to go. Stay and relax." She tried not to show her relief when he grabbed his coat. "Just an hour or two," he said.

For years Nina had actively disliked Finn Finnegan and his anemic spouse, Honey. When she and Sam moved to Cambridge Road, Honey was the self-appointed welcoming committee, offering opinions on everything from the color of the shutters on Nina's house to the best local dry cleaner to which liquor store delivered quickly. No matter how many times Nina mentioned that she'd been living in the neighborhood for years, Honey still showed up at her door more often than necessary to offer a phone number for a local sitter, a coupon, a heads-up on a new candidate for parish council or the school board. Nosiness dressed up as consideration. Nina refused to engage in chitchat as a warm-up to gossip. She didn't like Honey, and she didn't like Honey's husband, Finn, who was the muscle behind Finnegan Grocer's aggressive expansion over the past ten years, a strategy that meant the demise of so many small businesses, including some of Nina's favorites. Johannson's bakery and their exquisite cinnamon buns, Goldblum's deli, where she'd get pastrami and corned beef and bagels, Russo's tiny Italian grocer that offered freshly made mozzarella and imported tomatoes and the best chicken parmigiana sandwiches in town. Not to mention all the sundry mom-and-pop stores where the kids bought jump ropes and kites in the spring, beach balls in the summer, sleds in the winter, and penny candy all year round.

"It doesn't seem fair," Nina said to him once at a holiday party. "These people work all their lives to build something. They can't possibly compete with you. Doesn't it—keep you up at night?"

To his credit, she could admit, he didn't give a lighthearted answer. He was quiet for a long minute and then said, "If I thought about it only in those terms, I guess it would keep me up. My job is to feed people all over this city, to offer convenience and quality at a fair price. For example, the store nearest to the Kodak plant should have sandwiches ready to go every day, morning to night, so the shift workers can buy their lunch whenever they need. And while they're in the store, they can pick up light bulbs, a magazine, shampoo. Not everyone has a lot of extra time on their hands. I'm streamlining goods and services. Helping their dollar go farther."

"Okay," she said. "I see the value in that approach, but I miss the small stores. I miss Caruso's."

"That's a perfect example!" he said. "It took months of taking Vito Caruso out for coffee, for lunch, for an afternoon espresso down the street, to get him to trust me. To convince him to let us bring his cookies inside all Finnegan's locations. He was attached to the place, and I understood, but his kids didn't want the business. He was tired. After he sold, he and Connie were able to buy a place in Florida and retire down there and now everyone's happy."

"Most of all you."

"Me most of all. I have one of those half-moon cookies every afternoon."

Nina sighed. "The cookies don't taste the same, though."

"We use the exact recipe Connie got from her aunt in Utica, where those cookies were born."

She shrugged. "They're missing something. Connie Caruso's touch. A loving hand. Smaller batches, better quality control. I don't know, but something's missing."

"Maybe," he said, "but everything is fair in love and capitalism."

Nina hated him again.

She hadn't been looking for love when the trouble started; she'd been looking for lust. Barreling toward fifty, she felt she'd rounded a bend and could see through to the end of her life—a straight shot devoid of passion and desire and sex. The most surprising part of their women's group for her was hearing the truth of everyone else's intimate life. Hers was so pale in comparison. She'd been able to ignore the lack through the years because so much energy and intimacy and love had flown to and from her daughters. She couldn't blame that dumb book; she knew that was silly. By the time Bess came in blazing with her gift last year, their women's group was a lackluster thing minus any real discourse or conflict, which she imagined was the entire point of a women's group. But Bess had arrived not only with *The Joy of Sex* but with a list of questions for everyone: *How would you describe your sex life?* (Is that where it started? When the first word that popped into Nina's mind was *nonexistent?*) *How many times a week?* (Did it start then? When Nina realized that people counted their sexual encounters not over the course of a month, a year, a decade, but a week? *A week?*) *What have you not done yet that you're curious about?* (Everything?)

She was aware of but refused to consider too closely an additional factor: that living in a house with two teenage daughters who were in that delirious place between girlhood and womanhood had loosened something inside her. Something dangerous. She was grateful her girls were growing up in such a different world. And envious. Every day they shimmered a little brighter, while she felt herself curling at the edges. One thought clamored around in her head hour after hour—how much time left?

She wanted to have an affair. It started as a tiny gnat of an idea and wouldn't let her go. At first, it was like telling herself she wanted to color her hair or perfect her duck confit or paint the front door purple—idle entertainment. But she didn't want a different hair shade or door color, and her duck confit was pretty good. She wanted to transgress. She wanted something brief and intense and hassle-free. Maybe more than once.

For years she'd consoled herself with Sam's mostly amiable

companionship because it was more than many marriages had. He was a good provider and a great father, and shouldn't it be enough? But once she let herself accept the possibility of infidelity, once she let it seep through the cracks and disturb her carefully constructed identity, it was all she could think about. The how and the when and the where. Oh, and of course, the who?

After the first time at the lake, Nina had considered confessing all to Finn. But whenever she tried to rehearse the story in her own head, it was too mortifying. How could she make sense of that morning last April, when she'd looked out her living room window to see him stretching for his morning run? It had been months since his heart failed him so spectacularly, and he'd changed his ways. He'd quit smoking and cut back on beef and eggs and butter and alcohol. No more french fries or sugary soft drinks. An entire section of Finnegan's had been revamped as *Heart Healthy!* and the store sponsored weekend events at all its locations with nutritionists roaming the aisles and advising curious shoppers about what to eat for strength, health, and longevity. He started taking vitamins every morning, snacking only on apples, and running every other day. Honey had coerced him into going to Weight Watchers with her and they both—Honey would cheerfully announce to anyone who would listen—could fit back into their wedding clothes.

Nina noticed. And that particular spring morning, she'd taken in Finn's bright orange sneakers, the green gym shorts with white trim that were too short on his very long, very freckled legs. He touched his toes and grabbed one foot behind him to stretch a quad and performed a few jumping jacks and something inside of her had shifted so ferociously she could almost hear it, how she imagined the grinding of tectonic plates might sound if you put your ear to the ground. Tectonic plates were on her mind from the previous day when she'd helped Bridie study for the SAT, and they'd gone over an entire reading passage about the earth's subterranean movements. She liked the idea of the ground beneath her having life; she found the seismic possibilities exciting. She watched Finn through the window that day, a person she'd known forever, and thought, *Him*.

How to explain to Finn that Honey hadn't sent Nina to the boathouse that afternoon at the lake to help him collect folding chairs, but that she'd had her eye on him since the moment they'd arrived. She had tried to persuade herself for weeks that her fantasies involving Finn were just that. But when it had started to rain and he'd headed across the lawn, she'd recklessly followed him. She had not intentionally gotten soaked, but certainly understood what he would see when she walked into the boathouse in her drenched, white clinging blouse like a floozy on the cover of a drugstore Harlequin romance.

For years, the speculation in the neighborhood was that Finn and Honey's marriage was an unhappy one. Nina was never sure if this was true (although Honey was as close-lipped as she during their group's sex conversations) and even thought it might be unfair because Finn was a force. Handsome. Tall, long-limbed, sandy-haired, looking like he belonged on the tennis court or behind the wheel of a yacht, smart and doggedly successful. Honey was a complete contrast to Finn aside from looks—she could have been on the cover of a yachting magazine, too. Hard-edged where he was smooth, unforgiving when he was accepting, high-strung while he was easy in his bones. Finn was outgoing and garrulous, and Honey was—not. It was hard to imagine what they'd seen in each other.

But now, Nina had unleashed something far more complicated than her careless imaginings. What had he said that afternoon in the boathouse immediately after? The two of them breathless and stunned and vibrating like a pair of tuning forks. "This is going to be trouble."

And now trouble was crossing the street with a book in his hand. She didn't go to the door or the window because she wasn't ready to engage with him, not until she understood what he meant when he said, "I have a solution." He put the book into the mailbox. Lifted the little red flag and took off down the street at a light and steady jog.

Seven

What always occurred to Finn when he thought back to the night he met Honey, the night that changed his life because he'd done another girl a favor, was that she'd been a teenager. A *teenager*. Now that he had two teenagers, even allowing for how the world had drastically changed since the early 1950s, it was still inconceivable to him that he'd fallen in love with Honey when he was nearly thirty and she wasn't yet twenty. When he imagined Dune or Fern coming to him to say they were in love, he realized he'd have to pretend to take them seriously. But he had been in love, or something akin to love.

He'd been pressed into taking his cousin Maeve to the winter formal at his alma mater, the small all-boys college in Rochester he'd reluctantly attended after his parents were unable (or unwilling) to pay for his tuition at the University of Rochester, where he'd hoped to go. He wanted a big school where he could study not only business, as his father ordained, but literature and history and art and maybe even French. He'd doubled up on courses while living at home and finished a year early. Also decreed by his father: Finn went straight to work at Finnegan's Grocer starting as a floor manager at the smaller of the two stores they had open back then. Having to spend his days greeting his mother's friends in the aisles and, more often than was comfortable, former classmates home from college or faraway cities or shopping with the girlfriends who soon became wives who soon were pushing strollers through the automated opening doors was dispiriting.

That December, Maeve was visiting from Ireland and wanted nothing more than to meet an American boy to marry so she wouldn't have to return to her hometown of Sligo and work in the family store like her five older siblings. That she would trade her father's family store for her uncle's family store seemed not to matter to Maeve because one was situated in the place she'd lived her entire life and the other on the far side of the Atlantic Ocean. She saw the United States as her future, not Sligo, where her family still had an outhouse and a peat fire, and she shared a bed with her older sister. She had no intention of returning to Ireland without a solid marriage prospect, and the formal seemed like an opportunity. When Finn walked into the school's recreation center with Maeve on his arm he didn't have high hopes for the evening. He hated formal dances, where the opportunities for humiliation ran deep. He wasn't friends with any of the girls, and he didn't like how everyone in the room evaluated one another, the girls waiting to be asked to dance, the boys trying to figure out who looked enticing but also respectable. What he'd found exhausting at twenty-two was now depressing.

As Finn expected, Maeve was surrounded immediately by curious students enchanted by that lyrical accent and wanting to know about the village where she lived. Everyone in his Irish-Catholic world venerated Ireland unless they were the generation that fled. His peers, his friends, talked about the "old sod" even though they'd never been. He was standing against the wall, a glass of punch in each hand, watching Maeve laughing and dancing with his friend Roman. Nice. He liked Roman a lot. Roman was respectful and studious. Maeve couldn't have done better if she'd tried. He stood there, sipping the fruit punch—God, it was awful stuff—and scanning the crowd standing along the perimeter of the dance floor, when he turned and saw Honey.

Sometimes, on particularly difficult days or nights, Finn would replay that moment in his mind, asking himself if he'd do it all over again. In his memory, he turned and (had he embellished this part? Heightened the lighting? Lowered the music? Made that moment far more cinematic than it had been?) the door to the auditorium opened and standing there was the prettiest girl he'd ever seen. She wore a fitted black dress, and her flaxen hair wasn't teased or curled or tortured into some kind of unlovable force, unlike so many of the other girls in the room, but hung in loose waves around her shoulders. A black velvet ribbon held the hair away from her face. Finn couldn't stop staring. He didn't know why, but the ribbon captivated him. He imagined himself tugging on one end and watching this girl's hair fall around her face. She'd arrived by herself, which was unusual. Most of the women arrived in packs of five or six, not leaving one another's orbit until later in the evening when they'd determined who was worth their time. In a completely uncharacteristic move, Finn crossed the room in quick, long strides and handed Honey the glass of punch he'd been holding for Maeve. "For you," he said.

She took it, smiling but confused. "For me?"

"Yes."

"But I just got here. I'm sorry, have we met?"

"I'm Finn Finnegan." He put out his hand to shake hers. "Now we have met."

He called Honey at her home early the next morning. Their courtship was fast, and Finn surprised himself by how quickly he acquiesced. "Timberrrrr!" his cousin would say when Finn got dressed for a date. "The old-growth tree has finally fallen."

Both sets of parents were delighted at the couple's brief engagement. Once Finn proposed, he didn't want to wait for physical intimacy. Eight weeks until they walked down the aisle. Why wait? But Honey was an upstanding young woman, observant, and there was no way she was having sex with Finn before a priest declared them husband and wife in front of one hundred of their closest friends and family members on the altar of Saint Benedict's. No way Honey would allow his hand to hover in the vicinity of her breasts or somewhere lower until she had a ring on her finger and a smear of frosting on her nose from the cutting of the wedding cake and her name was Mrs. Fintan Finnegan.

Their reception went late into the night, so Finn understood when Honey fell asleep while he was brushing his teeth in the small hotel room where they stayed on their wedding night, the one close to the train station for their morning trip to New York City. He was patient, if taken aback, when Honey asked if they could take things slowly after their first dinner in New York.

"We don't have to do everything tonight," Honey said, sitting far away in the corner of the room, arms crossed over her ivory chiffon-and-lace peignoir. "We have our entire lives. Can't we work up to—you know."

"Sex?"

"Finn, don't say it like that."

"Like what? This is what married people do, Honey. I love you. I want to sleep with you."

"I want to *sleep*, too."

Honey's best friend Gina had come back from her honeymoon in Bermuda with a third-degree sunburn and a urinary tract infection. She'd detailed the unpleasantness to Honey and her other girlfriends over a long dinner recently, along with her belief that she would have truly enjoyed Bermuda if she'd had the wherewithal to ask her new husband to take everything a little slower. "I barely got to enjoy the things"—here she blushed—"the things he did that go along with, you know, making out, before he climbed on top of me and . . ." She shook her head. "I will only say that nobody should have to spend the first week of their marriage being pounded to death."

Pounded. It sounded terrifying. Honey didn't want Finn to pound her. She wanted them to dance and kiss and maybe midweek move on to more intimate encounters.

Confused, Finn said, "Honey, you have to give me a chance." That was the first but definitely not the last time Finn noticed that because Honey's first name was an endearment, it diluted any declarative statement that followed. She was born, the story went, with an almost full head of blond hair and after only a few days her newborn smoky gray eyes had turned the color of amber. According to family legend, she also smiled unusually early for an infant, and when her great-aunt Eleanor visited, she took one look at the baby's silky blond hair and bright amber eyes and gooey smile and said, "Well, look at her! Just like a teaspoon of honey." Honor was Honey's given name and the one that suited her better as she grew and took on the self-appointed role of judge and juror of everyone around her. Finn understood why her parents allowed the gentle moniker to stick. He sometimes wondered if anyone in history had been so ironically nicknamed.

Once they were home and settled, things progressed, and although Honey wasn't exactly a fervent or enthusiastic lover, she was dutiful in a way that Finn could accept. And the evening Finn came home from another frustrating day at the store, whip-tired after completing January inventory, and Honey greeted him with a smile and a lavish meal and told him she was pregnant, was one of the best days of his life. The pregnancy immediately softened her, opened her up to him, and that night they went to bed early, and she welcomed him in a new way. Maybe this was all it took, maybe the creating of her own family was the thing that would allow Honey to fully give herself to him.

The next morning, she cried for him from the bathroom. Although the doctor told them they hadn't done anything wrong, that sex was absolutely not the reason she miscarried, that first pregnancies often went that way, that it was nature's way of correcting a mistake, Honey refused to believe him. The following year, after Dune's uneventful pregnancy and safe arrival, all intimacy ended and didn't resume until Honey wanted to get pregnant again. After Fern's birth, Honey announced she didn't "need" any more children—"We have a boy and a girl! The perfect family." Finn inherently understood what she also didn't need or want—physical intimacy. He assumed everyone's marriage ended up that way.

He hadn't wanted to host a party last Memorial Day, but Honey insisted despite the iffy weekend forecast. Western New York's lake-effect weather was most pernicious during the winter, but the ever-shifting atmospheric systems over the Great Lakes could also bring in a sudden rush of clouds and thunderstorms to ruin a perfectly lovely summer day. Or not. *Lake effect*, in Finn's understanding, just meant you could never be sure what was coming.

The cobblestone lake house had originally been built by Finn's grandfather and, like many of the houses on the east bluff of Keuka Lake, was constructed as four levels built into a hillside, each level approximately seven hundred square feet. Cramming forty adults and an unfathomable number of kids—mostly teenagers—into one floor was impossible. Managing a party that spread over many levels ended up being more frustrating than fun.

On sunny days, when guests could congregate on the large outdoor deck Finn's father had added, larger gatherings gained some kind of critical mass. Left indoors, the parties tended to languish. And if the older kids couldn't water-ski or swim, they would gather sullenly in front of the television on the ground level watching game shows. Finn didn't think any of the kids were a bona fide couple, but the world of teens and sex frightened him, between the pill and the so-called sexual revolution (whenever he heard that phrase, he pictured a bunch of hippies marching naked down Main Street waving flags with a hammer and sickle).

The morning of the barbecue dawned bright and promising. Blue skies without a wisp of a cloud. Toward noon, surrounded by hungry guests, and just as Finn got the charcoals exactly right, the skies darkened, and the rain started. Everyone was well into their third Bloody Mary or screwdriver, and as Finn scrambled to move the food from the outdoor tables to the claustrophobic indoor kitchen, he realized they were going to need the folding chairs stored in the boathouse.

Much like the night he met Honey, he would replay that afternoon over and over, wondering if it had happened the way he remembered. He was in the slightly mildewy boathouse, wiping the spiderwebs from the metal chairs, when he heard someone banging at the door, saying it was locked. He pulled the door open—it wasn't locked, just sticky—and there was Nina Larkin, trying to cover herself with her hands because now it was pouring. She was soaked and grinning.

"Oh no," he said, seeing her state. He took her arm and pulled her across the threshold.

"It's freezing in here," she said.

"I know. It doesn't get any sun until the late afternoon, so it's always cold. Not that I expect the sun again today. We must have a towel around here somewhere."

"Oh, I'm fine until we get back upstairs," she said, shivering.

"Why were you out in the rain?"

"Honey said you might need help."

"She did?" Finn didn't even think Honey had noticed he'd gone. Nina tried to wring the water out of her long hair, and when she looked up, she said, "What's wrong?"

"Wrong?"

"You look like you've seen a ghost."

He saw Nina Larkin, soaked, her white blouse clinging to her body in a way that temporarily undid him. She pulled the blouse out from her jeans and away from her body, self-conscious. Embarrassed by the churn of feelings, he turned and looked around the room. He spotted a pile of old swim towels that Honey stored down here for when they needed to dry off the boat. "Here," he said, grabbing a few. "These are clean."

She took one of them and leaned over and deftly wrung the water out of her hair. "Better," she said, handing him back the towel.

He walked toward her and for the rest of his life would marvel at his boldness. "Let me help," he said. He undid the top button of her blouse and stared at her. She let her hands drop to her sides. They were both perfectly silent, but Finn could hear Nina's breathing change, and he didn't even try to conceal his erection. He kept unbuttoning until he could slide the blouse off her torso. He took another towel and wrapped it around her shoulders and pulled her close to him, and when she responded with fervor, not anger or reluctance, he was a goner.

He stepped away after many minutes. Her mascara was smeared from the rain, her face red from the kissing, but she didn't move. She stood, in her bra, pressed against him, and when he touched her nipple she groaned and said, "Don't stop." He didn't know what would have happened next if Dune hadn't started yelling for his father from upstairs. Nina quickly dressed and they each grabbed a few folding chairs and went back to the party. He went into the bathroom to wash his face, to wash *Nina* off his face, and wondered if he'd imagined the entire thing.

The contrast that imbued his life from that one kiss, that one spectacular grope, plunged his marriage, his daily existence, into bleak shades of gray. Things he'd been able to ignore were now like little fleas nipping at his bare ankles. The growing independence of his children. The hostility from his wife. The unlikelihood that anything would ever get better, and who was Honey going to direct her ire at when the children were all gone?

And this: was he done having sex? He was fifty-two. Fifty-two! Honey had indicated in many ways over many years that she was willing to endure his approach, intimacy, a few times a year. Hovering over the mother of your children trying to have an orgasm while that person literally braced herself against the onslaught was almost worse than nothing. He couldn't even masturbate. Where? Honey was on him every minute of every day. He had one constant, consuming desire and her name was Nina Larkin and he was determined to make her his wife.

Eight

Fern was paging through her French homework, figuring out how to get through the dreaded oral exam in school tomorrow without stuttering. Or, without stuttering too much, because not stuttering at all wasn't realistic. A little bit of a hesitation she could absorb, but sometimes—on vowels, always on vowels—her throat would constrict, and her muscles would tighten, and the vowel sound would not budge. Her first move was to try to cough the word out, but that rarely worked. A hush would descend over the classroom for one merciful minute, but soon she'd hear the snickering in the back. Her French teacher, Soeur Jeanne, was slightly hard of hearing or maybe just slightly cruel because she never acknowledged how the group of girls in the back of the room, her nemeses, her torturers, would start coughing into their hands in an imitation of her staccato stumbles (*eh, eh, eh, eh*) and eye one another while laughing as if they were hilarious even though those girls didn't have an original or truly funny thought in their brains. Ever. Once the coughing started, Fern was toast. The only way to get through the passage was to read so quickly her body didn't have a chance to notice the words. Not easy. And when the stream of sound was interrupted, her body did all kinds of other things. Her face flushed, her eyes teared (from anger!), her neck went blotchy, and she started rocking back and forth a little on her heels, or shifting her weight from side to side, jutting out a hip, almost like she could dislodge the word if she moved enough. It was never enough. Sometimes she could slur straight into a word that began with a vowel from the final consonant of the previous word, but the technique only worked occasionally and almost never worked while reading aloud because her eyes would always skip ahead and brace for trouble. Reading in French? When she barely understood the meaning of the sentence and often couldn't get the emphasis right? A complete nightmare.

One night, while cleaning the kitchen after dinner, she'd ventured a complaint to her mother. Everyone in the family skirted around her stuttering like the subject was radioactive. They all adopted a blank, patient look on their faces when her voice would snag, as if they'd never noticed before. What's happening over there? How interesting! When she confided to Honey how she struggled to read out loud in French class, hoping Honey might finally offer help, she could see her mother's shoulders strain against her cotton blouse, the set of her mouth descend. Honey rinsed off her soapy hands and said to Fern, "I have an idea."

"You do?" Fern was surprised. Honey only liked to hear good news, to talk about things that made her happy and proud, preferably both, when it involved her children. Fern and Honey were often at odds.

"Right before it's time to read in class, say to yourself, quietly, three times, 'Come Jesus, help me. Come Jesus, help me. Come Jesus, help me.'" She smiled at Fern, pleased with herself.

"I—I—I—don't think that's going to work, Mom."

"Have you tried it?"

"No, I haven't tried inviting Jesus into French class. I didn't know he was available on command like *I Dream of Jeannie*."

Honey turned away and started scrubbing the bottom of a pot. "I'm trying to help here, Fern."

"I know." Fern did know. This was Honey's idea of "helping." To suggest something supernatural, something so off-the-wall Catholic that completely excused both from any personal responsibility. The first time she'd brought up seeing a speech therapist, a few years ago, Honey had looked at her like she'd asked for a cigarette and lighter. "For what!" she'd said, affronted.

"To help with my stuttering."

"Nobody notices you stutter. You have to take your time, Fern. Go more slowly!"

"Mom, everyone notices. And going slowly is the problem." That was the day at the end of eighth grade when David Saunders signed her little handmade autograph book, a pile of pages stapled together with an elaborate hand-decorated cover that all the girls had made the final week of school. He wrote in big red letters on top of the second page: "F-f-f-f-ern. I h-h-h-hope you have a g-g-g-g-good summer. S-s-s-s-orry, I c-c-c-couldn't resist." She'd flushed with humiliation and wanted to cry because how could she ask anyone else to sign her book after that? They'd read what David Saunders had written, and what had been treated for years by her teachers and closest friends as implicit would become explicit. Out of the question. She couldn't even muster the nerve to confront David over his most egregious sin, that pathetic dope: She didn't stutter on consonants! Only vowels.

She'd been so looking forward to high school, to a new building with a whole new set of teachers who wouldn't have already had a dozen conversations about Fern's speech. But plenty of girls from her tiny Catholic elementary school class had matriculated to the same medium-sized Catholic high school and on the first day of the first class, when she'd had to stand and introduce herself and tell the class a little something about her interests, Jenny Grecco, her main female tormentor from eighth grade, had started the cough. *Eh, eh, eh*, every time Fern started to speak.

She stopped believing in new beginnings that day. Her life would follow her wherever she went. She stuttered, she weighed too much, she was the only member of her family who wasn't beautiful or athletic. They were fluid and she was granite: Fern, fat and faltering.

Nine

Honey wasn't unsympathetic. She hated the days when Fern came home from school visibly downcast and discouraged. She didn't know if the Jesus prayer would work, but wasn't it worth a try? Honey also believed, strongly, that if Fern could lose a little weight and feel confident in her appearance, the stuttering would improve. Wouldn't it? Fern walked around like she was trying to conceal something; that kind of posture couldn't help her esophagus. Larynx? If Fern felt more comfortable in her body, prettier, if her school uniform hung nicely, all of it would make a difference.

After Finn's heart attack, he begrudgingly joined Weight Watchers and so did Honey to keep him accountable. When they signed up, she only had eight pounds to lose. The women registering them argued that Honey's weight was in the normal range already and she didn't need to reduce, but Honey persisted. She lost eight pounds in three weeks and secured her lifetime membership as long as she maintained her weight within a few pounds. Weight Watchers had changed Finn's health and her entire life. She continued going to the meetings long after Finn had dropped thirty pounds and been given a cautious but clean bill of health from his cardiologist. She loved the meetings. She loved hearing other people open up about their weight and diet struggles. She was a cheerleader for all! She offered excellent suggestions about how to cut calories and still eat delicious meals. One night, her group leader asked her out for coffee after the meeting. As they both emptied multiple packets of Sweet'N Low into their black coffee and split a small scoop of orange sherbet, Lenore asked Honey if she would consider becoming a group leader. "You're good at this, and most importantly, you know how to lift the members' spirits. We need someone to cover a new meeting starting downtown."

Now, when Honey led her own meetings, she always started by talking about confidence. People could say beauty comes from within until they were blue in the face, but when a person went shopping for a new dress or slacks and nothing fit or they had to go up a size, they didn't leave the store feeling beautiful, no matter how appealing their insides. No, they left feeling defeated, unworthy, unattractive. Honey understood the ups and downs of self-esteem as they related to her bathroom scale, an object in the house that she'd anthropomorphized. She thought of the pale blue–and-silver scale tucked beside the pedestal sink as an older woman named Shirley. Sometimes, right before she stepped on the scale, completely naked, of course, and only after defecating, she would mumble a little prayer to Shirley. "Come on, girl. Come on, Shirl." She would hold her breath as the tiny needle hovered. She knew. She always knew. She could stand in her bathroom and feel her middle and her hips and know exactly what the scale would show. Up four pounds, down two, up three, down one. This morning the needle moved alarmingly to the right, farther than usual, showing a five-pound gain. Six, if she was perfectly honest—she'd kind of lifted one foot to nudge it back to five. Five! Only a few ounces until the scale went into dangerous territory. She would have to work extra hard for the next few weeks to get back down to where she felt her best. *Confident.* "I am not a little piggy," she whispered to herself as she stepped off the scale and pushed it back under the bathroom cabinet. She wanted to teach Fern the value of setting a goal and hitting it. She wanted to change Fern's world.

For the past year, she'd tried to slyly cut back on Fern's intake, with little success.

"Are you Weight Watching me?" Fern would ask, eyes narrowed as she prodded her fork at a pile of steamed broccoli or half of a baked potato, dry, with salt and pepper, while Dune was slathering butter and salt all over his potato and steak. He'd butter an orange if Honey would let him.

"Boys have completely different dietary needs and body makeup."

"I'm not one of your *members*." Fern put a little top spin on the word *members* and Honey let it slide. Fern and Dune made fun of her and her members behind her back and sometimes a little bit right to her face, but it was okay. She had found her calling. To deliver dietary advice and group support to whomever in Rochester needed her, to help those women and the occasional man reduce and reach their goal weight and, therefore, become the best version of themselves.

It's all she wanted for Fern—to become the best Fern possible. As she was running over in her head what the best possible Fern might look like, the real live Fern walked into the kitchen and made a beeline for the refrigerator. Honey stopped herself from commenting on Fern's outfit (an old pair of hip-huggers, a worn plaid cheesecloth blouse, both straining at the seams) and her hair (a veritable rat's nest in the back). "Can I help you?" Honey asked her daughter.

"I'm feeling a little peckish."

"I finished cleaning up after lunch. Kitchen's closed."

"I don't want a meal. I want a snack."

Honey walked over to the refrigerator, took an apple out of the crisper bin, handed it to Fern, and closed the fridge door. Fern sighed, but she could tell by the set of Honey's mouth that anything else would cause a fight and although sometimes she wanted nothing more than to poke at her mother, she didn't have the energy today. Besides, Clara was coming over soon to rehearse with Dune and they would definitely make popcorn. Clara would probably bring homemade cookies.

"You know," Honey said, facing away from Fern, taking the sponge from the sink and wiping down a spotless linoleum counter, "if the, the, voice issues are bothering you—"

Fern sighed and bit into the apple with her front teeth, spraying Honey.

"Fern!"

"Sorry! It was an accident."

"I swear. Sometimes I don't know where you came from."

They stood facing off for a second. Honey took the apple from Fern's hands and grabbed a paring knife and cut it into five neat wedges, one with a bite taken out of it. "Here. What I was going to say is if you really want to see a speech therapist, I will look into it."

Fern stopped chewing. "You will?"

"If you want."

"I do," Fern said. "I want that."

"Okay. Well. And there's another thing I was thinking about."

Fern knew there had to be a catch. "What?" she said.

"I think we need a two-pronged approach."

"Mom."

"I think that speech therapy might help. But I also would like you to start coming to my Weight Watchers meeting."

Fern sighed and looked out the window into the backyard. It was a beautiful autumn Sunday afternoon, and she could see the kids who lived in the house behind her running around their backyard, jumping into piles of vibrantly colored leaves, calling, "You're it! No, *you're* it!" She wondered if they got to eat whatever they wanted.

"I'll go. But if I hate it, I'm going to stop."

Honey clapped her hands. "Wonderful!" She gave Fern a hug. "You're not going to hate it. You might even make some friends! Some of my regulars have started bringing their daughters."

"Sounds like a blast. And speech therapy?"

"I'll investigate tomorrow. I promise. Deal?" Honey put out her hand as if they were business associates.

"Sure, Mom. Deal."

Finn walked in on the handshake. "What kind of toil and trouble is going on in here?"

"Not trouble at all," Honey said. "Fern is coming to Weight Watchers with me. Isn't that wonderful?"

Finn eyed his daughter and her lack of enthusiasm for the browning apple slices in front of her. "This was your idea?" he said.

Fern rolled her eyes. "What do you think?"

Honey glared at Finn. "You liked those meetings. Don't even try to tell me you didn't."

"It's okay, Dad," Fern said. She didn't want to risk losing the speech therapist before she'd even started. "I'll give it a try."

"That's my girl," Finn said. He had a copy of Leon Uris's *Trinity* tucked under one arm and was wearing his running clothes.

"You're going out now?" Honey said. Despite her encouragement around all changes concerning food, Honey was suspicious of Finn's recent running habit and the subsequent pile of sweaty clothes stinking up her laundry room.

"Quick run. After I'm done, I'll head into the store to check on things."

"Have you mastered reading and running?" she said, pointing to the massive tome under Finn's arm.

"Dropping it across the street."

"Would I like it?"

For the entirety of their marriage, Finn had never seen Honey read anything other than a magazine. "Maybe. It's about the Irish famine. Lots of people sitting around eating nothing."

"Finn!" Honey said, trying and failing to slap his arm as he started lightly jogging in place just out of her reach. "That's not funny."

"It is a little funny," Fern said, picking up an apple slice.

"Your lawyer has spoken," Honey said to her husband, sounding more resentful than she meant to; Finn and Fern had become two peas in a pod over the past year, Fern always ready to leap to Finn's defense in the face of any criticism.

He kissed Fern on the temple. "The verdict is in. I'm funny." Fern laughed as he ran backward out the kitchen door. "I'm funny!" he kept repeating until they couldn't hear him anymore.

Honey grabbed the plate with one apple slice left, emptied it into the garbage pail, and shoved the plate into the dishwasher. "Kitchen closed."

Ten

He tried, but Finn still couldn't descend his driveway without thinking about the morning of his collapse. The day after his fifty-second birthday. The previous night's party at their country club, a sit-down dinner for 120 guests, approximated a wedding, only with better food because Finn was Finn and the club let him bring in his own suppliers for the caviar, chilled shrimp, filet mignon, and lobster tail. The meal was decadent and the toasts plentiful, so when he woke the next morning, a bitter cold Sunday in January, to almost a foot of snow blanketing the street, he decided to pay for his sins and shovel the walk and driveway himself.

Even in his lingering sodden state—he'd consumed more than one person's share of bourbon—he was euphoric because he'd made it. His father had died of a massive coronary three weeks before his fifty-second birthday. Fifty-two loomed over Finn like a dare, the reason he'd eschewed a celebration at fifty. He felt—irrationally but obstinately—that if he could live longer than his father, usher in his fifty-second birthday, he would have won, and the prize was more time.

Honey wanted him to wait to shovel until Dune and Fern were up and could help, but he shook her off. He felt strong and the accumulation of lake-effect snow, the kind that rode in on a cold wind from Canada and dropped twelve inches in only a few hours, wasn't wet and heavy. He never remembered the exact meteorology, something about water content in the flakes, but the fallen snow was light and aerated. The kind of snow that frustrated the kids when they were younger because it was the consistency of confectioners' sugar, impossible to pack into a snowball or roll into a snowman or build into a fort.

"This will take twenty minutes," he said, zipping up his parka, pulling on leather gloves, jamming a wool beanie on his head. When he lifted the garage door he was assaulted by the cold and the glare of fresh snow sparkling in the sunlight. The street looked like the front of a Christmas card, all white and glistening and romantic. With the cars buried under the accumulation, you could imagine it was 1940, 1930, 1928—the year most of the houses on their block were built. He grabbed a shovel, ignored his headache and dry mouth, and tried to work up a sweat. Get the booze and meat and sugar out of his system. He'd gained weight in the last decades and didn't like how he felt. His clothes tight around his waist. Heavier on his feet.

No surprise, his father was on his mind this morning. Finn supposed he'd loved his parents the way most boys of his generation loved their parents—dutifully, respectfully. He wasn't happy when his father died, he missed his father, but at the funeral as he shouldered the front right corner of the weighted casket and processed out of the church to a lugubrious version of "Danny Boy" on the organ, Finn felt a physical sensation of relief, a disconcerting combination of joy at his pending ascendency and grief at his encroaching mortality.

His father had anointed Finn as successor and company president years ago but only in title. Fintan Finnegan Sr. and his brother—Finn's uncle Dennis—politely listened to Finn's ideas, often behaving as if they might act on the suggestions, but they never did. Finn's father was conservative in every possible way: politics, spending, store management, employee management, personal beliefs, religion. Vatican II broke his heart. He rued the cessation of the daily Latin Mass, thought it was outrageous when priests started facing the congregation. The advent of the birth control pill, civil rights, busing, feminism—all of it made him apoplectic. His last years were angry ones, and he coped by micromanaging Finnegan's into a state of stasis.

His father's intractability drove Finn crazy. He could see the potential of the stores so clearly—especially the opportunities for expansion. He lobbied for years to pay their employees more, get them invested in the success of the operation, introduce profit sharing. "Pay them more!" his father bellowed the last time Finn had brought it up. "If I had my way, I'd pay them less! Did you see the amount of produce that went into the garbage last Sunday?"

Well, sure. Produce went into the garbage because they needed to update the refrigeration systems and try to automate inventory. They needed to build and develop relationships with local fruit and vegetable suppliers and audit their use of wholesalers trucking products from down south and out west, crunch some numbers to see if it all made sense. A regional distribution center was inevitable and necessary and smart. His list went on and on. Finn could see how money was flooding out of the stores. If his father had his way, they'd still have everything behind a counter manned by female clerks wearing white aprons and ruffled caps, politely putting three pears into a brown paper bag, weighing them, and penciling the price by hand.

Finn didn't only want bigger, he wanted better. What was more central to the life of everyone around him than food? What was more satisfying than influencing how his community shopped for sustenance and pleasure?

The week after his father's funeral, when he was officially president of the company, Finn fired his uncle Dennis, handing him a seat on the board with an accompanying annual salary that was more than he deserved. He immediately announced that all Finnegan's locations would open on Sundays from eight a.m. to five p.m. When Monsignor Thomas at Saint Benedict's pulled him aside after Mass the following Sunday to register his displeasure, suggesting next week's homily might discourage parishioners from shopping on the Sabbath, Finn understood. He offered to donate coffee and donuts for the reception in the parish hall held the third Sunday of every month and for any other sanctioned church functions, and that was that.

Finn's second and smartest move was to recruit a young woman named Helen Harper from the MBA program out of Stanford. It wasn't easy. She'd grown up in California and was reluctant to relocate to a place that regularly appeared on the list of the gloomiest cities in the United States. He brought her out in June, when Rochester was at its greenest and sunniest and loveliest. He asked his neighbor Nancy

Tannenbaum, who was a realtor, to show Helen some houses on the market and a charming English Tudor right around the corner from the George Eastman house did the trick. "I would pay twice this for a tiny bungalow in San Diego, not even near the beach."

Bringing Helen into the fold meant breaking his father's golden rule: to keep Finnegan's Grocer firmly within the grasp of the family. No outsiders. If he'd heard the admonition once, he'd heard it a thousand times. But he knew his limitations, and he knew he needed help to execute his vision, and Helen Harper was a godsend. If Finn's preoccupation was roaming the stores and interacting with customers and envisioning how to improve the shopping experience, Helen's obsession was numbers. She would say every spreadsheet told a story about what was being done well, how they could improve, and where they were failing completely. Within a decade of her arrival, they'd opened four new locations and had plans for an additional three, including a renovation and expansion of the flagship store, smack in the middle of town. Expansion was thrilling, and Finn was just getting started.

He'd had about one-third of the driveway done when a pressure in his left arm distracted him from his musings. He stood up straight and was hit by a wave of nausea. Before he could stop himself, he vomited onto the snowbank he'd just created. His arm was throbbing. He tried to steady himself against the snowbank but it gave way and Finn slipped and fell. The next thing he remembered was waking up on a stretcher in the driveway and feeling worse than he'd ever felt in his entire life. The paramedics were talking to each other in urgent voices and injecting something into an IV line. They'd removed his jacket.

"I'm cold," he managed to croak out. "I'm sick."

"That's why we're here, friend," one of them said to him. A big guy with red hair and a full beard and surprisingly agile fingers given their size and heft. "But we've got things under control, and we'll head to the hospital soon."

He wanted to ask a million questions, but he was so tired. He felt like a prize idiot for not knowing the heart could fell him whenever it wanted. So he prayed. He prayed to live to see Dune and Fern graduate from high school. Marry. Have kids. In a disappointingly banal and predictable Ebenezer-like flash, he saw how single-minded and work-focused he'd been. He quietly bargained and promised: more time at home, better father, more understanding boss, better human.

He felt a quiet elation he assumed was the saline flooding his dehydrated body. Then he was floating above his street and could see the paramedics pummeling some poor guy on his driveway. He wanted to tell them to take it easy, but he was distracted by the view. Up here, everything felt lighter and clearer, even the blue of the sky. He could see the cars slowly making their way down Park Avenue and the steeple of the Episcopal church a few blocks away. And then he felt his mother beside him. She didn't say anything, but he knew she'd come to help. He looked down to see how the guy on the driveway was doing and saw Fern collapsed on top of that poor man. Fern. Sobbing and calling for him and he felt an unaccountable sadness not only because she was upset but because he knew he had to choose. He could go with his mother, or he could go to his daughter, but he couldn't do both. "Fern," he said. "Fern."

Hallucination, the doctors insisted. "These things—these premonitions or visions—can feel real," his cardiologist assured him. "You fainted and your brain was not getting enough blood, so strange things can happen during what we call *syncope*, things we don't even fully understand. But it's no surprise you would think of your children. Your wife. You'll have a greater appreciation for all of it."

But he hadn't *thought* about Fern, he'd *seen* Fern. From high above his body where she lay sprawled and sobbing. And he hadn't thought about Dune because Dune had slept through the entire incident. And he hadn't thought about Honey because—why hadn't he thought about Honey? Why, when he woke up in the emergency room, did he wish Honey weren't holding his hand? It turned out that feeling as if he were going to die didn't make him appreciate all he had—it made him wonder why, in this one critical way, he had settled.

He read a book called *Life After Life* full of case histories detailing experiences like his. So many people in the book who had near-death experiences said they now felt a peace about dying, an uptick in faith, but the opposite happened to Finn. He wasn't afraid of dying, he wasn't afraid of heaven or hell or whatever the church used as a brandishing tool to keep their followers in line, he was deathly afraid of wasting the rest of his life. He tried to broach his unhappiness with the doctor, who told him depression was normal after a cardiac event and would correct itself. Finn knew better. The correction was up to him.

Eleven

As soon as Sunday lunch was over and Clara was back in her bedroom, she started thinking about how to pitch her audition idea to Dune. She'd popped awake at dawn and couldn't go back to sleep because she'd experienced her first authentic creative impulse. Her drama teacher, Mr. Goodwin, was always talking about the human urge to create and the importance of channeling the inner self. He went on and on about Carl Jung and something about connecting to the conscious self or the unconscious self. Both? "Stop trying to figure out what other people want to see—including me, by the way," Mr. Goodwin would lecture them, tugging a little on his beard near the bottom of his chin, a nervous tic. "*Feel* what's right. *Feel* what's essential and authentic for *you*. Get out of your own way! Occupy your body," he'd say and then point to someone and tell them to take a lap. Taking a lap meant walking around the perimeter of the theater and trying not to *think*, trying to *feel*.

"Let me guess," Mr. Goodwin said to Clara one afternoon while particularly frustrated by her inability to memorize a series of dance steps for a scene they were doing in drama class, "you're a reader." He said *reader* pityingly, like he was saying, *let me guess, you're a stoner* or *let me guess, you're a Republican*, because Mr. Goodwin was extremely vocal about his hatred of the Republican Party and what they'd done to his country, a country he no longer recognized as his, he told them, shaking his head in sorrow.

"Reading isn't a bad thing exactly." He raised his voice a little, nodding at his own insight. "But it tends to put you all up here." He patted the back of Clara's head. "You need to work from here." He moved behind her and put his arm around her midsection, hand on her abdomen. She had her period and felt bloated and so she flinched a little.

"Oh, she reacts. She retracts!" Mr. Goodwin said. "Message received." He backed up, hands raised.

"No, no," she said, not wanting to fall out of hard-earned attention so quickly. "I liked it!"

"She liked it," he said to the rest of the class, taking an imaginary cigar out of his mouth and twirling it while he sent his eyebrows up and down, imitating Groucho Marx.

"I didn't mean it like that!"

"Don't worry, Larkin. I'm teasing you. Sit down. But remember what Priscilla taught us." Priscilla was Mr. Goodwin's yoga instructor girlfriend, who'd invited the drama class to her apartment a few weeks ago to teach the students how to breathe. He demonstrated now, inhaling slowly through his nose, hand on stomach, feeling it distend with breath and after holding for a few seconds, blowing the air out in a steady stream through his mouth. "From here," he said, patting his slim middle as it settled back into place. "From here."

"You realize he's a total creep, right?" Fern said later while they were packing up their things for the day. Fern had no real interest in drama; she took the elective for the theater tech part and because she thought it would be an easy grade and complained constantly because building sets was very time-consuming.

"He's not a creep. He's a creative."

"What's the difference?"

"He's an actor. He's not as uptight as everyone else we know. He operates on a completely different level, Fern."

"Really? Then why is he teaching *here*? Because Our Lady of Good Counsel is a hotbed of theatrical talent?"

Clara felt herself getting blotchy on her chest and neck. "He's in *A Christmas Carol* this year at Geva. And community theater is legit."

"What part?"

"The Ghost of Christmas Future."

"The one who wears a hood over its face and gestures with one finger? The nonverbal one? Sounds right."

Was this true? Clara'd only seen the movie once. "Lots of actors start at a small regional theater before they make it big."

Fern sighed and rolled her eyes, which was happening more and more lately. Clara and Bridie and Fern used to be joined at the hip, but things had been tense lately. All Fern wanted to do was talk to Bridie about college (they were only juniors!) and all Clara wanted to do was think about Dune, something she could not, under any circumstances, tell Fern or Bridie about. Not yet.

"I can't decide what to do for my *Godspell* audition," Clara said.

"Is there a worse musical on the face of the earth? *Jesus Christ Superstar* at least has something a little subversive in it," Fern said, slamming her locker door shut and turning to Clara. "Okay, what are your options?"

Clara had been in all the school plays since freshman year and almost always landed in the chorus, maybe with a featured line or two. She'd sung "Who will buy my sweet red roses?" in *Oliver!* (she would have brought down the house as Nancy) and was Gertie-with-the-annoying-laugh in *Oklahoma!* (she'd wanted Ado Annie) and though she'd been called back for Golde and Hodel in *Fiddler* last year, she wound up as the dead butcher's wife, Fruma-Sarah, who yells more than sings in a dream sequence from beyond the grave. Her voice wasn't powerful, but it was solid, she could sing on pitch, and she'd improved.

"As an avowed atheist, I'm not thrilled with doing *Godspell*," Mr. Goodwin, new to the school in September, had said while rocking back and forth in his Converse high-tops. Two girls in the back of the class angrily packed up their backpacks in protest and stormed out through the auditorium's swinging doors. "My right, ladies," he yelled at their receding backs. "My constitutional right!" He laughed and surveyed the rest of the group, half of them giggling (Would he go to *hell*?), a quarter clapping raucously in agreement, and the rest—like Clara—confused. "Anyone else need to leave? Go running to Mommy and Daddy and talk about the big bad unbeliever?" He waited and nobody spoke. "Okay, then! *Godspell*? Not my first choice. Not even my fiftieth choice. But let's look at this as an opportunity to step away from the rigid hierarchical structure of so many plays and explore what theater has to offer us in the form of the ensemble. Let's try to break free of *lead* and *supporting* and *chorus*."

"How many parts for girls?" Deirdre Connelly asked, raising her hand and speaking at the same time. As always, their all-girls school would join forces with the all-boys school right down the street for theater productions. As always, Deirdre would complain about how many of the leading roles went to boys instead of girls. Everyone in the drama club had many theories about Deirdre: Feminist? Lesbian? Plain old stage hog?

"Every part in this production is open to both sexes," Mr. Goodwin said. Deirdre Connelly clapped her hands and let out a little "Woo-hoo!"

"Even *Jesus*?" Greta Crane asked, hand to heart.

"Even the son of God. May the best human win the chance to be divine."

A female Jesus was all anyone talked about for days. Who could do it? What would the parents think? Some cheered. Some vociferously objected. Deirdre started wearing rainbow suspenders to rehearsal, and every time Clara walked past the practice rooms, she could hear her singing "Day by Day" at the top of her lungs. All the noise was for nought because it was crystal clear who would get the part, and that the messiah wouldn't be wearing a bra. Dune Finnegan was the Jesus to beat.

"Well, look what happened there," Clara's mother had said some weeks ago when they were pulling out of the driveway right after Labor Day and Dune was riding his bike home from his after-school shift at Finnegan's. "Dune Finnegan got almost handsome."

Dune, who'd been named after Finn and called Junior until Fern began to talk and could only pronounce his name as *Dune*, had spent the summer living at the family lake house while working for a local landscaper, and in the span of three months he'd transformed. He'd grown a few inches and acquired some musculature in his arms and back, his legs. He hadn't had a haircut since spring, and the longer length suited his blond hair, lighter from a summer of outdoor work. He wasn't exactly tall but was no longer short.

"That's *Dune*?" Clara said, gawking at the boy on the bike whom she'd known since second grade. Dune Finnegan with the constant runny nose until they figured out he was allergic to the family dog and banished it to the backyard. Dune Finnegan, who'd sung "Ave Maria" at the eighth-grade Christmas pageant and brought most of the parents to tears. Dune Finnegan, who'd won every spelling bee from second to eighth grade and had Coke-bottle glasses and ate a bologna sandwich on white bread with mustard and mayonnaise and one hard-boiled egg for lunch for as long as anyone could remember. "If it ain't broke!" he'd say cheerfully when mocked for the sulfur stink of the egg.

That Dune had disappeared, and *this* Dune—who'd also gotten contacts and had his braces removed—was a different creature entirely. And yet his youthful sweetness somehow shined through. He serpentined down the street, whistling as he waved at Nina and Fern, slowed the bike, bent to the curb, and picked up a piece of trash. The inside remained, but the packaging had been upgraded. New and improved Dune!

As it turned out, *almost handsome* was exactly what Clara wanted. She was fairly confident that by the limited and admittedly self-absorbed standards of high school, her kind of pretty (better than average) had more currency than Dune's almost handsome. She knew she wasn't a beauty. She'd heard two Spanish teachers in the hallway one day talking about a new freshman and Señora Garcia'd said, "She's a real beauty, isn't she?" and Clara felt a pang of sadness because the girl in question was quite stunning, and Clara knew nobody would call her a *real beauty* behind her back. But she also knew she was pretty enough.

She spent the ensuing days thinking about Dune and how best to signal her interest. Though they didn't hang out the way they used to during the days of hide-and-seek or softball on the block, they still found themselves together at family gatherings. He lived right across the street. Clara imagined how thrilled—no, how *relieved*—Dune would be when she made her interest known. She felt terrific about dating one small step down. Maybe a half step. It always seemed to her that having someone love you a little more than you loved them was the correct ratio for happiness and, my god, was she already *in love*? In love with her old friend Dune Finnegan?

While Clara was congratulating herself for how much she could improve Dune's life, rock his world, she failed to credit Dune's understanding of the shifting ground beneath him and his willingness to welcome in all possibilities. That one possibility would be Greta Crane would never have crossed Clara's mind because the one thing she and Dune had always laughed about was the lameness of Greta Crane.

Greta came from one of the wealthiest families in town. The Finnegans were up there and Clara's family was hardly poor, but Finn Finnegan was a grocer's son-turned-businessman and the Cranes were old money in Rochester, two different worlds. Greta's great-grandfather was a founding member of the oldest and most exclusive country club in town. Another of Greta's forebears had been instrumental in starting the Eastman School of Music with George Eastman. Greta's father published the local daily newspaper and partially owned Rochester's AAA minor-league baseball team. Greta's family had a house in Myrtle Beach where they went every spring break and one in Cape Cod where they went every summer, never mind the countless family vacations to Paris, Rome, London. Greta owned a dozen crewneck sweaters in various shades of sherbet, all with her monogram, GCE , embroidered on the front. She was medium height and had medium-length medium-brown hair and was medium smart.

Because Xavier ended classes a good thirty minutes before Good Counsel, the boys from Xavier who had a car or a friend with a car would already be hanging out in the parking lot when the girls were dismissed. One brilliant autumn afternoon, as Clara stood with a group of friends planning which movie to see over the weekend, she saw Dune open the door of his beat-up Buick and invite Greta into the passenger seat. As they pulled away, windows down, the Bee Gees' "More than a Woman" blaring from the car radio, Clara knew she had to act fast because boys were very dumb. Greta was cute and bubbly and laughed at everything a boy said even if she didn't get the joke. Even if she was the butt of the joke. And she was popular, which would hold sway over Dune. She was president of the junior class, the ski club, the New Year's Ball committee, and the girls' volleyball team. She volunteered at the local old-age home. Clara did not underestimate the power of Greta Crane with an agenda.

She instinctively knew she should avoid bad-mouthing Greta. "Did I see you in the parking lot the other day," she said to Dune one afternoon when they were hanging out after school, "picking up Greta? You guys make a cute couple."

Dune blushed. "We're not a couple. I just gave her a ride home." Clara nodded and lightly changed the subject. "Want to be my partner for *Godspell* auditions?"

From there, it had been a snap. They rehearsed together a few times a week, always at Dune's house because Fern was never home, and Bridie was always home and was nosy and annoying. Clara and Dune could talk for hours. About parents and teachers and college and their friends and who was smart and who was not and who was funny and who was just plain mean. They exchanged notes in the morning and collected little bits of gossip all day, proffering information like tokens. One afternoon when they were deciding which Bible parable they should use to improvise around for their audition, she could tell Dune wanted to kiss her. She looked at her watch and pretended she had to hurry home to help with dinner. She wanted to make him wait for that kiss. The next afternoon, the dirty Buick idled in the parking lot for her.

Today, she needed to head across the street and talk Dune into auditioning the way she envisioned. She pulled *The Joy of Sex* out from behind her dresser and started paging through when her door swung open. She shoved the book under the pillow, but it was only Bridie standing there with a board game. "Wanna play?" she said, holding a weathered version of The Bride Game, which they had played to death years ago but long abandoned. The game bored Clara because she'd swiftly figured out how to "shuffle" the cards so when her turn came, she got the coveted dress (formal daytime) and the right bouquet (extremely pink) and the three-tiered wedding cake and, most importantly, the desirable groom (formal evening, even if Bridie insisted the groom should be formal daytime, too). Bridie never knew Clara cheated.

"Where did you find *that*?" Clara asked.

"In the closet."

"No thanks, always-a-Bridie-never-a-bride." Bridie's face fell, and Clara felt sorry for resurrecting the old taunt. "Maybe later. I have to head across the street."

Bridie skulked away and Clara took the book out from behind the pillow. Clara knew her mother would soon figure out the book was missing, so she tried to sear most of it into memory, which was quite a feat because she simultaneously couldn't stop looking at the vivid illustrations in the book and was also repulsed by the vivid illustrations in the book. The woman in the drawings had a thatch of pubic hair so unruly that Clara kept raising her nightgown in the morning to look at herself in the bathroom mirror and make sure she wasn't sprouting some kind of wildness down there. The woman also didn't shave under her arms, which Clara knew she was supposed to admire but didn't. The man was short and squat and in some of the drawings he looked disturbingly like an apostle from one of her childhood Bible stories. In others he resembled Mr. McGivens, the grammar school gym teacher, who had tufts of hair coming out of every orifice. Mr. McGivens smelled like BENGAY and cigarettes and compulsively dribbled a basketball. He encouraged such ruthless behavior in dodgeball that the school fired him after Dominic Bianchi cleared the opposite court with three brutally precise hits on three different fourth graders, resulting in, respectively, a concussion, a broken collarbone, and a sprained wrist.

Some of the sections in *The Joy of Sex* frightened her (*Big toe?*) and some gave her a different feeling. Was this what everyone did at night under the covers? Or, if this book could be believed, on the floor, on a rug, on a blanket, in a meadow, in front of a mirror, standing freestyle, standing against the wall, standing on the bed? The bed, in fact, seemed almost an afterthought, a prop—like a potted Ficus or a lamp—that mostly served as support for acrobatic sexual positions. The single illustration with a bed was in the bondage or "gentle art of tying up your sex partner" section, which, like most things in the book, initially horrified Clara and then intrigued her and then was neatly incorporated into her index of self-pleasuring fantasies.

She and Dune hadn't had sex yet, but they were getting close. After the kiss, it was a short trip to allowing Dune to undo her bra. She hadn't let his hand venture below her waist, but she was ready. As for the rest, it was just a matter of time and making sure Dune had a box of condoms. The more she read and the harder she examined the photos, her shock and discomfort waned and it all looked—*thrilling*. She was going to get a good part in *Godspell*. She'd won the contest for Dune Finnegan—ha! Greta Crane never had a chance—and thanks, weirdly, to Bridie and this pilfered book, she was going to be very, *very* good at sex.

Twelve

Until recently, Dune Finnegan had had no qualms about spying on the Larkin sisters. Both houses had a family bathroom on the second floor, facing front, right onto Cambridge Road, with windows perfectly aligned. The Larkins' bathroom window, for reasons he could only thank a higher power for, was equipped with a flimsy, oft-broken shade that was rarely lowered except at night because the Larkin girls might have been unsuspecting, but they weren't dumb. One morning in eighth grade, while going through the ancient toy chest in the basement, Dune had found a tiny pair of collapsible binoculars and possibilities presented themselves. His father had real binoculars on the fireplace mantel, but one of his parents would have noticed if those went missing. He hid the toy binoculars in the vanity behind some ancient bottles of calamine lotion and Mercurochrome and a nearly empty box of Mr. Bubble. The only other person who knew was his best friend Christopher, and sometimes they'd stake out the Larkin bathroom together. The peeping was mostly innocent. The bathroom was large, and the girls only passed by the small window briefly and they almost always wore robes. When someone ran hot water, the window fogged. But on the occasional sacred morning, Clara would stand in front of the bathroom mirror in her underwear—back to the window, alas—and put her long hair up into a high ponytail. On some blessed evenings, Bridie would lower the shade while wearing her nightgown and if she turned just so, they could almost make out her backlit breasts. In what Dune considered an act of ultimate friendship, one morning after a sleepover, Christopher raced into his bedroom, handed him the binoculars, and said, "Hurry." Dune scrambled to the bathroom, locked the door behind him, brought the glasses to his eyes, and there was Clara. Clara in the nude. Clara applying some kind of lotion to her arms, her legs, her breasts. It only happened once, but the image carried Dune through many nights and many mornings. The only downside was seeing Clara in person because it was hard for him to look his old playmate in the eye. Until it wasn't. Until looking into Clara's eyes was all he wanted to do.

Now that she was his girlfriend (was she his *girlfriend*? Unclear), he was confused about the bathroom binoculars. On the one hand, he kind of had access to Clara's actual body right now, so what was the point in engaging in admittedly creepy behavior? On the other hand, wasn't it okay—because he kind of had access to Clara's actual body—to watch her sometimes? Admire her? Desire her?

He'd agreed with her plan to keep their burgeoning relationship secret until the New Year's formal not because their families would object, but because they'd completely overreact, watching and chuckling and in general being totally annoying. The formal was only eight weeks away and in some ways he would miss the subterfuge, the sneaking winks and smiles, how Clara would link her pinkie with his when they were in the car and nobody could see, the glorious late-night make-out sessions when they'd sneak into one of their respective backyards after dark. She'd made him wait for those, and though he supposed they could continue, they probably wouldn't. He was eager to publicly declare Clara as his. They could sit together at basketball games and rehearsals for the play and hold hands. He could pick her up in the parking lot after school and watch her burst through the doors and rush toward his car and they wouldn't have to play it cool, just a couple of neighbors riding home together because it was convenient. How could any amount of sneaking around feel better than that?

He decided to ditch the binoculars. Someday it would be a funny story to tell Clara, but only if he did the right thing now. He brought his backpack into the bathroom, and before he put the binoculars into a side pocket to carry down to the garbage, he took one last look for auld lang syne. He squinted and turned the tiny knob with its minimal focusing ability, but the Larkin bathroom was empty. The front door beneath him slammed shut, and he saw his father, dressed in jogging clothes, trot across the street with a book in his hand. Before his father put whatever book he was carrying into the Larkins' box, he reached into his windbreaker and pulled out a thick manila envelope. He looked around almost as if he knew he was being watched. Dune stepped back from the window but kept his father in his sights. His father wedged the envelope into the middle of the book. Put the book in the mailbox. Secured the latch. Bent to touch his toes a few times and took off down the street.

The scene he'd witnessed wasn't particularly odd; his father and Mrs. Larkin exchanged books all the time, so why did Dune feel queasy? He was sure it was nothing, but the only way to know was for him to take a look at what was inside the envelope. While he was trying to decide whether to snoop in the mailbox or rid himself of the binoculars first, the Larkins' front door flew open and out came Clara. Clara! She was heading for his house to practice. She stopped halfway across the street and pulled off her thick sweatshirt and tied it around her waist, revealing a shirt he'd never seen before. Tight and low-cut. He groaned in pleasure. Mailboxes, binoculars, they could all wait.

Thirteen

Unlike most of her peers, Nina hadn't come to her marriage a virgin. She wasn't a virgin the morning of her first wedding, either, the one that did not result in marriage. She was to wed her high school boyfriend. He'd finished college and was working in his father's accounting firm. The years of heavy petting in the front seat of his car had progressed in the last months to quick and furtive sex in the back seat. They were careful, but it was still nerve-racking, counting the days between periods. Nina couldn't wait until they were married and could go to sleep and wake up together and do all the other things married people did in an actual bed. The wedding was scheduled for a brilliant Saturday in May on the North Shore of Long Island. They planned a small ceremony at church and a cake and champagne reception in her parents' backyard. She'd stood in her bedroom window the morning of the wedding and watched her father and a neighbor unfold rental chairs nearly levitating with happiness. When Patrick showed up at the door of her bedroom as the photographer was taking a picture of Nina pinning a corsage onto the lapel of her mother's pale blue suit, she still didn't suspect a thing. "You're not supposed to be here," she said, shooing him out of the room, laughing. "Where's your tux?" Then she noticed his eyes were red-rimmed. He'd been crying. And she knew. She knew because he didn't look at her in the white organza wedding gown embroidered with tiny shamrocks, a nod to his family, and whistle or grin or even say, *You're beautiful*. He said: "I'm so sorry."

After they made all the phone calls, and her father quietly asked the rental company to come pick up the chairs and tables and they distributed pieces of cake to the neighbors, after she returned all the gifts and spent so many hours crying in her room it seemed impossible her body could still produce tears, after she'd gone by herself to see *Cheaper by the Dozen* and as the lights went down spotted Patrick walking down the aisle with two buckets of popcorn and a tall blonde, she asked her boss about transferring out of Manhattan. She was a secretary for a medium-sized advertising agency in Midtown, and she was good at her job. "You like snow?" her boss asked her, out of the blue, a few weeks later. "There's an opening in the office in Rochester." Nina wasn't even sure she knew where Rochester was. Before Syracuse? Before Buffalo? It didn't matter. She said yes.

In the years between Patrick and Sam, Nina made a good life for herself in Rochester. She was happy enough. Not that happiness was ever a conscious goal, it was more of a gentle hope, a belief that if she worked hard to make good choices, practice kindness, rise up to meet her own personal moral code—based on the only thing about Catholicism that made perfect sense to her, *do unto others*—that the universe wouldn't reward her exactly, but might smooth the path a little. Both she and Patrick had come from families who went to church every Sunday, and when he pressed for sex, she was terrified by what might happen if they were caught, or worse. "Nina," Patrick had pleaded with her for weeks and weeks, "there is a difference between believing in God and believing in the church. We break rules all the time because they're dumb. What do a bunch of celibate priests and nuns know about love? You think God is sending them special information? These rules were made-up. We don't have to follow them." And so they hadn't and she would forever be grateful to Patrick for releasing her from the fear that had been instilled in her by the church. What he said made more sense to her than any ponderous sermon. She became a cheerful C & E Catholic—only attending Mass on Christmas and Easter. She'd released herself from the cycle of sin and forgiveness because Patrick was right, she was a good person, a person with a conscience and a heart. She didn't mind that at twenty-eight she was "over the hill" and still single. She dated, but most men annoyed her. They'd come into her apartment—a place she loved and worked very hard to afford, a space she kept tidy and welcoming—with their booming voices and dirty shoes. They'd put their feet on her coffee table and freely rummage through the refrigerator, leaving dirty plates and empty beer bottles wherever they'd sat. She had the occasional overnight guest but always woke up in the middle of the night and wanted to ask whomever it was to leave. Having a man in her bed felt like a violation of her feminine space: the snoring, the rank night breath, the tossing and turning and tugging of sheets and blankets. She'd prefer to share her space with a cat or a dog, but abandoning a pet all day while she worked seemed cruel.

"Aren't you scared to be alone?" her married friends asked, but she didn't feel she lived alone. She lived on the second floor of a beautiful building in an old, historic part of Rochester, close to downtown, where her office was located. Some of the older homes had been renovated into apartments and hers had a working fireplace in the living room and a bay window in the bedroom. The street she lived on had a wide grass median in the middle of the road, and every spring a line of magnolia trees would burst into magnificent pink bloom. Her downstairs neighbor, Margaret, owned the building and had become a friend, almost like a sister, to Nina, who had two actual sisters back in Long Island who were much older and completely uninterested in Nina, confused by both her career and lack of a husband and children.

Margaret gave her a taste of something new, a life built only around herself, not around some nebulous concept of husband and children. Nina didn't know any adults who were happier than Margaret, who ran her father's bar downtown, keeping books, managing purchasing, occasionally filling in behind the bar, where she was a no-nonsense verbal executioner of the overly drunk regulars when they needed to be put in line. She drove a light blue–and-white Dodge pickup truck that was at least fifteen years old and rumbled so loudly when Margaret turned the ignition that it served as Nina's morning alarm. The souped-up muffler extension meant that Nina could hear Margaret arriving home minutes before she pulled into the driveway. Margaret was going to take over the bar when her father was ready to retire and had an entire notebook full of ideas and plans for how to update it—"Bring into the nineteenth century," she'd joke. "But not until Pops gives the go ahead. When he's ready, I'll be ready."

Nina'd heard the murmurings about Margaret, and she wasn't blind. She'd seen the young women leaving Margaret's apartment early in the morning wearing last night's clothes. Some of the men who came to Margaret's regular Sunday dinners brought other men. It was all fine with her. She wasn't a prude, and she wasn't judgmental. All these people had taken her in; she was part of their ad hoc family.

Nina was happy. So nobody was more surprised than she when she started dating Sam Larkin. He was one of the creative directors at her agency working mostly on the local phone company and Xerox—two huge accounts. As the office manager, she scheduled all the conference rooms. He never sent his secretary to schedule his meetings; he came to her desk to do it himself. The first time he asked her out to dinner, she thought he was teasing.

"Teasing?" he said, confused. "Why?"

She politely declined and he bided his time. He kept stopping by her desk. Pointing out certain local art shows or telling her about the new restaurants he'd tried. When they talked about their pending weekends, he was always doing something interesting. Going to the art museum or the planetarium or to see the philharmonic or to a local park. Or he was taking the train to New York City for a show or the ballet. She assumed he brought dates on these occasions. He never asked her to join him, but he would recap the events on Monday. She didn't know anything about opera or classical music, but he never made her feel dumb. He made her feel like telling her about Brahms or Verdi or Tchaikovsky was the best part of his day. He was a perfect gentleman. He wooed her with information and good manners. After a few months, by which time she was dying for him to ask her out again, when he suggested she might want to accompany him to the local awards dinner—Sam and the agency were nominated—he barely got the sentence out before she blurted, "I'd love to."

By then, they knew each other more than a little. And after six weeks of dating and dinner with his parents, who seemed both nervous and thrilled that he'd brought someone home to meet them (had he never brought anyone home before?), they were engaged. He proposed with his grandmother's opal-and-emerald wedding ring. Sam's mother was frail, and his father had heart problems, and Sam wanted a small and quick wedding, before he lost one of them. They would both be dead before Clara was born, barely two years into marriage.

At the beginning it was easy to tell herself that the awkwardness of living with Sam was getting to know each other, that they had both lived alone longer than most people who married, and of course it was an adjustment, and Sam was being respectful. She tried everything she could think to send the right signals, let him know she was eager for a greater intimacy. Lingerie, alcohol, candlelit dinners, breakfast in bed, which she hoped would segue into something more romantic. He was appreciative and enthusiastic, but they never quite got beyond their initial unease. They had sex, but it was quick, and whenever she tried to get him to slow down, pay attention, it seemed to have the opposite effect.

It made a peculiar type of sense to Nina that her growing love for Finn somehow made her a better wife to Sam. Her love for Finn seemed to take shape overnight and feel both inevitable and thrilling and had created a valuable distance, a kind of airlock, between her and her marriage. When she stopped longing and hoping for a different intimacy, she fully appreciated what a great father Sam was, his nimble mind and good looks, his professional ambitions. Sure, he was occasionally distant and moody. He was human. But then she would be jerked back to the reality of her situation. She couldn't occupy this forlorn space forever. Finn was pushing them to do something, anything. Well, not anything. He was pushing for the universal undo, and he was antsy. He was done with Honey, and he was going to move on—with Nina or without her. Nina knew she had to choose between staying rooted in the life she'd built with Sam or giving up Finn. Once he managed to get a divorce from Honey—and she had no doubt he would—he wouldn't be single for long. She wasn't so lovestruck that she couldn't see the inevitable. But completely blowing up her life to create a new one with Finn *and* her daughters *and* his children *and* somehow incorporate their ex-spouses into the mix? Who did she think she was? She was a housewife with a food column in Rochester, New York, and maybe divorce was "sweeping the nation," as *Newsweek* had just put on the cover, but not in her world. Not in any way that looked exciting or desirable or, frankly, even tolerable. Custody battles and squalid apartments and downsizing and kids who walked around looking drawn and confused. Bitterness, anger. She didn't know a single person whose marriage had ended who didn't seem more miserable than before. Or if they were happier, their circumstances were reduced—the quaint phrase from Jane Austen always came to mind.

Sam would not only be blindsided by her request for a divorce, he would never agree to one, and on what grounds? Lack of ardor? Not enough foreplay? Kissing wasn't hot?

"Aren't you *angry*?" Bess used to ask her. "Aren't you just furious all the time at how unfair it all is?"

If Nina was angry then, she couldn't locate it, and Bess seemed angry enough for everyone. A small scandal on their block had erupted earlier in the summer when Bess was quoted in the newspaper after leading a workshop as part of a regional conference for women called "Speak-out." Her session, "Women and Anger," had sold out so quickly the organizers asked her to hold three more and there was still a waiting list. "Why," a local reporter asked Bess, "do you think so many women are angry?"

"Where do I begin?" Bess said to him, rolling her eyes. "We're indentured servants in our own homes, forced to obey the whims of children and husbands. It's exhausting and maddening. We can't catch a break. We've been told we have more opportunity, but nobody's giving us a hand with our existing opportunity. How are we supposed to do all these new things liberation has brought into our lives and find the time to still run everyone else's lives? It's not like you can drop your kids off somewhere for a few days or weeks or months. There is no Lollypop Farm for children," she said, referencing the animal adoption farm that held regular tours for elementary schools. The backlash had been swift.

"NO LOLLYPOP FARM FOR CHILDREN"
Says Local School Nurse

The headline was splashed across page two of the front section of the next day's paper. The letters to the editor went on for weeks. Even Bess, who seemed to have a spine of steel since her divorce, was cowed. She had to meet with the principal and the head of the school's board to explain herself and apologize. Her kids were mortified and Bess was a social pariah for months and she hadn't even *done* anything, she'd only *said* a thing.

She suspected Bess knew what was going on with her and Finn. Bess walked in on them one night having a heated argument in Finn and Honey's kitchen during a party. In the midst of all the confusion, Nina had allowed herself one fantasy: that once all the children in both of their houses were safely off to college, they would do something. "Three years," she said to Finn that night. "We can hold on for three years."

"Three years is—" Finn said. "No."

"No what?"

"No, I'm not waiting. I'm leaving Honey at the end of the year."

"She agreed?" Nina felt a queasy combination of hope and fear.

"No, but I've found a way. I'm moving on with my life before I drop dead in the produce department like my father."

"You're not your father."

"Unless I am."

"Three years will go by so fast," she said even as she knew it wasn't true. Rochester was small. Their world was even smaller. They were bound to be caught. It was a miracle they hadn't been spotted somewhere yet. She was pleading with him, whispering, when Bess opened the door. A startled Nina blurted out, "I'm annoying Finn about the type of produce he carries." It was such an absurd sentence, so dumb given her tear-streaked face and his heightened color.

"Okaaayyy," Bess said, looking back and forth and raising an eyebrow to Nina as if to say, *Do you need help here?* after which Nina quickly shook her head. "Then I will leave you two to continue discussing—*produce*."

Bess, bless her, never brought it up again.

After the produce incident, they'd agreed to take a break. Think. Regroup. But Nina couldn't think or regroup. She was miserable and couldn't see her way through to any kind of resolution. She didn't want to be this person: guilt-ridden, traitorous, impatient, distracted, unhappy, occasionally mean. She broke it off with him but suggested they could still be friends! Still have their lunches! They could still talk about the kids and politics and his stores and her column but could not touch each other. They could not have sex.

"Nina," Finn said when she laid it all out for him. They were standing by their cars in Ellison Park on an unusually cold day in late September, both wearing winter coats still smelling of mothballs. He stared up at the sky for a long time, and she had the completely demented thought that he was going to hit her. Instead, he breathed in deeply and exhaled and looked at her and said, "I don't want to be your friend. I love you. I want to marry you. I want to live with you."

It took her breath away. It was simultaneously the only thing she wanted to hear and the last thing she wanted to hear. It was an impossibility. It was a dream. "I can't see the path," she eventually said. "I can't even fathom how we get from here"—she looked around at their pathetic rendezvous spot—"to a world where we're together. Married. I can't. Aren't you guilty? I feel awful all the time. A terrible wife, a worse mother."

"I don't believe in guilt," he said.

She laughed, a sharp, bitter sound. "How convenient."

"I don't believe guilt is helpful, how about that?" He grabbed both her hands, pleading, "Don't you think we deserve to be happy?"

"I think *everyone* deserves to be happy. I don't think I deserve happiness at the expense of other people I love. My girls. Your kids. What are we teaching them if we just take off and put ourselves first and upend their entire lives? What does that say about vows and duty and obligation?"

"That a mistake should not be a life sentence. We show them how to correct."

She hit him, a joke of a punch. She'd never hit anyone in her life; she'd never even gently slapped the girls on their bottoms. She tried to punch him in the solar plexus, make it hurt, but it landed softly and he grabbed her wrist and said, "Nina, please. Marry me."

She started sobbing. She couldn't look at him. "Don't be cruel. I can't marry you."

"But do you want to?"

"That's not the right question."

"It's the only question."

That was four weeks ago.

And now, this envelope tucked into a book. This madness. Had he lost his mind? She wasn't entirely sure where the Dominican Republic was on the map, but it looked pretty. She went into her office and spread all the documents out on her desk—the hotel brochures, the article clipped from the *New York Times* about divorce tourism, the airline tickets with open-ended dates to and from Santo Domingo via New York City, the photos of the hotel rooms and balconies and restaurants leading out to a bright blue swimming pool—and started to read.

Fourteen

Within minutes of her arrival, Clara was angrily pacing his bedroom, and Dune realized they were on the verge of their first argument, and although he didn't have experience in these matters, he was pretty sure their first argument should not happen this soon. Clara arrived idling at ninety, going on and on about some late-night creative impulse, and after an overly long windup, she'd revealed her choice of audition song.

"'Send in the Clowns'?" Dune said, perplexed. "I don't see how it can work for the audition." He'd set Clara off.

"Well, let me draw a picture," she said, putting the Judy Collins album on the record player and choreographing a performance where she mimed blowing up a series of balloons, tying them into a bunch, and being pulled around the room by the balloons. Clara tugged the balloons in one direction and the balloons pulled her back. She'd sit and the balloons would lift her back up. "See?" she said, dropping the pretend balloons and turning to him triumphantly. "Like that."

"Okay. Cool. But I do have a technical question."

"Shoot."

"Those balloons wouldn't have helium in them, so how could they float up by themselves and pull a, you know, fully grown human?"

Clara sighed. Pursed her lips. Looked away. Looked annoyed. "Creative license," she said. "Remember when Mr. Goodwin said we should think of the apostles as *clown-like*? Remember how they all dressed in the movie?"

"I don't think he meant us to be so literal."

"Well. Do you have a better idea?"

"I don't have one. Not at all," Dune said, even though he had about ten better ideas. He wanted to kiss Clara. He was afraid of Clara. "If we brainstorm together, we'll figure something out." She sat on the edge of his bed. She seemed to soften. "I mean," he said, "I'm thinking out loud, but maybe we should stay away from show tunes. I think everyone else will sing something from a musical, and if we don't, Mr. Goodwin would appreciate it."

Clara nodded. "Interesting."

Dune was so relieved he almost capitulated. But he loathed "Send in the Clowns." What did it even mean?

"What about," Clara said as Dune held his breath, "something by the Beatles?" She knew Dune loved the Beatles, and he recognized this as an offering. "Which song?" he asked.

"I don't know. Something we can have some fun with." She stood and started pacing back and forth, brow furrowed. She snapped her fingers. "Beatles. Godspell. 'My Sweet Lord.'"

"Interesting," Dune said, instead of what he was thinking: *No*. "A George song could work. But for the record, technically, it's not a Beatles song."

"What?"

"I mean, George wrote it, but not while he was in the Beatles. It was his first solo single. The Beatles were basically over in April of 1970 and George released the song in November." He watched the enthusiasm leach from her face with every word he said. What *was* he saying? What was wrong with him? But he couldn't stop. Clara was stone-faced. "Everyone thinks it's a Beatles song. It's a George song, but it's—it's not"—his voice started to fade—"a Beatles song. For the record, I mean."

"By all means, let's keep the record straight on these things."

"He probably started writing it while he was still a Beatle. I guess it doesn't matter."

"Okay," Clara sighed. "What do you think about the song 'My Sweet Lord,' written by the Beatle George Harrison but released by the *former* Beatle George Harrison?"

"I mean—I think—good? Maybe?"

"Too on the nose?"

"Maybe, yeah," he said, relieved.

"I'll think of something else."

"You just keep thinking, Butch. It's what you're good at." He was pleased he remembered the line from the movie; he knew it would make her laugh. It did.

"You're funny," she said.

"I am?"

"And cute. I don't care what song we use. As long as it's something fun and we get the parts we want." Dune was looking at her, but she could tell he wasn't listening to what she was saying. "Is that a new top?" he said.

"Kind of."

"It's really nice. You look really pretty. I really mean it."

"Three reallys. You must *really* like me." This kind of flirting was still new to them and the charge in the room was thrilling. "How come you're sitting all the way over there?"

He jumped up and walked over to the record player and put on a song he knew she loved, Elton John's "Your Song." He reached out to her as the first notes filled the room.

—It's a little bit funny
—this feeling inside

She took his hand. She didn't think anyone had ever looked at her so pleadingly in her life. "Come here," she said, linking their pinkies and pulling him back toward the bed. "Come kiss me right this second."

Fifteen

Because Sam was working late, Nina made breakfast for dinner, something she and the girls loved. Pancakes, bacon, lots of butter, and real maple syrup from Vermont. A bowl of strawberries. She loved the easy evenings when she didn't have to put up an entire dinner for Sam, complete with a salad to start and dessert to finish. Some nights the girls would hang out with her well past cleanup and have a cup of tea and become a little chattier than usual. Not tonight. Bridie had a test to study for. Clara had run upstairs the minute she was done eating, claiming homework and needing to practice for her *Godspell* audition.

Nina settled on the sofa with a book, enjoying the quiet of her living room. The next thing she knew, someone was banging on the door, and she woke with a start; she'd fallen asleep in front of the fireplace. She had been dreaming one of the girls was outside and locked out and Nina's legs were like molasses and she couldn't get to the door to rescue her daughter. As she sat up, she realized the banging wasn't in her dream but at her door, and she had the irrational thought that it was Sam's mother or father pounding on the door, back from the dead, "The Monkey's Paw" come to life thanks to the universal undo. Who would bang on the door at two in the morning? As she reached the vestibule, she heard Sam's voice and almost tripped over the rug with relief. She turned the lock and opened the door to find Sam with someone who looked vaguely familiar. A very young, very good-looking man. "Well, hello there," she said, looking at Sam whose arm was slung around the stranger's shoulders. He was quite drunk. "What have we here?"

"He's okay," the young man said. "A few too many Manhattans. He was insisting on driving home, so I took his keys. Can we come in?"

"Of course." Nina opened the door wider and took one of Sam's arms as he tripped over the threshold. "Sam, sit down."

"Love to!" he shouted.

"Quiet. The girls are sleeping." She turned to the young man. "I've never seen him like this." They each took one side of Sam and sloppily maneuvered him into the living room and onto the sofa, where he promptly passed out. The man started untying Sam's shoes. "You don't have to do that," Nina said.

"Not a problem."

"I'm sorry, but your name—"

"Garret."

"Have we met?"

"We have. At the conference in California. I work at PARC on the development end of things."

"Right. Yes. Nice to see you. I didn't realize you were in town. Sam didn't say. You could have come for dinner."

"That's kind. We had a meeting run late and everyone wanted a nightcap and some"—he gestured at Sam—"wanted a few nightcaps."

"He'll be mortified. Nothing like this has ever happened before. Where were you all?"

"I don't remember the name of the place. I'm not exactly stone-cold myself."

"Then you must stay. I don't want you driving."

"Someone else drove us. I'll head out now," Garret said. "Have Sam call me in the morning."

"Will do," Nina said. "Thanks again." As she walked out onto the front step with Garret, she recognized the rumble of a truck's engine. She looked over to see the familiar blue-and-white pickup that used to sit in the driveway in front of her old apartment. It couldn't be. She followed Garret and, when he opened the passenger door, bent down to see the person behind the wheel. That familiar face.

"*Margaret?*"

"Hi, doll. Long time, no see."

Sixteen

In December, the sun hightailed it out of town. Eleven days and counting. "256 Hours Without Appreciable Sunshine," the *Democrat & Chronicle* reported on its front page beneath a too-cute line drawing of an enormous gray cloud with Popeye-sized biceps, threatening a frowning sun saying, "My turn!" The article included the popular and empty reminder that Syracuse got even less sun than Rochester, as if trivia made anyone feel better during the interminable stretch of gloomy days.

Nina had relocated to Rochester during a glorious spring. Blue skies, soft breezes, lengthening days leading into comfortable nights. Everyone joked about the winters, and though she'd been told to prepare herself for the cold and the snow, no one had warned her about the unrelenting gray, about how the sky seemed to have a physical weight to it. About how damp and biting the days felt when the sun refused to show itself. Nina felt the lack of light in her bones.

Today, she was chaperoning Bridie's French class on a school trip to MAG, the Memorial Art Gallery. She often volunteered for these jaunts because she loved spying on the girls within their school configuration, but Honey was a near-constant parent chaperone and Nina was dreading seeing her today. Last month, a group of students had gone to a yoga studio run by the new drama teacher's girlfriend, Priscilla. Fern and Bridie had loved Priscilla and everything about her: her tights, her long braid and bare feet with painted toes, the quiet but forceful way she spoke. They loved the apartment with its bay window and a wicker chair that hung from the ceiling alongside a bunch of dangling spider ferns.

Nina was fascinated, too. Is this what her life would be like if she was still single in Rochester right now? The first thing Priscilla taught them all was belly breathing. She made the girls put their hands on their stomachs to make sure their bellies expanded on the inhale, "the opposite of how most people breathe." Honey fidgeted throughout the entire demonstration, angrily eyeing the dust balls in the corner of the room and complaining she couldn't possibly expand her stomach. "It's not how I breathe," she whined. And when they all got into Nina's car to drive home, Honey told Fern and Bridie to ignore what Priscilla had said.

"Why?" Fern asked. "Why can't we breathe to expand our horizons?"

"Because it will make you look pregnant."

"Mom!"

"Well, it will. You girls need to stand straight and suck your stomach in, keeping it flat and firm. You won't get a husband otherwise." Honey's favorite threat.

As Nina stood in the soaring Fountain Court, in front of the namesake fountain, which a little plaque told her was a replica of a Renaissance-era piece in Florence, she vowed to visit this elegant, peaceful space more often. The teacher was speaking to the girls in French, and though Nina could make out a word or two, she didn't pay attention until the docent arrived and they started their tour and Soeur Jeanne fell back with Nina and said to her, with concern, "Are you okay? You look pale."

"I do?" Nina said, genuinely surprised. She believed she was doing a great job with her exterior self, acting normal, looking normal. "I am a little tired," she said to the nun. "And these gray skies—"

"*Bien sur*," said Soeur Jeanne. "But when the sun does reappear, we will appreciate it so much more." She gave Nina a self-satisfied pat on the arm and Nina had to steel herself not to flinch. She gestured that she was heading to the ladies' room. "I'll catch up with you," she said.

If Bridie's teacher hadn't said anything, she might have assumed her pallor was due to the horrible lighting in the restroom, but she could see she looked terrible. She hadn't been eating or sleeping well since she'd told Finn he would have to move forward without her. And now this thing with Sam.

When Nina replayed the days at the conference, looking for signs she might have missed, she couldn't remember a single one. No kind of palpable energy between Garret and Sam. Sam wasn't nervous around Garret or vice versa. Neither of them seemed to pay more attention to each other than anyone else. What she did notice that weekend was how cultish the whole thing felt. It was the same at all those places: the Kodaks, the Xeroxes, the Finnegan's Grocers—they all declared themselves *families* as if they were engaged in some kind of higher purpose and not peddling food or film or paper. These paternalistic organizations run by men who seemed incapable of saying they were out to make a lot of money and protect their respective fiefdoms. No, they had to attach emotion to it, a sense of belonging to a greater good, a greater God. Funny how organizations mimicked religions. They all had mottos and retreats and acceptable clothing and spun highly specific visions and dreams for the future, all in the service of something they deemed noble. She guessed they forgot about the money changers in the temple.

Had she misinterpreted her entire marriage? Could it be that Sam wasn't attracted to any woman, ever? In a way it was a relief. In another way it was devastating. The morning after Margaret brought Sam home, Nina pulled *The Joy of Sex* off the shelf where she'd put it after liberating it from Clara's room (she was relieved Clara had filched the book; the illustrations would have terrified Bridie) and searched the index for homosexuality. But even that book, with its pages of prose and illustrations devoted to heterosexual relations in the tiniest and most enthusiastic detail, had barely anything to say about men having sex with men, except that men who wanted to "become" straight would need help overcoming "nonrelations with women." This seemed to place the blame squarely on Nina, which couldn't be right. She knew Sam loved her, in his way. She even believed he admired her physically. He liked her hair a certain way; he bought her beautiful clothes and jewelry. He just didn't want to touch her. She knew from her years living above Margaret's that plenty of gay men had made peace with their choices. She knew some of them were divorced. She knew some of them maintained a pretense of a heterosexual marriage. But none of them were her husband.

The morning after Margaret brought him home from the bar she'd inherited and made into a welcoming space for gay patrons, Sam apologized to her for *overdoing it.*

"Overdoing what?" she asked coolly.

"The drink. You know, when out with clients you have to match them one to one."

"Really?"

"Not a rule, but an unspoken practice," he said. "And that guy from PARC can really put it away."

"Garret?"

"Yeah. Garret. He's quite a drinker."

"And Margaret?"

"Margaret?"

Did he look genuinely surprised or was he feigning surprise? "My old landlady Margaret. Remember her?"

"Not really. What about her?"

"She drove you both home. I assumed from her bar."

"God, I don't know. I'm embarrassed to say I don't even remember coming home."

She believed that part. "She has a bar downtown."

"I don't know. There were a bunch of us and we went to a few places. Nowhere I'd ever been before."

She didn't push. She pocketed the information and for a few delirious days believed she had a free pass out of her marriage. But then she would imagine Clara and Bridie home alone with Sam, an image that always brought her up short, and now was even more complicated. She was stymied and confused, and the only tolerable option was staying with her girls. What other choice did she have? For all she knew, the drink with Garret really was nothing.

In the days immediately after telling Finn he needed to move on without her, she was elated, brimming with nobility and sacrifice. And then the sun disappeared, and the gray invaded the city, her house, her corporeal being. She imagined her insides as completely leached of color, and, looking at herself in the mirror of the bathroom at the museum, she saw she was fading on the outside, too.

The bathroom door swung open and in came Honey Finnegan. "Oh, hello!" Honey said. "I was wondering where you disappeared to."

"I'm right here." Nina took a lipstick out of her purse and applied the color to her lips, but it only made her look worse. She had the fleeting notion, standing next to Finn's lawful wife, that sex with Finn was a magic elixir her body couldn't do without. It certainly felt that way. And it certainly looked that way.

"I'll see you upstairs, Honey," she said to the bathroom stall where she could tell Honey was layering the toilet seat with paper.

Upstairs, she caught up with the class in front of a Monet, one of the museum's prized paintings. The museum's docent was an overly enthusiastic woman in her sixties wearing a sensible shirtwaist dress and flats. She explained how Monet had painted Waterloo Bridge in London multiple times during the winter of 1901. How lucky, the docent trilled, that one of them landed at MAG so anyone in Rochester could come see it for themselves. This one, she said, is called *Waterloo Bridge: Veiled Sun*. Of course it was. Not even the paintings in Rochester were allowed full sun.

"You can line up in pairs and get a bit closer," the docent said. She pointed at the piece of tape on the floor marking the point beyond where visitors' feet should not transgress. Bridie and Fern and Nina were last to approach the painting, Nina behind them. Bridie leaned in and as she did her toes went past the tape.

"Not too close!" the docent snapped.

"Sorry, sorry," Bridie said, cheeks turning scarlet. "The colors are so pretty."

Nina put a hand on Bridie's shoulder. "You're good. I wish I could touch it, too."

"Okay." The docent clapped her hands and motioned the girls out of the room. "Moving right along."

Nina stayed behind. Monet wasn't her favorite. All those water lilies. But this painting drew her in. Imagine seeing this bridge at night—the rain, the shadows, the warm lights of Big Ben in the distance. She could almost hear the rumble of the London taxis and the rush of pedestrians on the bridge.

"It's beautiful, isn't it?" Honey appeared beside her.

"Yes. Have you been to London?"

"Years and years ago. Before Fern was born. We left Dune with my mother and Finn and I took a few weeks in Europe. London, Paris, Rome, Venice."

"Sounds magical."

"It was," Honey said. "Of course you couldn't get a decent cup of coffee anywhere. And the food was quite rich. Don't get me started on the toilet paper!"

Nina stared at her and forced a laugh. "I guess you were happy to get back to the good ole USA."

"I was." Honey nodded, oblivious to Nina's sarcasm. "I'm going to find the girls. You coming?"

"In a minute." She stood by herself and looked back at the painting. She'd love to go to London. Or to France to see Monet's garden. Or anywhere in Europe. Or anywhere that wasn't the Finger Lakes. She was in the room alone now, so she crept even closer to the painting than Fern had. She tried to understand how someone could do what Monet did, how a bunch of brushstrokes could become this seductive image. What did it feel like to make something so alive and satisfying by squeezing tubes of color onto a paint palette?

"Our children are nearly adults," Finn had repeatedly argued. "They will be out of the house so soon. This will be a tiny blip in the story of their lives, and you know what else?" God, he was so sure, so confident. "When they're older, they'll understand. They'll get why we did what we had to do." Sometimes his arguments made sense. She hadn't told him about Sam and the night with Garret. Finn would only see Sam's behavior as an advantage to exploit. He would go scorched earth. She couldn't do it to the girls.

How could Honey, a person who didn't seem interested in anything extraordinary or beautiful, belong to Finn? How was it possible for her to go through the rest of her life, ceding the love of her life to a woman so vacuous and unappreciative? Well, someone else would get him. Finn would eventually find someone else.

She thought about how little she'd traveled, how much of the world she hadn't seen, and tried to imagine doing it with Sam once the girls were gone and was overcome with regret and sadness. She thought about Finn and his nameless, faceless younger new wife taking the kind of grand vacations he'd promised Nina. Hawaii. Japan. Rome. Athens. She thought about sitting home while he escorted the second Mrs. Finnegan into an elegant restaurant in Paris. She thought about what Finn had said the first day at the lake: "This is going to be trouble."

When she and Finn had met briefly last week, he'd made an undeniable argument. "You think we've stopped, but we are never going to stop, and we will get caught, which will be much worse than taking this thing into our own hands."

She hadn't replied, but his words had wormed their way into her head and reverberated constantly. He was right. She knew, deep down, that the same thing that had happened in June, in early August, in late August, for most of September, and again in October was barreling toward her again. A phone call. A furtive meeting. A release.

And yet.

Still alone in the room with *Veiled Sun*, she slid her feet past the tape on the floor. She extended the tip of one finger out in front of her and let it hover right above the painting, right above the brushstrokes put there by Monet's hand so long ago. She let her finger get closer and closer to the canvas, until she could feel the edge of one of the white crests of the Thames, the one right above Monet's signature. She pressed lightly. Then harder. She heard footsteps in the corridor and quickly stepped back, feeling intoxicated and fearless. Touching the painting had felt fine. Better than fine. It had felt incredible.

Seventeen

Fern was the first to know. She woke up early. Her bedside glow-in-the-dark clock said quarter to five in the morning. She tried to fall back asleep, but she had to urinate, so she pulled on her robe, slid her feet into her pink terry-cloth slippers and went down the hall to the bathroom. She didn't turn the light on because she didn't want to rouse herself to wakefulness. She reached for the toilet paper only to find an empty roll. Her brother. He never ever replaced the toilet paper. It was infuriating. She gingerly crept forward in the dark, underpants at her knees, to reach the under-sink cabinet. She grabbed a roll and scurried back to the toilet, finished her business and pulled up her pants. As she was repositioning a fresh roll of toilet paper into its holder, she heard the front door open and close.

She went to the window and drew aside the curtain. A cold front had moved in, and the lawn was silvery with frost. A light snow falling. She couldn't see who was in the car. It was awfully early for anyone to be awake and driving somewhere, but sometimes her dad had to get to one of the stores extra early for a shipment or a problem that had cropped up overnight. Smoke was rising from the exhaust pipe, the frantic rhythm of the windshield wipers not helping much with the layer of ice on the windshield. The car wasn't warm enough. And then the strangest thing happened. Fern saw Mrs. Larkin hurrying across the street carrying a mint-green suitcase with an ivory leather border. She recognized the suitcase because she and Bridie used it when they pretended to be Maria von Trapp leaving the convent and marching through town singing and swinging her luggage. The inside of the suitcase was also light green except for one corner where beige powder from a compact had spilled, staining the fabric.

The driver's door opened, and her father stepped out. Dressed for work in a suit and tie. He hurried down the driveway and met Mrs. Larkin halfway. Took her suitcase and opened the trunk. Fern stood still as a statue, but her teeth started chattering even though she wasn't cold. She watched as her father opened the passenger door and Mrs. Larkin slid inside. Her father bent down to kiss Mrs. Larkin right on the lips.

"Dad?" Fern said quietly. Her heart started beating erratically. Her palms started to sweat. She couldn't possibly be witnessing what it seemed like she was witnessing. She put both her hands on the window, started banging with her flattened palm. But he didn't hear her. He got into the car and adjusted his rearview mirror. Reversed down the driveway.

"Dad!" She raised her voice a little but not so much as to wake her mother or brother. Between the bathroom window and the car windows, even if she screamed they wouldn't hear her through the glass and across the lawn. She waved both hands, trying to get her father's attention. She didn't know what was happening, but she knew if she didn't stop it, it would be very bad. She ran down the stairs and flung open the front door just as the car turned out of the driveway and onto the street. She ran across the lawn in her bare feet.

From the passenger side, Nina Larkin turned and saw Fern. Fern instinctively waved and saw Mrs. Larkin raise her hand and quickly drop it and turn her gaze forward. Her father said something to Mrs. Larkin, smiled, but he didn't notice Fern. He put the car in drive and slowly drove down the street.

"Dad!" Fern started running, but her feet were so cold and the road so slippery and it was still dark. "DAD! STOP!" she yelled. She couldn't run as fast as the car was moving, and her father didn't hear her. She kept going—she'd never run so fast in her life, and even though it was freezing, she kept going and going, but by the time she was halfway down the block, whimpering and shivering, the car was out of sight. They were gone.

Eighteen

Clara knew the minute she walked into the kitchen that something was wrong. The only time their mother wasn't already up and making breakfast before Clara came down was when she was sick, which Clara could remember happening maybe three times in her entire life. She could hear her father knocking around upstairs, whistling along with the radio. The note was sitting on the kitchen table, propped up against a wooden bowl full of apples, the glossy beige envelope looking like a wedding invitation. Clara's and Bridie's names were carefully written on the outside in their mother's distinctive Palmer method script and in the royal-blue ink she favored. Clara ripped the envelope carelessly and skimmed the sentences quickly, not able to take it all in at once, but catching fragments of the whole.

My darling girls—with Mr. Finnegan—I'll explain in person—need to see your beautiful faces—don't believe what other people say—be kind to your father—be good to each other—I'm home Saturday—promise all will be well—love—love—love

Clara stood rooted in place. She heard someone laughing and looked up and realized she was laughing. This wasn't real. She tried to make sense of what she'd read. She walked into the living room, still holding the note, and looked across the street to the Finnegans' house. Dune! Was Dune awake and reading a similar madness from his father? But their house was completely dark and though that was the least strange thing about this morning it nagged at her. Her father was coming down the stairs and she wanted to run out the front door to Dune's house or to the fire alarm box at the end of their street to pull the lever and signal this emergency. She lurched toward the door and stopped when she realized she was wearing torn gym shorts and her faded purple T-shirt from seventh grade that said, I CAN'T BELIEVE I ATE THE WHOLE THING! She looked dumbly at her father as he entered the living room.

    She handed him the note.

Nineteen

By the time they'd reached the Rochester airport, a speedy twelve-minute ride, Nina realized she'd made a terrible mistake. All she could see in her mind's eye was Fern. Fern flying out of the house and down the front walk. Fern standing in her bare feet in the falling snow. Fern frantically waving. Those terrible seconds when she locked eyes with Fern. She'd almost waved back until she remembered what she was up to with Fern's father. In that moment, she could have said something to Finn, who hadn't seen Fern, but then he took her hand, smiled reassuringly, and said, "Here we go." And they left.

As they landed in New York for their connecting flight, she made a beeline for the departures board, looking for the next flight back to Rochester. Three from JFK in the afternoon, the first only a few hours away. He could go on without her, get his divorce, and start over, but her life couldn't transform into a cacophony of heartbreak.

But Finn took her arm and led her to the Pan Am terminal with its flying saucer–like roof, up a flight of stairs, and through a door marked CLIPPER CLUB, which even at this early hour was full of businessmen drinking screwdrivers and tall glasses of beer and other beverages that seemed more appropriate for a smoky bar late at night. She could see how the airport existed in suspension. What time zone had all these people come from and where were they going? You couldn't tell much by looking at a person. Nobody would suspect that Finn, walking toward her holding two extravagantly garnished Bloody Marys, a perfect picture of a successful businessman in his pin-striped suit with the wide lapels, white shirt, and neatly arranged hair, had just run out on his wife. Nobody would look at Nina in her black A-line shift and tidy ballet flats and think, *That's a woman who just abandoned her family.*

After the second drink, Nina let herself be guided once more to their connecting flight. On the plane to Santo Domingo, an upbeat Finn acted as if the confounding betrayals and confusing legalities were behind them and this was a honeymoon, fully sanctioned by their loved ones and friends, blessed by state and church. Nina recoiled from his smugness. She turned her head to the small window. Finn opened his briefcase and went through piles of memos and what looked like inventory sheets while she tried to stop the distant beat of a Bloody Mary headache. She was queasy. She tried slow, deep breaths like the silly yoga teacher had instructed and mercifully fell asleep until they landed.

When she woke and woozily stepped off the plane into the Caribbean sun, she felt as if she crossed into Oz. The heat and humidity hit her like a punch. She didn't know where her sunglasses were. She shielded her eyes and grabbed the railing to walk down the steel staircase leading from the door of the plane.

The heat on the tarmac was brutal. Finn was carrying her winter coat, and though she'd picked a lightweight worsted wool dress to wear on the plane, she immediately broke out into a sweat. She looked at her watch. Two p.m. Last period. Bridie had math and Clara would be in AP American History. "Lord, it's hot," she said. She'd expected the bright sun but thought the air would sit light on her skin, not this thick, weighted atmosphere.

"Wait until we're sitting by the hotel pool. You won't mind the heat." Finn stopped on the tarmac and turned to her, took her in his arms in front of everyone and kissed her on the lips, deeply, brazenly. It was the first time they'd been affectionate in public, and even though the other people watching them were complete strangers, the kiss was electric and reassuring. When they arrived at the hotel and she opened the door to their room, she was overwhelmed by the scent of roses. Finn had filled the ocean-view suite with roses of all colors. Red and white and pink and yellow. In the middle of it all, a silver bucket with condensed water droplets on the outside, an expensive bottle of champagne cooling. She froze, stood holding her purse. Finn unlatched his bag and reached in for a camera and film. The bright yellow box with the Kodak logo was such a familiar sight from home (it was not her home anymore; it had stopped being her home when she left this morning) it startled her.

"You're taking pictures?" she asked.

"Of course. Don't you want to remember the first days of the rest of our lives?" He fiddled with the lens a little and brought the camera up to his eye. "Smile."

That photo was the first one they'd see when they developed the roll: Nina, still in her traveling clothes, backlit from the light coming in from their balcony so her face was somewhat shadowed, though you could see the furrowed brow, her lips slightly parted but not smiling. One hand clasping her handbag. The toes of her left foot grinding into the carpet. She looked more like a hostage than a bride.

Twenty

Sam hadn't believed her. He'd thought she would never leave the girls. But as soon as he came down the stairs and saw the bewilderment on Clara's face, the note in her hand, he knew he'd underestimated Nina's unhappiness. And her strength. Because Sam had spent his entire life perfecting the art of looking away, the sidelong glance, he understood the courage it took to face your life dead-on and walk out the door.

His ability to craft a story that sometimes ran concurrent to truth and sometimes briefly intersected with it was why he was so good at his job. He could make an audience see what he wanted them to see. You could convince most people of anything if you offered a highly specific narrative. His was easy to summarize: Only child of two loving older parents. Lively bachelorhood until he met the one person he couldn't pass up just as he was ready to settle down. Two daughters—one the spitting image of him, one of his wife, both smart as a whip. Highly successful advertising executive until Xerox lured him away to work in-house and lead the marketing team. Tough but fair boss. Loved good food, nice wine, the occasional game of tennis. Hated golf. Hated the country club even more. Dutiful if disinterested churchgoer. Nobody suspected he had any secrets. He'd been careful.

As a kid, Sam understood it was not okay to openly desire boys but was foggy on whether it was okay to desire them secretly. For many years, he didn't have a word to define his feelings but knew he was lucky in specific ways. He was handsome and athletic and smart. Girls liked him. He wasn't the target of verbal or physical abuse like Billy Jensen, who lived on his street. Sam tried not to join in when the other kids called Billy a fairy or a homo or a fag. When he asked his mother what the words meant, she'd been annoyed. "Don't repeat those things. It's not nice. Billy's okay," she would say. "Just a bit peculiar." *Peculiar* became the word he mentally applied to the boys who seemed like him. But even that was guesswork.

The year he entered Amherst, Alfred Kinsey's *Sexual Behavior in the Human Male* posited that 37 percent of adult American men had had at least one orgasm with another man and, of even greater interest to Sam, claimed that having erotic feelings for people of the same gender was an ordinary human impulse. Ordinary! The campus babble around Kinsey's claims—even though they were decried as outrageous by his fellow students—gave him a glimmer of hope. Was this a phase? Could he learn to desire women? He had tried. He was a virgin in spite of having been dragged along to a brothel in high school by his friends on the tennis team where a kinder-than-he-deserved, scantily clad woman gamely tried to make him hard and promised his difficulty was "perfectly normal," and when they all reconvened in the entryway of the house of ill repute, had waved and said, "Bye-bye, stud. Thanks for the ride." He'd wanted to run back and give her another $5, but he hadn't had it.

Everyone on the Amherst campus was warned not to use the men's bathrooms at the bus station because they were populated by deviants and perverts. Returning from his first trip home from Thanksgiving break, he casually strolled into the fetid lavatory and back to the storied last stall, which, indeed, had a middle-aged man sitting on the closed toilet seat smoking a cigarette and waiting for company. The man dropped his cigarette on the floor and ground it beneath his unexpectedly professional black wing-tipped shoe. He gestured for Sam to come closer. He was wearing a suit, not a particularly expensive one, but well-kept. Sam stepped into the stall and closed and latched the door behind him. The man unzipped Sam's pants and started to fondle him. It was so fast and so welcome that all Sam could do was place both hands on the surrounding metal partition and try to muffle his cries. As he was finishing, another person entered the restroom and went straight to the sink to wash his hands while singing "when Johnny comes marching home again, hurrah, hurrah," and the man on the toilet seat put a finger to his lips, motioning Sam to keep quiet while he lifted his feet off the floor to conceal his presence. They both held their breath until the interloper exited, and as the man on the toilet reached back out for Sam he panicked. He flew out of the bathroom and didn't even bother trying to find a cab to campus. He ran back, his duffel banging against his thigh, terrified of nothing in particular and everything at once.

He didn't go to class the next day, he was so ashamed. He took three showers and went to the barber for a crew cut, as if his hair had borne witness and might give him away. He went to church first thing in the morning and knelt in the wooden pew, praying for forgiveness and strength, silently begging God to make him different. He vowed abstinence and promised he would only think of women, practice self-abnegation. It didn't work, of course. He'd return to the bathroom in the bus station every time he came back to school and the man in the wing-tipped shoes told him about a nearby park where Sam would also go, terrified each and every time he would encounter someone dangerous, familiar, or, worst of all, an undercover vice cop.

He became furtive in action and thought, barely admitting to himself what he was doing before, during, and after, which gave the encounters a dreamy quality and allowed him to compartmentalize the touch, the arousal, the sometimes-violent orgasm not as a part of his life but as part of a smaller Sam that lived in a tiny place buried deep inside.

One of the hardest parts of all this was denying his parents something they wanted very much. A daughter-in-law, grandchildren. If his parents suspected anything, they never let on. His ongoing bachelorhood started to not only exhaust him—he was mildly shocked by the number of women he dated who were eager to have sex before marriage—but to get him a reputation as someone who was not serious about relationships, a careless lothario. When he was promoted to creative director of his advertising agency at only thirty-two, his boss took him out to lunch and said that although dating a lot of women was perfectly well and fine and fun, there came a time in life when a man needed someone at home. A partner. A spouse.

So when Nina Larkin waltzed into the office one morning, all long legs and swinging brown hair and with a vibrant bemused smile, he felt something inside him stir and thought, *Finally*. She'd been hired to assist the soon-to-retire office manager, but she was so competent her predecessor left earlier than expected—out of relief or embarrassment. Nina not only had a way with organization and systems, but she had good creative instincts. Once, taking notes during a meeting where he and his staff were brainstorming ideas for a campaign for the local telephone company and talking about using animated cartoon characters, he said, "I don't know. What are we missing here about telephones?"

"They connect people," Nina said, looking up, not hesitating to contribute in the slightest. "Cartoons are funny, but they're not emotional." She was right. Sam won his fifth Clio for the "Only Connect" campaign. He invited Nina as his date and they got tipsy and laughed all night, and when the winner was announced, she leaned over and kissed him on the cheek before he took the stage.

He thought, *I'm saved*. By the time he knelt at the altar on his wedding day, he'd stopped believing that God would come to his rescue. Praying felt like calling someone who never answered, but he believed in himself. He believed he could harness temperance, fidelity, and change with Nina by his side.

But of course—

He was always careful, but he wasn't always scrupulous. Once, in Chicago on business, his hotel was near a small bar called the Wagging Wheel, and he noticed a lot of men—only men—going in and out. One night, he had three quick drinks in the hotel bar and strolled down the block. He stood on the sidewalk watching the bar's door for nearly an hour until he worked up the courage to walk in, head lowered, ready to cut and run if the scene was wrong, but it wasn't wrong at all. Men of all ages, casually talking at the bar, some playing pool in the back room. Ella Fitzgerald was on the jukebox, and a few couples were slow dancing in the corner. The feeling of the place was warm and curious. He ordered a drink and talked a little to the bartender who recommended an exhibit at the art museum and to another man who told him about a great rib joint near Wrigley Field. He left quickly but went back the next night and the night after that and both times brought someone back to his hotel room. The encounters left him briefly exhilarated and swiftly flattened by shame.

He told himself every time he was getting it out of his system, but what happened instead was that he took in the full possibility of himself, and that self was growing larger. After Chicago, things got sloppier. Like his frequent visit to the third dressing room on the right at the JCPenney downtown, which had phone numbers of interested men scrawled in pencil near the hook to hang clothes.

He told himself that because what he was doing was purely sexual in nature, a necessary release, it was okay. Something that allowed him to focus on being a good father and provider. He endured sex with Nina until she seemed to lose interest, which he assumed was normal after having two babies. She was tired. He was tired. Sometimes they'd hold hands. Kisses became pecks. He'd believed he could probably continue with the bifurcated life he'd created for a long time. Forever. Until he met Garret.

Twenty-One

Honey knew the second she woke up that something was wrong. Finn was always up ahead of her. She'd never been a morning person, and even when the kids were very small, he would let her sleep in an extra thirty or forty minutes and wake her by placing a steaming mug of coffee on the bedside table, the gentlest alarm. Even when they were arguing, even during the past weeks, when a foreboding chill had settled over the house, he'd brought her morning coffee. Black with two packets of Sweet'N Low.

That morning, not only was there no coffee, but the house was unusually cold. Finn always turned the thermostat up when he woke. The sky was lightening. Why was the house so quiet? Where was her coffee? She flew out of bed and down the stairs. "Finn?" She went into the kitchen and turned on the lights. "Finn? Are you here?"

"Mommy." Fern's voice from the corner of the room. She was sitting in the breakfast nook, wrapped in a blanket.

"Fern. What are you doing sitting here in the dark. What's going on? Where's Daddy?"

"Gone," Fern said, pushing an envelope across the surface of the small wooden table.

"YOU WOULDN'T DARE" WAS WHAT Honey'd said to Finn weeks ago when he brought up divorce over lunch at the diner nearest his office—a burger platter for him, a plate of cottage cheese with tomatoes for her. At first, she didn't understand the gravity of the situation. She thought he was complaining about work or maybe something to do with the kids. She started out sympathetic, telling him he should take some time for himself. Maybe get back into golf, which he'd neglected since he started jogging, a pastime she loathed because his running clothes never seemed to get as clean as she wanted. "Maybe we should plan a week at the lake," she'd said.

"I'm not talking about taking up a hobby," he said.

"What are you talking about?"

"Significant changes."

"Like what?"

He looked over toward the door of the restaurant and gave a little nod to someone he recognized. He took a healthy bite of his burger and said, "I'm not happy in this marriage."

She froze. Not happy? What was that supposed to mean? All she could hear underneath the whoosh of blood rushing from her heart to her head was her father and one of his favorite and most irritating responses to her younger self: "Who ever said anything about *happy*?" which was the exact sentence that burst out of her mouth. A misstep. He started to respond, and she raised her hand and lowered her voice to a whisper. "I am not having this conversation here."

He nodded, motioned for the check and they drove home in silence. She started marshaling her arguments beginning with the obvious. "We took a vow before God," she said the minute they were back in their house and alone. "Lest you forget, for better or worse, *until death*." She winced, hearing herself. She sounded like a schoolmarm or like one of the nuns at the elementary school. He took a deep breath and ushered her into the dining room, where they sat. He started out slow and careful but quickly gathered steam. He was angry. He was dissatisfied. Times were changing, and he realized he needed more from his relationship.

"We don't have a *relationship*. We're married!" Honey pleaded.

"And this marriage is enough for you? We almost never talk about anything significant. We never do anything different or exciting. Most everything I do seems to annoy you. I can't remember the last time we had sex—"

"Please don't use that word."

"Christ, Honey. You are my wife, and you can't even say the word, much less welcome the—" he broke off in exasperation. "You're good with this?" he asked, gesturing to take in the room, the house, the two of them, and the entire state of New York for all she knew. She should have taken his hand. She should have said something about love and companionship, asked why he was unhappy. She should have done a million things, but as her panic rose, she defaulted to threats. Duty. God. Retribution.

"You aren't going to be able to receive Communion," she said to him, her voice hushed and ominous. "Think about that, Finn. Think about what it's going to be like to go to Mass and sit there like an outcast—like Bess!—as we all receive."

He shook his head almost sadly. As if she were a particularly thick student or a cashier at the store who couldn't remember any of the produce codes. "I go to church because it's good for business. My faith is a personal thing. Me and God. I don't need the middleman. Nobody does."

She gasped, genuinely afraid for him, for his soul. But she also recognized, staring at him across her highly polished colonial dining table, that he had a light behind his eyes, a fire that she'd rarely seen. She recognized she was dealing with something she didn't fully comprehend. "Well, what about business?" she finally asked, tacking into the wind. "What are people going to think? What are your employees going to think? What about *your children?*"

"I think it's going to be a nice bit of gossip for a few weeks. I think it's 1977 and the world is changing and, ultimately, nobody is going to give a shit. And I will take care of Dune and Fern. For that matter, I will take care of you. You don't have to worry about money or the house or any of it. I mean that."

The following weeks were horrible. A frustrating round-robin of Honey pelting Finn with questions (Was there someone else? Had he cheated on her? How long had he felt this way?) and Finn turning it all around on Honey ("This is about you and me and only you and me"). They spent most of their time quietly hurling accusations at one another, stewing in opposite corners.

One day, Honey wrote down a list of all the things she did for him and their family in a typical day. It had thirty-two line items, everything from laundry to managing the annual physicals to hosting the company Christmas party. He took his time looking at the list. Nodded his head in affirmation. "I agree. You do all these things, and you do them well." *Finally*, she thought, *we're getting somewhere*. "But," he continued, "where's the romance?"

"Romance?"

"Where's you and I having dinner alone? Going to bed early *together*? Taking a walk? Traveling? Show me something on this list"—he let the page flutter to the floor—"about love and affection."

Later, she would regret how she'd stonewalled. She refused to even discuss divorce, and when he intimated that if she didn't concede to see a lawyer, he would take matters into his own hands, she'd ignored him. She buried it deep and waited for it to pass like she always had.

She had been scared on her wedding night. What she'd told Finn was true—her friend had warned her sex was unpleasant and painful—but she would never tell him the whole truth. About the weekend she and all her cousins were having a sleepover at her aunt Millie's house the night before Easter Sunday. The next morning the older kids would hide eggs and help the younger kids with the Easter egg hunt. Honey was only fifteen and her aunt had let her assemble the Easter baskets. One big chocolate bunny, a fistful of chocolate eggs and jelly beans scattered around. The whole thing wrapped in colorful cellophane. When they were done, all the older cousins—including Jake and Janet from Chicago—settled into the rec room to play Hearts. Jake asked her to help him bring some sodas up from the basement. She and Jake had not gotten along when they were younger. He was two years older than she was, with better grades, a spot on the hockey team and a quick wit. Honey resented how he moved through the world with such ease and charm. "I like that dress," he said as they were rummaging through the extra refrigerator in the basement, putting bottles of Coke into a large carton to carry upstairs.

"I made it," Honey said. She was thrilled Jake had noticed. She was proud of the dress, turquoise-and-white gingham with a full skirt and white sleeves. You couldn't even tell she'd messed the hem up a bit on one side.

"Cool," he said. "How do you make a dress?"

"You start with a pattern," she said. "Then you pick the fabric."

"You picked this out?" He fingered the edge of one cap sleeve. "It's a good color. It's very soft," he said, moving closer. Then he ran his finger down her arm. "This is soft, too."

She froze in place. A boy had never touched her. Never approached her so familiarly, and this wasn't any boy—it was her cousin. She laughed a little and took a step back.

"Don't go," Jake said. "I want to hear more about the dress. How do you figure out how to make it do this?" He pulled on the button placket in front of her and one of the buttons came loose.

"Stop it," she said, feeling the tears build, feeling panicky.

"I'm admiring you," he said. Everything moved quickly. He pressed her against the wall made of concrete bricks. It was damp, and she could feel the back of her dress absorb the moisture. Jake started kissing her and at first, she liked it. It felt good. But just as she was starting to enjoy the kissing part, he pushed his hips against hers and moved his hand down to her breast and started kneading it. "Don't," she said.

"I'm *admiring* you," he'd insisted. The whole thing was confusing, alternately terrifying and titillating. She had liked kissing him, she had. But she hadn't liked the other stuff, any of it. He'd lifted her skirt and shoved his hand down her underpants with such force her knees buckled. She'd grabbed his forearm to steady herself and he took that opportunity to slip a finger inside her. "God, you're so ready," he said and she wanted to ask what he meant, but he was slobbering all over her face and between his tongue and the hand in her pants rummaging around like he was looking for a lost penny, she was so overwhelmed that she closed her eyes and tried to figure out what to do with her hands, which were now hanging limply at her sides.

"Kiss me back," he said to her.

"What?"

He put his other hand on the back of her head and pulled her closer to his face and said, "Kiss me back. Like you were before."

Whenever she would think about that day, she would mark this moment as the one when she could have stopped him. Why hadn't she stopped him? She would never forgive herself for not screaming or pushing or resisting. If she'd given him a hard shove and run up the stairs, the thing that happened next never would have happened. He pulled her underpants down and even though she pressed her knees together, he was able to get himself inside of her. That's how she remembered it, as dispassionately as possible. A part of him went inside a part of her. He pinned her against the wall for what felt like forever but was probably less than five minutes. He'd extracted himself and grabbed a roll of paper towels and wiped himself off. Then he'd raised a single paper towel streaked with blood and said, "I thought so. You're a good girl, Honor."

Him using her given name in that moment was awful. She was sad her cousin had attacked her, sad she would never want to look at him again, sad she wasn't pure anymore. But she was mostly sad that by calling her *Honor* his disdain became manifest. He hadn't forced himself on her out of some kind of misplaced affection but out of contempt. He'd taken her honor and made it into wordplay.

"Careful," he said then, pinching her waist until it hurt. "Looks like you've had a few too many jelly beans." He leaned close to her ear again. "Don't be a little piggy."

She never told a soul what happened. Jake brought the carton of Cokes upstairs. She'd cried a little and fastened the front of her dress as best she could with a missing button. She ran up to her aunt's powder room and washed her face. She couldn't believe how normal she appeared. Her lips were redder than usual. She had to redo her mussed ponytail. But looking at her you wouldn't know anything was different. She walked through the kitchen, where her mother and aunts were putting pastries and cookies on a tray for tomorrow's brunch. Her aunt Millie looked at her and frowned. "Everything okay, Honey?"

"Sure," she said breezily. On the kitchen table was a bowl full of Easter eggs dyed pink, green, blue, purple. Only hours ago, she'd showed her youngest cousin how to write with a crayon so the words "Happy Easter" appeared on the side of the egg when it emerged from the dye. It seemed an impossibility, something she couldn't get her head around, how she had been a different girl, intact, when she'd dropped the egg into the vinegary solution.

"Look, Honey," her cousin Linda said. "It worked!" Honey took the egg and brought it over to the sink. She blotted the end where the dye had pooled with a napkin and slipped the egg into her pocket. For the rest of the weekend and the following week, she kept the egg close. Whenever she remembered, she'd pick up the pink egg from *before* and hold it until her breathing steadied. She kept it until she got her period a week later, and when she did, she brought the egg to the backyard and threw it into the woods. She couldn't stand the smell of vinegar for the rest of her life.

On her wedding night, when Finn had gently tugged on the pretty white lace underpants she'd bought for her trousseau, she couldn't help feeling queasy. She panicked and started to cry. He was gentle and understanding and although it took a few nights to consummate their union, she was okay. As the months passed, she didn't start to enjoy the intimacy exactly, but she didn't always dread it, either.

Then she lost the baby. In her head she knew the miscarriage didn't have anything to do with what had happened to her in the basement with Jake, but in her heart she believed it did. She couldn't shake it, and every time Finn approached her in bed, she tensed up. She loved being with him, but she never learned to love the intimacies of marriage. She endured, of course she endured—it was her duty as a wife. Their union was sanctified in the eyes of God and their community and opening herself to her husband and welcoming children was what she'd vowed to do. But when Finn's intimate advances stopped, she assumed they'd come to a mutually satisfying unspoken agreement. She was relieved and giddy. She thought he was, too.

"Aren't you going to read it?" Fern asked Honey, standing in her nightgown, holding the note.

"Later," Honey said, in a voice so chilly Fern didn't dare ask again. "Get your brother. We're going to the lake."

Twenty-Two

When Finn first started confiding in Helen Harper that he was unhappy in his marriage, she told herself not to read too much into his ramblings. As a person who'd spent most of her working life in male-dominated rooms, she was used to a whole string of odd confessions and personal remarks. Some of them had intent behind them—sexual, romantic, malicious, condescending—but most were simply because men were accustomed to dumping their frustrations and anger and grievances onto the nearest woman, no matter who that woman was. No matter if she was their secretary or boss or coworker. What Helen was to Finn—he often told her—was his right hand, the other half of his brain, the person (unsaid but implied: *other than him*) most responsible for all the good things happening at Finnegan's Grocer.

Shortly after Finn took over as president of the stores, after he soft-retired his uncle into a seat on the board with a handsome salary but no real responsibilities, he was forced to admit that he'd underestimated both how stagnant the business had become and how far it had to go to grow and stay competitive. He also had to admit that he wasn't the strategic visionary he'd imagined, he wasn't even as good as his uncle Dennis. He was more like his father. He was a people person. He was great at walking the aisles, talking to employees, plumbing them for ideas and suggestions. He had a million opinions on the flow of the store and how the displays should look and where they would best be situated. He knew how to meet and nurture and manage relationships with suppliers and when he had to cut someone loose. He loved interacting with customers even when it was listening to their complaints about prices (and it was 95 percent listening to complaints about prices). He thrived out and about in the community, showing up to a benefit with a big fat check and glad-handing the local politicians, whom he might need a favor from someday. He was good at product and relationships and although he liked thinking about the future, how to expand and leverage the latest technology and become more profitable, he was sometimes fuzzy on how to get there. His job, as his father told him thousands of times, was to keep the stores profitable and keep those profits in the family. *Expansion* was a slightly dirty word for his dad because it involved risk. Loyalty, steadfastness, family, serving the community they occupied—those were the things Fintan Sr. cared about. Finn didn't get jazzed by figuring out neighborhood real estate sales and traffic patterns and the possible optimization of empty parking lots in the right places. He liked targeting small businesses that would be better off folded into Finnegan's, but he didn't spend a lot of time thinking about how the vacated factory next to the huge parking lot on Culver Road might become a new Finnegan's location.

The best thing he ever did was hire Helen Harper, who loved nothing more than getting into the nitty-gritty of any kind of spreadsheet. She was a math prodigy who'd gotten into college at sixteen and blazed through graduate school before she was twenty-three. As he told her again and again, they had a beautiful professional marriage. Many nights, he hung out in her office later than needed, shooting the shit. Many weekends, she'd find him roaming the aisles of one of the stores. Chatting up the cashiers and then joining her for lunch.

Helen had had her share of romantic entanglements. None of them lasting long because there was always a moment when the man in question would make it clear he didn't approve of her job and ambition. "When we're married," "When we have children," "When I get a promotion,"—all phrases concluding with the assumption she would leave her job. Helen would smile and nod and stop returning phone calls and that would be that. She loved her work. She loved the life she'd made for herself in Rochester. At first, Finn Finnegan was a father figure to her, but it became apparent he needed mothering much more than she needed fathering. She would remind him to have something to eat midday and gently steer his sometimes-wrongheaded ideas into good ones and his good ideas into better ones. She commiserated over how nobody could understand the demands of running a business that had so many moving parts and touched so many lives in town. People took it for granted, he'd passionately lecture her, the choir, how they could stroll into one building and find everything they needed to provide for their families. Then, seemingly overnight, the complaints about Honey became less frequent and his demeanor took a turn for the brighter, the livelier, the slightly more flirtatious. *Interesting*, she thought. She didn't want to *be with* Finn—he was too old, they were colleagues—but a workplace fling? A little affair? She could make that work. She would bide her time until he made a move. She was patient.

When Finn called her into his office on a Monday morning and closed the door, she knew something was up. He loved trumpeting his open-door policy, which he'd read about in a business magazine and implemented immediately and which mostly meant everyone could hear his booming voice all day. He gestured for her to sit and was uncharacteristically hesitant as he started talking. "I'm leaving town tomorrow for a few days," he said.

"Okay," Helen said. "Business or pleasure?"

He smiled briefly. "A little bit of both, I guess you could say. I wanted to give you a heads-up because it's going to impact you. I'm leaving Honey." Helen had a lot of practice not reacting to the things men said in meetings; she knew how to look interested and nonjudgmental and conceal any expectations. "A lot of things are going to change when I get back. Not for the stores necessarily, but personally, and I wanted you to be one of the first to know."

She lowered her head to hide her smile. She was surprised but not surprised. She could hear her heart thumping a little harder. He picked up a sealed envelope and handed it to her. "If you need to get in touch with me, that's where you can reach me." Helen nodded. "Only in case of a real emergency. Something you can't handle on your own."

"Got it," she said. "I can't imagine needing to disturb you."

"Great."

"And there's something else, Helen. Something I'm only telling you. I hope I'm not jumping the gun."

"Yes?"

As he finished his explanation and stood, looking relieved and more relaxed than when their conversation began, he opened the door and saw the note taped to its surface. He read it and looked back up at Helen. "Want to check those new refrigerators they installed yesterday? Might be an issue here."

"Love to," Helen said. "Give me a minute. I'll be right down."

Twenty-Three

Nina needed to make a friend on this trip the same way she needed another hole in her head, but here she was, lolling in the shallow end of a hotel pool in the Caribbean on what should have been an ordinary December morning in Rochester (Clara was in AP Bio; Bridie had a free period). She was wearing last summer's swimsuit, a navy one-piece with a thick ivory stripe down the center, which the salesperson at Sibley's had assured her was slimming. The suit was cut higher on the leg than she was used to, and she'd had to shave her bikini line before they left. She'd already secreted her pink disposable razor in the suitcase hidden in the back of her closet, so she borrowed Sam's silver-plated razor, the one he'd had since they met. Unused to the instrument's weight, she'd given herself a tiny cut at the bikini line. Wading in the pool now, the chlorinated water made the cut sting in a way that felt soothing. She wanted something on the outside to hurt.

Finn was sitting at an aluminum poolside table beneath a brightly colored and tasseled umbrella, deep in conversation with their local attorneys and someone named Mr. López, an American from Miami who was an attorney and a kind of expediter as far as she could gather. Finn wanted to speak to the men alone. Nina knew but refused to *know* how he was going to persuade the courts to grant their divorces without spousal consent, which even in this place designed for quickie divorces they were supposed to have secured. She knew it had to involve money. She knew he'd been talking to Mr. López for weeks. She knew they had to live in this hotel for forty-eight hours to "establish residency" in the Dominican Republic and that on Thursday morning they would go to the courthouse and these men sitting across the concrete patio, drinking iced tea, and quietly murmuring, heads bent, would go in front of the divorce judge. Finn and Nina would marry the following day. Unbound and rebound in the span of twenty-four hours in a courthouse on an island she would never want to return to again.

Finn didn't care that the church wouldn't recognize their divorce and remarriage, and neither would Honey or Sam. He considered their recalcitrance a tiny technicality. Once they were married and living together as husband and wife, his argument went, Sam and Honey would have no choice but to capitulate and grant them official divorces in New York State. And then they'd simply marry one more time. "I'll marry you in every goddam state in the country if I have to. Fifty weddings, fifty courthouses."

Although his argument was heartless, he was correct. Honey would be hostage to Finn's finances ("Don't you worry about Honey," he'd said dismissively when she brought up her concerns. "She'll be well provided for.") Sam would probably never speak to Nina again, but he would want the scandal and its resultant heat in his rearview mirror as quickly as possible.

In the days after Garret delivered Sam to their front porch, he and Nina warily avoided one another. She wanted to wait him out. Every day that went by without him coming to her to offer an apology or an explanation, she became angrier. On the following Saturday, when Bridie and Clara were out of the house, she put together a salade Niçoise, one of Sam's favorites. She made a baguette and a tarte tatin.

"What's the occasion?" he said, coming into the kitchen, pleased.

"You tell me."

He squinted at her, confused.

"Don't you think it's time we had a conversation about the other night?"

Sam's face shuttered, the tiny muscle in his jaw twitching as his color drained. And the persistent suspicions she'd tried to quiet erupted into something undeniable and solid.

"What about the other night?" he said, turning away from her. "I'm sorry I drank too much."

"And Garret? And Margaret?"

"I told you, it was a client thing just like—"

She put her hand up to stop him. "Please, let's not do it like this," she said.

"Like what?" She could see him gearing up for combat. In that moment, his and Clara's resemblance was destabilizing it was so familiar: Chin up. Lips thin. Eyes blazing.

"Like I'm dumb. Like you're dumb," she said. He sighed and sat at the table and picked up a fork and speared half of a hard-boiled egg. "Sam? I'm talking to you."

"Sit. Since when are you not able to talk and eat at the same time?"

She would try to figure it out later, why that particular comment made her livid—the casual dismissiveness, the lack of contrition, the inability to engage honestly for the duration of one lousy lunch. Standing there, watching him shovel haricots verts and tuna into his mouth like he didn't have a care in the world, untethered her from whatever it was—a silent pact? A tacit agreement? Willful ignorance?—that had kept them loosely, unquestioningly in lockstep. She almost felt herself floating away. She could hear him talking, but the words coming out of his mouth were gibberish. He sounded like he was speaking to his staff.

First, he stated the problem: she was misreading things. Then he asked a question: What was she implying anyway? Followed by an observation: Did she know how ridiculous she sounded? He wrapped up with a recommendation, a *specific action*, as she often heard him suggest to coworkers: she should sit down and have some lunch and stop acting crazy. He spoke deliberately and calmly, but his eye contact was aggressive, and his entire demeanor made it clear her responses were unwelcome and unnecessary. "You know," he said, sopping up the vinaigrette in his bowl with a piece of bread, "people say this time of life"—he looked up, gestured aimlessly with the baguette—"*the change*, can cause strange symptoms. Not just physical but mental."

She started to feel insane. She folded her hands in her lap and said: "I want a divorce." He laughed at her.

"SO," THE WOMAN SHE WOULD come to know as Judith said, slowly wading toward Nina sitting at the shallow end of the pool, "are you one of us?"

"Pardon?" Nina wasn't in the mood to talk to this woman or anyone.

"One of the fallen? Holding the forbidden apple? Hester Prynne?" She took a finger, wet the tip with her tongue, and traced a letter *A* on the swell of her left breast. Nina laughed despite herself. "I guess I am," she said.

"Welcome," Judith said. She was spectacularly beautiful. She shook the water out of her long black hair like a sleek wild animal or someone in a Pepsi commercial and sat down next to Nina on the stairs. "I'm going to order a drink because you look like you could use one."

"What do you recommend?" Nina said. Was she going to drink her way through this entire inexplicable trip? Maybe.

"Something called tropical punch. It's good and strong. Lots of vitamin C, too." She waved prettily toward one of the pool attendants, who were all young, skinny locals looking slightly absurd in their dress whites, like they'd come straight from the deck of a naval ship. It was hot and they were wearing long pants and long-sleeved shirts and navy ties. Nina realized her bathing suit matched their uniforms. One of the attendants came over, cheerfully wiping his brow. "Hi, Cyrus," Judith said. "A couple of punches?"

Beyond the deep end, Finn stood and shook the hands of the men he'd been meeting with. He had a manila folder under his arm. He turned to look for Nina, spotted her, and waved. She smiled back. He was beautiful. Something in her settled a little.

"That your guy?" Judith asked. Nina nodded.

"Mine's over there." Judith pointed to a heavyset balding man sitting on one of the lounge chairs with a big book on his lap. From where Nina was sitting, she recognized another big potboiler. "Is he reading *Trinity*?" Nina asked.

"*Exodus*," Judith said. "Get it?"

"Very appropriate."

"That's Danny. That's my guy."

Nina couldn't help but like this woman, who was acting like they were all at a table at the high school cafeteria, pointing out their crushes. Cyrus hurried over with two tall sweaty glasses filled with a coral-colored liquid, red straws, and fat wedges of pineapple on the rims. Nina took a sip. It was cold and sweet and delicious and tasted mostly of rum. "This is good," she said to Judith. "This is extraordinary."

"There's a smile!" Judith said. "I was going to ask why so glum."

"Oh. It's complicated."

"Sweetie, if it weren't complicated, we wouldn't be here. Danny's been trying to divorce his wife for ten years."

"Ten!"

"Ten and three months. You know how many days? I do. It's 3,739. Or close. I don't do leap-year math."

"A lot of days," Nina said.

"His wife's a real bitch. Got to hand it to her, though, she made us work for it." Judith drained her tropical punch in one noisy slurp and waved her empty glass toward Cyrus, who nodded.

"And your husband?" Nina asked. It hadn't occurred to her last night that she might find comfort in talking about the thing they were all doing in this place. "Oh, I never had one," Judith said. "Thank god. Only one furious spouse to deal with. How about you?" she said cheerfully, taking her second drink from Cyrus, as if they were talking about local tourist sites or restaurants.

"We're both married" was all she was willing to offer Judith in terms of details.

"Not for long! When's your hearing?"

"Tomorrow," Nina said. She'd woken up in the beautiful hotel room, palms outside the window, the sky a kind of vibrant pink she'd never seen before, and told herself once again to get back on a plane to her daughters. And yet here she sat, sipping a rum drink. (Bridie in math; Clara, creative writing.)

"We're tomorrow, too! Finally. He's a dentist and I'm his assistant. We're together all day and we want to be together every night. Who could walk away from that?"

Later, at dinner on the veranda of the hotel, surrounded by the chatter of other guests, the bustle of the staff, and buffeted by the sea breezes, Nina and Finn were quiet, awkward, speaking but not really.

"Pass the butter."

"How's your fish?"

"I like your tie."

"Pretty sandals."

"Look at the moon, would you?"

The conversation superficial, but the undertones complex. Nina understood how easily everything they'd put into motion could melt away, as quickly as the scoop of mango sorbet in the silver dish in front of her, a tiny, dissipating yellow sun.

"Ready?" Finn said finally.

They'd just crossed the threshold of the room when Finn grabbed her, pulled up her long, floral skirt, and bent her over the bed the way she sometimes liked. Usually, he defaulted to sweet and gentle, but now he was quick and desperate and as he plunged into her, she reached behind him and grabbed his buttocks and said, "Fuck me."

It was like she'd flipped a switch. She felt herself become hollowed out. He didn't go soft as much as evaporate. One moment he was inside of her, the next gone. They didn't move for a minute. Two. Finn sat down on the edge of the bed.

"Sorry," he said.

"It's okay. We're tired. Today has been hard."

"You've never said anything like that before. During sex, I mean. The—the swearing."

"I thought you'd like it."

"I was—surprised, I guess."

The bed was across from a full-length mirror, and she could see how vulnerable and middle-aged they looked, how exposed. As she collapsed on the bed, she started to sob. Finn covered her with a sheet, patted her back, said, "Shhh, shhh," as she cried herself to sleep.

Twenty-Four

For most of the felled, the vomiting started Tuesday night, but the trouble had been planted the day before, when Robert Pavone, new to the deli department, noticed a strange noise coming from one of the new refrigerator doors when he clocked in in the morning. He walked up the stairs to tell someone, but Miss Harper and Mr. Finnegan were behind a closed door in his office. He left a note taped to the door, brief and to the point: *Hi. Third refrigerator from the left making a weird noise. Wanted you to know. Sincerely, Robert Pavone from Deli.* He reread the note and felt a little strange about the *sincerely*, but figured it was best to err on the side of polite. He gently placed the note on the door, not wanting to disturb the meeting inside.

When he went back downstairs, the noise was gone. He walked into the fridge. The temperature felt fine. Just like last night. He checked the interior thermostat: also fine. He could hear Mr. Finnegan's voice coming closer as he stepped out of the walk-in.

"Are you Robert Pavone from deli?"

"Yes, sir."

"What's this about a weird noise?"

"Well, sir, I'm not hearing it anymore. But I did earlier."

Finn and Helen walked in and out of all the new walk-ins, checking gauges, opening and shutting doors, putting a gloved palm onto various food items.

"I think everything looks okay," Helen said.

"Good." Finn needed to get home before Honey did so he could pack and put his suitcase in the trunk of his car without her noticing. "I'm going to take off, then."

"Sorry for the trouble," Robert said.

"Don't ever apologize for paying attention. You're doing a good job. And you don't have to call me *sir*. I'm Finn to everyone here." Finn put out his hand and Robert shook it a little too vigorously.

When Robert came into work the following day and went to grab the tray of cooked roast beef out of the walk-in, the refrigerator felt warmer than before, even though the gauge displayed the correct temperature. When he told his boss, Eddie checked the gauge himself. "Right where we need it," he said. "You're getting used to the cold."

Robert grabbed a tray of cooked round roasts and brought them over to the slicer. Adding a "beef on weck" to the prepared foods had been Robert's idea. He'd grown up in Buffalo and his father had worked at a deli where the local sandwich—roast beef on a Kimmelweck roll with horseradish cream—was a big seller for the lunch crowd. When he suggested Finnegan's add them to the deli case, Finn agreed and put Robert in charge, which was a big deal for Robert, who had nearly flunked out of high school but was thriving at the store while living with his grandmother. If he kept saving, he could afford a place for himself in a few months.

He quickly assembled and wrapped the dozens and dozens of sandwiches for distribution to three store locations by lunchtime. As he was cleaning up, after the sandwiches were safely on their way to their destinations, he had enough beef left to make another few dozen. He decided to cut them up and offer samples ahead of the weekend. They always did a brisk business in premade when the Bills were playing, even though the team was pathetic this year. Nine losses, two shutouts at home. Didn't matter. People still bought food to watch the game. He arranged the wedges of sandwich on a platter and decorated it with pieces of parsley and put it in front of a huge royal-blue-and-red cardboard cutout that said GO BILLS!! He stood back and admired his creation.

Twenty-Five

What Helen Harper would run over in her mind again and again was the number of times she'd walked by that plate of fucking sandwiches and thought, *What a brilliant idea!* Free food always thrilled the customers, and Helen had believed for months that with the proper kind of push and a little more creativity, they could make the deli department one of the most profitable areas in the store. Every time she walked the floor that morning, Robert was replenishing the platter. By the time he got back to his grandmother's house at the end of his shift, he was queasy and feverish. His nana put him straight to bed. "It's that time of year," she clucked around him. "Poor Robby. Try to get some sleep. These bugs are quick. You'll feel better tomorrow."

But he didn't feel better the next day. He felt worse. His grandmother Concetta, who, truth be told, wasn't feeling great herself, called the store to say he was too sick to work. When Helen got the note, she called Eddie at home to see who they might find to replace Robert for a day or two. "He's real sick, Miss Harper," Eddie's daughter said. "He's in the bathroom throwing up."

"Oh boy," Helen said. "I think there's a stomach thing going around. Tell him I hope he feels better." Losing a bunch of people to a stomach flu was not something Helen needed ahead of a busy weekend in December, especially not a weekend where she was the solo person in charge. She might need to move some employees from one store to another. "Lizzy?" she called to her assistant. "I need employee names and phone numbers. Anyone who's not already scheduled this weekend."

Right around then, Viv and Sally, two of the cashiers who had snuck pieces of the sandwich several times the day before, both called to say they couldn't get out of bed, that they'd been up all night.

Back on Cambridge Road, Nancy Tannenbaum had let her daughter Lisa have a few friends sleep over, all girls from the volleyball team. She woke up to them screaming, absolutely *screaming*, at five in the morning. Lisa came tearing into the bedroom, "Martha is puking! And so is Missy!" At first, Nancy thought the girls were experiencing some kind of collective hysteria via disgust. They saw one person vomit and that was it, they were all sick. But it quickly became clear they were all suffering from something. Donna opened the trash and saw the wrappings of sandwiches from Finnegan's. She called the store to report what was happening and helped all the girls into her van and headed for the emergency room. A few blocks over, Melissa Anthony, who owned a dress shop next to the Finnegan's on Clover Street and picked up lunch at the store every day for herself and her husband, a tailor, woke up at three in the morning with a queasy feeling that quickly progressed to full-blown diarrhea and vomiting. Her husband followed an hour later, and they spent the night vying for the only toilet in their apartment.

By Thursday morning, Robby was feeling a little better. He went downstairs, but his grandmother wasn't in the kitchen. He found her in her bed, moaning and delirious. She looked awful and couldn't seem to string more than a few words together. He called an ambulance.

BEFORE SHE HAD A CHANCE to pour her morning coffee, Helen got a call from one of the doctors in the ER at Rochester General. He suspected something more than a stomach virus. Twelve patients who needed antiemetics and IVs all reported having bought prepared food at Finnegan's.

"I'm sorry to hound you when you're not feeling well," Helen said to Eddie when she got him to the phone. "But I'm hearing a lot of people are sick and—"

"It's the beef," Eddie said, his voice weak.

"The beef?"

"I don't want to say the name or I'll heave. The sandwiches. Robert's sandwiches."

"Shit. Okay. Any idea what I should do?"

"Check refrigerator number three," he said, dropping the phone and heading, Helen assumed, back to the bathroom.

Helen made sure the sandwiches were pulled from all the shelves in town and instructed the two unaffected employees in the deli department, which she temporarily closed, to trash all the inventory from refrigerator number three. After she called the refrigerator manufacturer demanding a service visit by end of day and notified Dennis and the board and the New York State Department of Health about the incident and instructed the local emergency rooms to notify her about any additional cases of food poisoning, she closed the door to her office and opened the envelope Finn had left. She eyed the number with its unidentifiable exchange. Should she call him? What could he do from wherever he was that she couldn't? What a mess.

What an opportunity.

"Where in the hell is my nephew?" Finn's uncle Dennis asked, storming into Helen's office, freshly shaved and showered and wearing a suit. Outfitted for battle.

"Somewhere in the Caribbean."

"The Caribbean! What's he doing there?"

"Getting a divorce from Honey."

"Are you kidding me?"

"I'm not." She handed him Finn's note. "He's with his neighbor Nina Larkin. They're getting married. The newlyweds are expected home tomorrow."

Helen wished she could have taken a photo of the look on Dennis's face. "Has he lost his mind?" Dennis asked. Helen shrugged.

"Helen?" Lizzy poked her head in the door. "Robby's grandmother is in intensive care."

"From the sandwich?" Helen put a hand to her forehead.

"Apparently. She has a heart problem or something and they can't get the infection under control."

"This is not good," Dennis said.

"And," Lizzy continued, "both the *Times Union* and the *Democrat & Chronicle* need a quote from you. Unless Mr. Finnegan is available."

"Mr. Fintan Finnegan is not available," Dennis barked at Lizzy. She backed out of the office and closed the door. Dennis turned to Helen. "We have to keep this out of the paper."

"Dennis, that's impossible and unwise. This is a public health issue. We have to say something about it and find a way to reassure people about the food in the store. Honesty is the quickest way to get past this. Should I call Finn?"

"Do you want to call him?"

"I feel confident I can handle the situation as well as anyone. With your help, of course," Helen added, which was not true, but Dennis Finnegan was not her biggest fan. He never forgot the unceremonious way he'd been ushered out the door.

"Okay. I agree," Dennis said.

"What do I say when the reporters ask about Finn?"

"Tell them the truth."

"What do you mean?"

"The truth. Honesty in all things. Right?"

She stood there, confused. This was not her job. "I don't know."

"It's simple," Dennis said. "Say it like it's no big deal. Like you've given them a little scoop for the society page."

She was still a little bruised by her last conversation with Finn, still smarting from his revelations and from how badly she'd misread the cues and how easily he'd tossed off his ludicrous plans, but she didn't want to expose Finn to the local press.

"Think about it," Dennis said. "If there's an article about our sandwiches making people sick and another piece about Finn eloping with his neighbor, which do you think people will talk about all weekend?"

Both, Helen wanted to say. But she was tired and needed to start putting out fires and Dennis had a point. "Okay," she said, picking up the phone. "I'll get to work."

Twenty-Six

Finn had arranged things so if they wanted they could divorce in the morning and marry the same afternoon. But Nina refused to share the date of their respective divorces with their wedding anniversary. On Thursday morning, she put on her traveling dress. Black, simple, demure. The perfect costume for an unraveling. She removed her wedding rings and slipped them into her cosmetic bag. Maybe the girls would want them someday. Probably not, but maybe. She didn't even wear makeup. This ritual was a necessity, not a joy. She'd been told everything that was going to happen but was still nervous in the courtroom when Mr. López started speaking in his rat-a-tat mixture of English, Spanish, and French (imagine having all that vocabulary at your fingertips!). She was sure someone was going to stop the proceedings and catch them out. But the judge reviewed the documents impassively and asked a few questions of Mr. López and then everyone was shaking her hand and saying congratulations. Mr. López led them to another office, where they submitted the papers and were handed an official divorce decree. Within minutes they were standing outside on the sidewalk. She was single, a free woman.

In the car on the way back to the hotel, Finn asked how she wanted to spend the afternoon. Looking out the car window, she pointed at the market they were passing in town. "I'd like to go there. See what they're selling. Taste some food that isn't made for Americans in a hotel for Americans." Finn groaned. "I wasn't expecting a busman's holiday. The last thing in the world I want to do is inspect produce."

"It's crowded and hot in the market," Mr. López said, immediately siding with Finn, who paid his bills.

"Then I want to see the water," Nina said, disengaging her hand from Finn's.

The beach was wide and the sand an otherworldly white, like someone had poured bags of sugar up and down the coast. The water was a color blue she'd only seen in magazines and movies. They had two chaise lounges with thatched umbrellas to protect from the sun. The tropical drinks tasted better, the food more delicious touched by the salt air. She felt herself getting drunk—day drunk for the third day in a row, was this her new persona?—and feeling deliciously tired. They went for a long swim, and when she was falling asleep on the hotel towel carefully laid out on top of the cushioned chaise, she licked her forearm. It was salty.

When she woke, the sun was lower in the sky and a breeze had kicked up. She could hear Finn faintly snoring next to her. She picked up her watch from the sand beneath the chair, where she'd woozily placed it before falling asleep. Two forty-five p.m. Clara would be heading to Drama Club and Bridie probably walking home with a friend. She wanted to call them, but Finn had convinced her they needed to wait until the wedding was over to open that Pandora's box. And what could she possibly say to them over the phone that would do anything other than make them feel worse? Going home was the start of a process, Finn kept reminding her. A bumpy process that would lead everyone to a greater happiness. She had to believe him.

She sat up and considered another swim. For the first time since leaving Rochester, she felt herself relax a little. The deepening blue and green of the water as the sun shifted in the sky made her wish she could paint or watercolor. She pulled on flip-flops and grabbed her straw hat and took off down the beach. Her empty ring finger felt strange, and she kept rubbing the place where she used to feel solid gold. She stood at the shoreline and let the gentle waves break and crest and foam around her toes.

She had not been nice to Finn since they'd arrived, whatever *nice* even meant—but she didn't care. Stepping into his car two days ago had brought her to a place beyond sense and rules, a place that required its own vocabulary. She needed a new language, one she couldn't conceive of yet or one, ideally, they would build together, syllable by syllable. The old words were useless: betrayal, destruction, selfishness. They'd acted in service of something bigger. A greater love. A way to move through the world honoring what she now knew was the purpose of love: that you would not feel alone all of the time, just some of the time. In a perfect world, everyone would see—Finn and Nina were bringing their world *more* love.

And yet, strolling back toward the beach hut, she wondered what would happen if she left. If she went back to the hotel and packed her bag and got on a plane and returned to Rochester a single woman. Still scandalous but in a simpler way. Like Bess. Bess would let her stay in her house until she found a place for her and the girls, not the temporary, furnished house Finn had rented for them in an adjacent neighborhood, close enough for all the kids to walk to but not too close to their former spouses. He said they'd start looking for a bigger place to buy soon. But what if she—*left*? What if she didn't marry anyone else? Ever?

She could picture the little house she and the girls would make together. She'd let them paint their rooms any color and pick their own bed linens and furniture. She could imagine the three of them around a small table in the kitchen, laughing and eating more casually than they ever did when Sam was home. The scene filled her with joy, but then reality rushed in. She didn't have her own money. A Christmas Club account with $375 in it waiting for her to do her holiday shopping. A small savings account where she deposited her meager pay from the newspaper had a balance of almost $500. Not enough to start a new life, never mind maintain one. Sam would never finance this fantasy of hers. She and Finn had already set off this little bomb. How could she change course now? What agency did she have without him backing her? She realized, glumly, she was thinking of herself as one of Finn's acquisitions. She reminded herself she was here because she was in love. She was here to build a new life with a specific person, not just shed the old one. But what if last night's dinner was a harbinger of dinners to come? What if, in ten years' time, she found herself with a wandering eye again? As she returned to their spot on the beach, she motioned to the waiter to bring two more drinks and a check.

Next to her, Finn let out a loud boozy snore and startled himself awake. "God," he said, rolling over to face her, "that was loud. I don't usually snore." His face was creased on one side and his lovely hair all akimbo. He hadn't properly applied sunscreen to his beakish nose, and the ridge of it was bright red. The waiter appeared with their drinks and Finn sat up and said, "Ah, you are a goddess." He took a greedy gulp and put the glass down and reached out for her hand. She took a sip, sat up, and said, "Come with me."

"Where?"

"I want to show you something. Bring your drink."

The sand was hotter than they expected, so they ended up dashing over to the slight strip of grass that led to the changing stalls and restrooms. "Where are we going?" he asked.

"You'll see."

She led him into one of the stalls. It was small and hot and smelled faintly of mildew, but she'd changed in there earlier and the latch worked. She closed the door and struggled to get the slightly rusty latch to close. Finn, beginning to get the picture, gently moved her hand away and engaged the latch with one pound of his fist. He turned to her. She slipped the straps of her swimsuit off her shoulders, one at a time, as he watched. She paused before she pulled the blue serge fabric down below her breasts. He was transfixed. She kept tugging and kicked the suit to the side with one foot. She could hear him breathing harder, more deeply, and she nodded at him. He pulled off his damp swim trunks and lunged for her.

"Stop," she said. He stared, confused. She put her hands on his shoulders.

"I have a question."

"Now?" He sounded desperate. He would have done anything she asked.

"What if I want to go home?"

"What?"

"If I want to go back home now, before we get married. What would you say?"

"Nina." He tried to pull her closer, but she resisted.

"I need to know."

"What do you need to know?"

"If I want to go home tomorrow morning, what would you say?"

"You're not my prisoner."

"But what would you say? What would you do?"

She could see him straining for an answer, not comprehending the questions. "I would say, don't go. I would say, I love you. I would say, if you need to go, go. But I wouldn't give up on you." He cupped both of her breasts in his hands and whispered, "You are so beautiful—"

"Shhh," she said. She gave him a light shove and he sat on the cushioned bench behind him, looking up at her.

"Do you want to go?" he asked, confused.

"Maybe. Maybe I do." She knelt on the bench, legs on either side of him, until she was straddling him, but he wasn't inside her. She kept herself there for a bit, teasing, until he started to groan. With one hand on his chest, she took her other hand and lightly wrapped her fingers around his cock and held it firmly. He moved his head back and forth, wild-eyed. "Look at me," she said, as she put him inside her and started to move slowly up and down and up and down. "Look at me."

She had never looked another man in the eyes during sex. Not even Finn. And what they were doing in the slightly mildewy, damp cabana took on the same otherworldly quality of the past few days. It was sex and it was something else. He had his hands around her waist, but she was controlling the pace of the friction, how their bodies moved, and he was following her. It was slow until it was furious. They moved with each other in a kind of fever, an exorcism and a baptism, stopping and starting until—and she would never fully embody this word again—until they were utterly *spent*. Collapsed onto each other but not moving. Sweaty and giddy and tearful. They were reconstituted in what she would always think of as their real union. The moment when she chose him despite and because of it all: The pain. The sacrifice. The beauty.

The wedding the following morning took exactly twelve minutes. I do, I do. Man and wife. Kiss the bride. Judith offered to come and take photos, and they said yes. The only photo they would ever display in their home was the one Judith took that day. Nina in her white linen shift, Finn wearing his divorce suit, both hand in hand, grinning at each other like a couple of fools. Behind the viewfinder, Judith had laughed. "Now there are two people in love," she said as the shutter clicked.

As they packed for home the next morning, Nina took the pretty pink soap shaped like a scalloped shell from the hotel bathroom and tucked it into a corner of her suitcase. When they got home, she would place the soap into a box with the rest of the photos from the trip, a few seashells from the beach, a matchbook from the hotel, and for many years to come she would take the box out when she needed a reminder and bring the soap to her face and breathe deeply.

Twenty-Seven

Clara and Bridie had talked about skipping school, their father seemed willing to let them do whatever they wanted, but Bridie was such a mess that Clara wanted to keep them on some kind of schedule until their mother returned. She walked around in a daze, not quite believing what was happening to her. To *them*. Her dad didn't want to talk about anything. Not the note. Not the reason for their mother's departure or where she was or what she was doing. Not the bewildering fact of Mr. Finnegan. Mr. Finnegan! Their mother was *with Mr. Finnegan*. Her father was tight-lipped, and she gave up trying to get anything out of him other than the banal cliché he insisted on spouting: *everything will be fine*, which was so blatantly untrue. He acted as if their mother were off visiting a relative or friend and would reappear soon and they would all reconstitute as a family somehow. Clara had a million questions and not a single soul to ask. The one rule Sam insisted on was that she and Bridie weren't to say a word to anyone about what was going on. Not a word. And the only person she could have talked to about all of it was Dune, and he was gone, too.

The morning of the note, while Sam was upstairs explaining to a hysterical Bridie what had happened, Clara had pulled on her winter boots and run across the street holding her ski parka tight around her shorts and T-shirt. It was freezing. The morning flurries had given way to a bright winter day. Clara could smell the moisture in the air and the burning wood from the houses on the street that had stoked their fireplaces against the chill of the first true winter morning. She pounded on the Finnegans' front door, but nobody answered, and the house was dark and felt hollow. She tried to peer through the glass panes flanking the doorway. Nothing. Then she realized Dune must have left her a note in their hiding spot, the old galvanized steel milk box still sitting at the side of the garage even though hardly anyone had home delivery anymore, not since Finnegan's bought out all the bigger dairy farmers, consolidated operations, and effectively put the smaller farms out of business. But no. The milk box was empty. Clara was confused.

If the Finnegans had left town, why wouldn't Dune at least call her? Why hadn't he run over when their family had presumably received a letter much like the one her mother had written to see how she was doing? To commiserate. To talk down this extremely fucked-up thing their parents had done? Clara trudged back into the house, where Bridie was standing in the kitchen in her nightgown looking utterly lost. She went straight to Bridie and took her in her arms and Bridie resumed sobbing.

The next morning, as they rummaged through the fridge for lunch supplies—ignoring the packed bags Nina had left for each school day she'd be gone—she asked Sam about taking Nina's car to school. "I don't know," he said, looking flummoxed for the first time since Nina had left. Decisions about when the girls were allowed to do certain things was strictly Nina's territory. Clara pressed her advantage. "Dad," she said, moving close to him and lowering her voice, "we can't take the bus today. We can't. Bridie will *lose it* the minute she sees her friends. If I can drive us, we have a way to leave early if she has a complete nervous breakdown." Sam reluctantly handed Clara the car keys with a series of safety warnings and a promise they'd come directly home after school.

"Do not," she said, pointing her finger right in Bridie's face as they were buckling their seat belts in Nina's dirt brown Volvo, "tell anyone at school what's going on."

"What if Fern says something?"

"I'll take care of Fern." In truth, the only reason Clara wanted to go to school was to find out where Fern and Dune were hiding. She would never forget the strangeness of the day, the feeling of being in a place that was completely familiar but didn't offer any comfort. She stood at her locker staring into the messy space until the bell rang for class. She hid in the bathrooms during lunch because she couldn't possibly sit at a lunch table with her friends discussing the holiday break or Christmas or a television show or sharing homework. Everything had changed, but she was moving through an unchanged world, and it made her dizzy. She needed to find Fern. Clara went to the principal's office after first period to talk to the school secretary, Mrs. O'Neill, who liked Clara and who was also a terrible gossip if she trusted you. One of her favorite expressions being *You didn't hear it from me, but—*

"Hey, Mrs. O'Neill," she said, "Fern Finnegan borrowed my history notes the other day and I need them to study for a test. Can you tell me what class she's in next period so I can find her?"

"Fern's not here, hon," Mrs. O'Neill said.

"Oh," Clara said, doing an excellent job of looking confused. "I hope she's okay. I guess I'll stop by her house after school."

Mrs. O'Neill raised a brow. Clara stood wide-eyed. "Well. You didn't hear it from me, but . . ." She walked closer to Clara and lowered her voice. "Family emergency. Out of town."

"I didn't tell *anyone*!" Bridie said to her when they got in the car at the end of the day, beaming with accomplishment. Clara'd had what her mother called a rumbly tumbly belly since lunch, wondering if Nina might be back early, hoping they'd walk into the house and she would, what? Be unpacking? Cooking? Apologizing? But when they pulled into the driveway the house was dark.

"She's not home," Bridie said, chin trembling.

"Stop being such a baby, Bridie!" Clara also wanted to cry but wouldn't.

In the mess of the remainder of the week, Clara had forgotten Mr. Goodwin was posting the cast list for *Godspell* the day before Christmas break started. Even though Clara could barely allow herself to think about what her mother was doing with Mr. Finnegan, she did realize that, intentionally or not, they'd planned the trip to end just as the holiday break began. Starting Friday afternoon, school would be off for nearly a month. A small mercy.

On Friday morning, only one day before their mother had promised to return, they sped to the drive-through at McDonald's to get Egg McMuffins and coffee. The line was long, and they were running a little late. They wolfed the food down in the car and raced into the school cafeteria minutes before the bell rang for first period.

"Clara! Clara!" Her friend Miranda was waving her down in the hallway. "You did it!"

"I did what?"

Miranda rushed up to Clara and hugged her. "You're John the Baptist!" Miranda was squealing and jumping up and down. "I got 'Day by Day'!" She started twirling in circles around Clara, singing and clapping. Clara slowly approached the cast list posted on the bulletin board in the cafeteria, and there it was. *John the Baptist: Clara Larkin.* Right beneath the outcome that only days before had been a dream and now was something entirely different—*Jesus: Dune Finnegan.*

"Larkin!" Somebody was yelling to her from a lunch table. "Hey, Larkin!" She turned to find Missy Grunwald waving her over. She and Missy were friends in grammar school but once they got to Good Counsel went their separate ways. Missy was funny and loud and mean. She had no interest in Clara once she had a whole bunch of girls to pick from who were more like her. "Hi," Clara said, suspicious.

"Congratulations on the play."

"Thanks." Missy was playing to the table, to her friends, who were all wearing school-mandated navy cardigans but had had them monogrammed at the fancy sweater shop in town in contrasting colors. One pink. One lilac. A few red and green. "And condolences, I guess."

"Huh?" Clara squinted. Missy was up to something. She pushed a copy of the *Democrat & Chronicle* across the table. "Food Poisoning Scare at Finnegan's Grocer," the headline on page one read. Food poisoning? "What about it?" she snapped.

"Page seventeen," Missy said. "Check out your mother's wedding announcement." Two of the girls at the table laughed but wouldn't look at Clara. A few of the others looked down at their hands and had the decency to be embarrassed. Clara felt the McDonald's coffee rise in her gullet. She swallowed hard. If she vomited in front of these girls, in the middle of the school cafeteria, she would have to move to a different state. Possibly another country.

She turned the pages slowly until she saw what they'd all read. A small item in a column on the society pages: "A little bird tells me that as I type this, Finn Finnegan and his neighbor, Mrs. Samuel Larkin, who writes for a competing paper, are honeymooning in the Dominican Republic after leaving their respective spouses this week. We wish the newlyweds the best upon their return to the snowdrifts of our town."

"Are you okay?" Missy said, not sounding the slightest bit concerned. "I can't believe you've been coming to school. It's crazy."

"What's crazy?" Clara said.

Missy laughed. "All of it! Your mother is a fast operator. Gotta bag the grocer when you can, right?" Someone tapped Clara's elbow. She turned, and Bridie was standing there looking like a ghost. Like someone had drained every ounce of blood from her body, and how had Clara not noticed the circles under Bridie's eyes? She hadn't been sleeping. A rage so pure and cleansing rose in Clara that for the first time since their mother left, she felt a sense of purpose, almost elation.

"Missy?" Clara said. "Go fuck yourself."

When they returned to their empty house and the dark kitchen, the dirty dishes in the sink, the garbage piling up in the corner, the funky odor of spoiled apples, something in Clara snapped into or out of place, she couldn't tell. How could the house smell completely different already? It didn't smell like her mother's house anymore. Like beef stew and marigolds from the yard and the cedar candle she liked to burn during the holidays and the Jean Naté After Bath Splash she used every morning. It didn't smell like care. It smelled like indifference.

She turned on all the lights. Told Bridie to hang her coat in the front hall. The beginning of Christmas break. No homework. No nothing. She started filling the sink with sudsy hot water. Cleared the counter of crumbs.

"What do we do now?" Bridie said, her lower lip resuming its daylong tremble.

"We cook."

Twenty-Eight

Nina was already fidgety when they landed. The flight from JFK to Rochester had been delayed—they wouldn't see any of the children tonight. After a brief awkward call to Sam they'd both agreed Nina should wait until morning to see the girls. At the baggage carousel they bumped into Finn's old friend Hugo, who came right up to him and clasped a hand on his shoulder and asked if he was okay.

"Sorry?" Finn said.

"Tough business, this," Hugo said, shaking his head. "But one small incident can't take down the Finnegan legacy. You all will get through it." As Nina was about to ask what he was talking about, Finn shook his head slightly, indicating she shouldn't say anything.

"Thanks, buddy," Finn said. "I'll be right back," he told Nina and headed for a newspaper vending machine, dropped two dimes into the slot, opened the door, and took out a paper. Nina watched him read the front page and then rub one palm over his face. When he turned to walk back, he was pale. "What's wrong?" she asked. Finn had smeared newsprint all over his left cheek, and she took a hanky out of her handbag and tried to wipe some of it off. He handed her the paper.

> "Salmonella Outbreak Linked to Finnegan's Grocer
> Sickens City Residents"

"Oh no," she said. "You didn't know?"

"Of course I didn't know," he snapped. "You think I wouldn't tell you? Helen knew where to reach me. I can't believe she didn't call. I need to call Dennis." He found a pay phone on the other side of the baggage area. Nina spotted their bags coming out and collected them. Waited for Finn to finish his phone call. She paged through the paper, not really paying attention to what she was reading until she got to the Society section and saw the headline at the top left of the page, right above a brief missive on Princess Margaret's recent escapades—"Finnegan Remarries"—and started to read.

"What were you thinking?" she said once they'd loaded their bags in the car and started driving toward the rental house, their new home.

"I had nothing to do with that."

"But who knew?"

"I had to tell Helen. Our families know."

"I hardly think Sam or Honey called the papers. Why would Helen do that?"

"Dennis did it."

"Shit, shit, shit."

"It might not be bad, in the long run."

"Pardon?"

"He did it to embarrass me, but why not rip off the Band-Aid? Get it all over with."

"But the kids must have seen this. Their friends. What was Helen thinking?"

"I don't know what got into Helen in the space of three days."

Nina sighed. Put her head against the freezing car window. She didn't want to start a fight on their first night home, which was already feeling disastrous.

"I have to stop at the store," Finn said, referring to the one nearest their old houses and now the new house. "This is bad," he said, as they pulled into an empty parking lot and a deserted supermarket that at nine p.m. on a Saturday night should have been open.

"Dennis wouldn't even talk to me tonight. He's called a board meeting for Monday."

"We need food."

They pulled out of the parking lot and drove ten blocks to the *other* supermarket in town. "I can't show my face in there," Finn said. And for the first time since they'd left for Santo Domingo, Nina saw a flicker of concern on his face. He'd been so assured, so confident, from the moment the plane lifted off the runway. He was chewing his lip now, which she'd never seen him do before. She put a hand on his shoulder. "I'll go in. I'll be quick."

She took her time getting to the door, grabbed a cart and slowly started cruising the aisles. She'd popped in here a time or two when she was driving by and in a hurry, but she didn't really know where anything was. "Can I help you?" one of the cashiers asked her, sensing her confusion.

"Campbell's soup?" It had to have been her imagination—there was no picture of them in the paper—but she saw the woman hesitate. Nina smiled reassuringly and said, "And makings for grilled cheese?"

"Let me show you," the woman said. "Not very busy right now."

They walked around the store, and Nina swore she could hear the gears churning in the woman's head. RITA, her name tag said. "How are you tonight, Rita?" she asked. She and Finn were in for some rough weeks, months, but she was going to hold her head high.

"I'm good," Rita said. "A little surprised." Ah, here it was. "Why so?" Nina stopped and faced her.

"I would have guessed the Ravenous Gourmet made a three-course meal every night."

They both laughed, Nina with tremendous relief. "Sometimes you have to keep it simple."

"Amen," Rita said, stopping in front of a shelf of canned soup.

Nina got what she needed and bought some breakfast items. Coffee and cream and eggs. She didn't know how this hadn't occurred to her before, but even when Finnegan's Grocer was back in business, she was probably going to have to steer clear for a while. She loaded the bags in the back seat and got in beside Finn. "Well, I made a friend," she said. "Might come in handy."

Finn put the key in the ignition and started the car. Shook his head and sighed. "My father is rolling over in his grave right now."

Twenty-Nine

The first morning of their married life in Rochester, the phone rang at the inauspicious hour of four in the morning. Helen Harper was on the other end of the line, calling to say Robert's grandmother Concetta had died.

"Dammit," Finn said, wanting to get into it with Helen Harper about a host of things, but not during this call. "Should I go to the hospital?"

"No, I just left. Everyone else is going home for a little sleep."

"Why didn't you call me earlier? I would have come over."

"Well. Honey was there, for one thing."

Finn practically jumped out of bed. "Why was Honey there?" Behind him, Nina groggily turned over. "What's wrong?" she said. Finn waved her off.

"We needed someone from the family on-site, and we didn't want to bother you during your"—Finn swore he could hear an ugly smirk in Helen Harper's voice—"honeymoon."

"'We'?" Finn said. "Who exactly is 'we'?"

"Dennis and me. We decided."

Finn heard it all in one sentence—*we decided*—and within minutes of walking into the conference room at the main office Monday morning at eight, looking around at the faces of the board, he knew he was toast. He felt like a ghost at his own funeral. Nobody directed a comment or question toward him; they talked around him. All questions from the board about the salmonella incident, its aftereffects, the strategy going forward, were directed to Helen and Uncle Dennis. When they got to the part about who could be the public face of this new strategy and Finn said he'd like to volunteer for the role, his uncle Dennis all but rolled his eyes.

The discussion moved onto his "package." He wasn't given much of a choice. A person had died, a mother and grandmother and soon-to-be great-grandmother, and someone had to be held accountable. He could retire early. ("With a handsome compensation package that will set you up beautifully for the rest of your life," Dennis relished telling him. Only he and Finn knew those were the exact words Finn had used all those years ago when he retired his uncle.) Or he could take a reduced role as the director of the Finnegan's charitable arm, the Finnegan Community Foundation. He'd draw a smaller salary, but his private stock options would be safe. "The truth is," Uncle Dennis told him when they had an awkward attempt at a conciliatory coffee many weeks later, "if Helen is as good as we both suspect, she's going to make this family quite wealthy."

"What if I'm not interested in either of those options?" Finn said. "What if I want to fight this decision?"

"Take one of those packages," Dennis said, "and I will guarantee you, in writing, that Dune's future here as the eventual head of this company is solid and assured."

"And if I don't?"

"Leave it to chance," Dennis said. "And fate. And behavior, of course."

Finn looked around the room at the stone-faced board, most of them old friends or distant cousins. Not a friendly smile in the bunch. Not a suggestion of a little wink and nod that he didn't have to worry about Dune. Dune, according to Honey's clipped phone recriminations, was drinking too much and regularly passing out and oversleeping and missing school.

"I'll take the foundation."

Thirty

After the new year, still on their endless holiday break, Clara started cleaning. She cleaned with a vengeance, an unholy concentration fueled by rage and more than a little fear. If her mother was going to move out, fine. She would scrub her mother right out of the house. She started with the upstairs closets, reorganizing and donating and refolding and discarding whatever was ripped or yellowed beyond fixing. She scoured the wooden floorboards on hands and knees as if she were excising something. She rearranged furniture and flipped cushions and vacuumed woodwork. She cooked and cooked and cooked. She only slept on the nights she fell into bed bone tired.

"I don't want to see her," Clara told Sam. Nina had only been inside the house twice, including for the most awkward Christmas morning in history. Sam chilly. Nina overly chipper. Bridie, the traitor, quietly thrilled their mother was there, following her around like a puppy. Nina had arrived with a ludicrous stack of gifts and the pan of hot cinnamon buns she made every Christmas morning as if nothing had changed. *As if nothing had changed!* Clara locked herself in her room until Nina left, and she refused to open her gifts.

"Why are you so awful?" Bridie pleaded. "It's like you want to hurt her. Clara, she's our *mom*."

"I do want to hurt her," Clara said matter-of-factly. Clara didn't want to think too hard about why she was spending all her time setting the house in order because the answer was embarrassingly obvious. As if she could scour away her pain. As if alphabetizing books would vanquish the emptiness she felt. As if arranging the spice shelf would somehow lead to Dune returning to her, on bended knee, hat in hand, asking for her forgiveness instead of what he was doing now—refusing to speak to her.

"What I don't get," she said to him during their one awful conversation, the conversation where he called her mother unspeakable names and blamed Nina for ruining his senior year, a charge Clara had leveled at her mother herself but that sounded ridiculous coming from Dune's mouth, "what I don't get," she'd said, "is how you can be this mean to me."

She pierced his composed furor for a second. But then he shook his head sharply and said, "What I don't get is how you are making this all about you and me." They were in his living room. She'd tried going upstairs when she entered the house, but he stopped her. "We can talk here," he said, feet apart, arms crossed, in the middle of the living room. She approached him now where he was standing next to the fireplace that clearly hadn't been used in weeks because his father was the one who always built the fires. The room was bitterly cold. "Dune," she said meekly. "I love you. I miss you *so much*. You are my best friend. You are the first boy I've loved."

His eyes welled up. She would hold on to that moment for far too long, but there was no denying it. As he stood saying nothing, she could almost hear his brain worrying the problem. His face softened and her heart lifted. She took another step closer, and he didn't back away. He didn't flinch when she gently linked her pinkie with his. She remembered the illustration in *The Joy of Sex*—the woman in her disheveled dress and fancy updo. She started to slowly unbutton her blouse. For a moment Dune stood rooted in place, stunned. Then he grabbed her wrist. Hard.

"Stop," she said, "you're hurting me."

"Have you lost your mind?"

And apparently she had because she went for it. She shook off the top and grabbed his jeans around the waist and tried to get her hand inside his pants.

"Stop it!" he said. She reared back and sat down on a chair and hid her face in her hands. He picked up her blouse and put it on the chair next to her. "You can go now," he said.

"But what's going to happen to us?" she asked, heartbroken. "What about the play?" She could tell by the look on his face he hadn't considered the play. Rehearsals wouldn't start until after winter break. "I don't know," he said. "I have enough problems now. Go home, Clara. Go. Home."

The day after school resumed and right before *Godspell* rehearsals would begin, Mr. Goodwin asked her to meet him after school. He told her Dune had threatened to quit the play unless she was replaced. She'd barked a quick, indignant laugh. "He can't. Who does he think he is?"

"I guess he thinks he's—Jesus?" Clara's mouth fell, flabbergasted. "Sorry. Sit down, Clara." He took her arm and gently led her over to the beat-up sofa he'd dragged off the street and installed in his office. It was mustard-colored, and the fabric was dingy and worn where it had been sat upon the most, but the seat cushions were deep and comfy and whenever they had bigger meetings in this office everyone jockeyed for a spot on the couch. Even now, Clara enjoyed having one side all to herself while Mr. Goodwin sat on the other side. He was avoiding looking her in the eye. He released a long sigh. This wasn't good. "You aren't going to fire me, are you?" she asked.

"I'm not."

"Oh, good. For a minute—"

"But we do have a problem. A conflict needs to be sorted."

"Sorted how?"

"Here's the thing," Mr. Goodwin started then stopped. Put his hands on his knees and looked toward the door like he was wishing someone would burst through and save him. "Dune has made it clear he won't participate in the play if the two of you have to work together as a team."

"But in the play, we are a team," Clara said.

"And therein lies the problem."

"Who's the director of this play anyway?" Clara said, she could see how the conversation was going to unspool; she could feel it in her bones.

"I'm the director, and that's why I'm speaking to Dune and to you. I want you to know I've had many, many conversations with Dune. He's not completely unreasonable. If you want to stay, he will quit. But he's not willing to, in his words, 'rat-a-tat tap around the stage with someone he hates.'"

Clara winced. Dune did not hate her. It wasn't possible.

"I'm sorry if that sounded harsh. For what it's worth, I think Dune doesn't know where to put his feelings right now and he's dumping them on you. He also believes people in the audience will gawk at the two of you given—given recent developments."

Clara was rubbing the arm of the sofa where the fabric had worn away and morphed into a bunch of slender threads barely covering the foam filling, looking like a balding man valiantly trying to cover his pate. Dune was right. She hadn't fully considered that part. It did sound awful. "I don't hate Dune," she said quietly. "I don't hate him. I miss him." And to her complete horror she burst into sobs for the first time since Nina walked across Cambridge Road carrying her suitcase and sat herself in Finn Finnegan's car and then flew south. Mr. Goodwin slid over a little and awkwardly patted her back. Then he stood and got a box of tissues and waited patiently while she blew her nose for what felt like one hundred times and tried to collect herself. As her sobs became hiccups, he started to speak. She had to look awful; she was an ugly crier.

"This situation stinks," he said. "I tried to talk Dune into being more accommodating, but you're both confused and angry. He admits you're a victim of this situation, too, but feels he won't be able to—"

"To *act*?" Clara said. "Isn't he an *actor* and isn't that what actors do even when they have to work with someone they hate?" She put a little spin on the word *hate* and Mr. Goodwin slumped a little.

"Clara, here's the thing. You and Dune? You're still . . ." Clara could see him biting back a word. Children? "You're teenagers" was what he landed on. "I'm sorry you have to deal with this situation. It's not right. But I can't fix any of it."

"Dune thinks it's all my mother's fault. He called her a whore."

"I'm sorry about that, too. I'm sorry this play that should have been a highlight of your senior year has become something quite the opposite. But Clara, I will do whatever you decide. If you want to stay, I will find a replacement for Dune."

Did she want to stay? For many weeks it was the only thing she cared about. Getting a part where she and Dune could perform together. But if she was honest, as outraged and furious as she was with Dune, when she imagined getting onstage with him wearing their dumb straw boaters and carrying canes and singing the big number—

When you feel sad (heel-toe, step, step) *or under a curse* (walk, walk, pivot)
Your life is bad (shuffle tap, ball change) *your prospects are worse*

—she dreaded it, too. How could they sing those lyrics cheerfully, jauntily, and look at each other and ham it up and not cry. Or take a swing at the other person. And practically everyone in the auditorium would know what had happened and might show up out of morbid curiosity because Finn Finnegan's son and Nina Larkin's daughter were performing together. Every one of those people would have an opinion on recent events, and if some people felt sorry for her, an equal number didn't. "I don't know what to do," she said.

"Do you want to talk it over with your parents?" Mr. Goodwin asked. "Do you want me to talk to your parents? Yours and Dune's?"

"No!" Clara said. The only thing that could possibly make this situation worse was to involve Mr. Goodwin and the parents. He would want them all to sit on cushions on the floor and *access their feelings.* So far, the Finnegans had successfully avoided the Larkins and vice versa, except, of course, for the two newlyweds.

"Take tonight to think it over," Mr. Goodwin said. "Talk to your dad or your mom or maybe even Dune. But I need to know tomorrow."

"Okay," she said as all energy and anger drained out of her at once.

"Clara," Mr. Goodwin said. "I know this is hard for you, and I'm not taking any sides here, obviously. I don't know your parents and I don't know Mr. and Mrs. Finnegan. The former Mr. and Mrs. Finnegan, I mean," he added.

"Yeah, I figured," Clara said.

"I imagine right now you think you're never going to get over this, but you will. You all will. And I hope I'm not stepping out of line by saying this, but you're going to be okay, and you can come here and talk to me whenever you want. Let off steam. Whatever you need."

"Thank you," she said. She felt like she could sleep for weeks. How delightful to pull a Rip Van Winkle and take a decades-long nap and wake up sometime in the future when her entire world wasn't exploding.

"I'd also like to recommend yoga," he said, perfectly straight-faced.

"Sure," Clara said, needing to get out of the room. "I'll consider yoga."

"Feel free to reach out to Priscilla. She would love to help, and the practice opens up so much."

"Okay. Well, I better get home." She stood as Mr. Goodwin sat up straight and took a deep long yoga-y breath, his hand on his stomach, and raised his eyebrows as if to say: *See how much better I feel?*

Clara gave an anemic thumbs-up and grabbed her backpack and walked out to the school hallway, which was deserted at five p.m. She didn't want to go home. She didn't want to stay. She had the sinking feeling that this floaty emotion of not belonging anywhere—existing in the in-between—wasn't going away anytime soon. As she got to the parking lot, she saw Dune's car idling. He was sitting behind the wheel. Her heart lifted. He was waiting for her. Maybe they could get through this. He was vibrating with anger the last time they spoke, but maybe he was equally as tired, missing her as much as she missed him. She was carrying her winter coat over one arm, but she didn't stop to put it on. She hurried across the parking lot only to come up short when Dune looked up, put the car in drive, and peeled out of the parking lot, leaving her behind, alone and shivering from the cold.

Thirty-One

Fern tiptoed down the hall to her parents' bathroom. She didn't want her mother to know she pre-weighed herself before the Thursday-night Weight Watchers meeting. She disrobed and stepped on the scale, forgetting to breathe. Down two more pounds! She hopped off and did a little dance in front of the mirror. Even she could see she was much less jiggly, although not exactly firm. Not firm Fern yet. Oh, how her tune had changed since last fall.

If Fern had planned on ditching Weight Watchers as soon as she could, her father's leaving had upended that possibility for the foreseeable future if not for her entire future. At first, Fern sat through those meetings clutching her food diary in one slightly sweaty palm, picturing herself as an old woman sitting in the same room, probably wearing the same jeans and sweater because nobody stepped on the scale in an outfit that might add ounces—pounds!—to their original weigh-in number. She sat in disbelief every week as some of the members slipped into the restroom to change into the outfit they had worn for their first weigh-in. Not even Honey was that crazy. "We need to start, ladies and gentlemen!" she would holler to the back of the room where weigh-in took place monitored by a volunteer, sometimes Fern, who would watch as person after person removed shoes, sweaters, belts, jewelry before they stepped on the scale. "You're not losing a pound; you're losing a bracelet!" Honey would yell to no effect. One memorable week, one of the regulars, Stella, hit her lifetime goal wearing a pair of shorts she had to hold up with two hands and a dangerously loose tube top. In the middle of January. In Rochester.

Fern could even admit she enjoyed the version of Honey who ran the meetings. That Honey was quick and confident and sometimes funny. She would introduce herself the same way at the top of every meeting. "Hi, everyone, and welcome. My name is Honor, but I've been called Honey since birth, so I was born into this kind of work." Everyone would laugh every week, even the people who remembered when she used to say: "And then I married a grocer! If I can keep my figure trim and healthy, anyone can!"

Honey wouldn't acknowledge it out loud, but the spike in attendance since the scandal was quietly thrilling to her. She knew people had come to see if she was a mess, if she'd mention Finnegan's all the time as she used to (the answer was no), but most of them stayed and became members. Fern's attendance, and attendant weight loss, was such a bright spot in Honey's life right now that Fern couldn't consider leaving. Not yet. She'd even made some friends as Honey had suggested she might. Two girls from her school: Phoebe was a senior ("big-boned," declared Honey) and Jenny a sophomore ("Those thighs will be obstinate," Honey predicted). They would compare notes on what they were eating at the school cafeteria and trade tips for best snacks. Fern and Phoebe seemed to have a similar trajectory. They'd lose a pound one week and gain two the next. Lose three, gain two. Up and down, up and down.

But their friend Jenny dropped weight every week. She'd already lost twelve pounds and had a hot pink achievement ribbon that she wore to school every day like a veteran decorated for extreme bravery in the face of a bowl of potato chips. One Saturday, the three of them went shopping and out to dinner at a place Honey had recommended that had an enormous salad bar. "Measure the dressing!" she told Fern, slipping a set of measuring spoons into Fern's backpack. "So many calories. And don't forget to refuse the breadbasket, and diet soda only."

They all obediently filled their plates with salad greens and raw vegetables, passing by the macaroni salad, potato salad, bins of shredded cheese and hard-boiled eggs. They measured their lite Italian dressing and cut their food into smaller pieces to make the meal last longer until Jenny said, "This stinks." She returned to the salad bar and piled a plate with actual sustenance and plopped it down at the center of the table.

"How do you lose weight eating all that?" Fern asked. Jenny raised a brow and pursed her lips, like Fern was thick. "What? What is it?"

"Okay, well, if you *must* know." Jenny opened the little zippered compartment on the front of her navy Champion backpack and pulled out a small brown bottle with an eyedropper.

"Eye drops?" Phoebe said.

"No, moron. I put a few drops of this into my coffee every morning and I don't get hungry until the end of the day. Then I have whatever I want for dinner. Also? I have tons of energy. I've cut ten seconds off my sprint time in track."

"How do I get some?" Fern said.

"My mom gets it from her doctor," Jenny said. "She calls it pep juice. I'm sure she'd get some for you. She wouldn't care. Whatever it takes to be thin! That's what she always tells me."

Within days both Phoebe and Fern were equipped with a little brown bottle of their own and it was, indeed, magic. Fern dropped five pounds in one week. She hardly thought about food most days, just like she'd always imagined was possible. She assumed every skinny person she knew didn't think about the next meal the minute they finished the one they were eating. Honey was over the moon. "See! Sometimes it takes a bit for your body to adjust to your new way of eating." She proudly pinned the hot pink ribbon on Fern's blouse two weeks later. Fern wouldn't wear it to school, of course, but she liked having it.

Phoebe told them they were crazy. "That shit is speed," she said to them after a couple of days of taking it. "It's going to wreck you and your metabolism. I'm done with Weight Watchers." Phoebe was a candy striper and planning on becoming a nurse, and loved lecturing anyone who would listen about "the societal pressures surrounding women's bodies and internalized negativity." She showed up at school one day with her heavily underlined copy of *Fat Is a Feminist Issue*. She wanted them all to read and discuss. Jenny snorted and handed it back to her. "Uh, no thanks."

"She's *British*," Phoebe told Jenny, who had an unhealthy obsession with the royal family, magazine photos of Prince Charles lining her locker. Jenny wasn't swayed.

Fern was torn. She liked Phoebe. She wanted to read the book and discuss with Phoebe. But she also liked losing weight and reluctantly admitted her mother had been right. It had helped her self-confidence. She still stuttered, but she talked so quickly now thanks to the pep juice it wasn't quite as noticeable.

One night she opened the book, and the things Susie Orbach wrote about resonated with her. Why was she always trying to make herself smaller? Why did women have to be *small*? She considered telling her mother about the drops and talking to her about body image and feminism and how thinness was a tool used to control women within a patriarchal structure, but she knew how that conversation would go. But she and Phoebe started having lunch together every day, and although Phoebe looked askance at Fern's lunch, a plate of lettuce with undressed tuna and cucumber slices, the low-calorie dressing in a little cup on the side so Fern could lightly dip each forkful into the tasteless vinaigrette, they never ran out of things to talk about. Phoebe invited Fern to come to visit her at work, and soon Fern was working as a candy striper at Rochester General. One Saturday morning, she ran into her pediatrician. "Fern!" he said, surprised and pleased and a little confused. He eventually mentioned her weight. "It's a lot to lose in a short amount of time," he said. "Are you doing it in a healthy way? Getting all the nutrients you need?"

Phoebe was standing behind him and Fern glanced at her quickly. "I'm doing Weight Watchers" was all she said. Phoebe shook her head dismally and Fern felt awful. But the only time her mother didn't look distraught these days was when she saw Fern's diminishing body. True, because of the drops, she was having a horrible time sleeping, but what was Jenny's mom's motto? *Anything for thin?*

One night, unable to sleep and hearing Dune moving around downstairs, she put on her robe and went to find him. He was sitting in the living room in the chair she used to think of as her father's. He had a heavy cut-glass crystal tumbler in his hand with some kind of brown liquid in it.

"What are you doing?" she said as she entered the living room.

"Man of the house," he said, raising the glass in a toast. "Haven't you heard? Having a man-of-the-house beverage. Want some?"

"No," Fern said. "Empty calories."

He nodded. "How's school going for you these days?"

She laughed. "Aren't you taking this dad thing a little far?"

"Aren't you taking the mom thing a little too far? Going to those meetings? You know you don't have to if you don't want," he said kindly.

"They're not bad," she said. "I've made some friends."

"Do you ever hang out with, uh, Bridie?"

"Yeah. Not Clara, though. She's—I don't know. Weird."

"Weird how?" He tipped the glass back and emptied it.

"I guess she's taking the mother thing too far. She's, like, cleaning all the time and cooking and won't let Bridie go to—the other house for dinner." None of them had come up with anything better than "the *other* house" to refer to where Nina and Finn now lived.

"Weird."

"Do you miss her?" Fern and Dune had never talked about it, but Fern knew about him and Clara. She had from the very start.

Dune stood up abruptly. "No," he said, walking toward the bar for a refill.

"Should you drink that much?" Fern asked. "Isn't that stuff really strong?"

"I can handle it," he said.

"Sorry I asked about Clara. What happened wasn't fair to you guys."

He replied without looking at her: "I could give a *flying fuck*."

"Okay," she said brightly, even though she had a bad feeling as he sloppily refilled his glass. "See you in the morning."

Thirty-Two

Saturday morning, late February. Gray, gray, gray. Dune slept straight through the lunch he was supposed to have had with his father at noon. He'd been out late the night before, drinking himself into oblivion, or, more accurately, attempting to drink himself into oblivion. His problems felt so insurmountable that no amount of Budweiser would wash them away. Sometimes he could temporarily forget he was miserable. Miserable at school because nobody asked about what happened but everyone's eyes were full of pity, unless they were full of glee because Dune Finnegan wasn't on top of the world for a change. Miserable at home because his mother told him constantly, in an increasingly urgent and hysterical tone, that he needed to be "the man of the house," a statement that pierced him straight through, heart and soul. He wasn't even eighteen! Miserable rehearsing for the play, which he'd been so fucking stubborn about and now hated and would have given anything to leave but how could he after he'd made Clara quit? Why he'd chosen to punish her in that way now seemed incomprehensible to him, but he'd done it, and he had to live with it or face even more humiliation.

Dune never imagined Clara would leave the play entirely. He didn't think Mr. Goodwin would seriously entertain his objections. Now he was stuck performing with Deirdre Connelly, who was not fun, not pretty, not Clara, and who had very strong and wrong opinions on every little step they took. His life was exhausting.

He rolled over and looked at his watch. He could probably still catch his father if he hurried. He made himself stand up and assess the internal damage. His head hurt. What else was new? But his stomach seemed okay. He pulled on the shirt he'd worn out last night; it reeked of cigarettes. He went to the kitchen. He hoped the leftover coffee in the pot was from this morning. He casually rinsed out a mug, filled it with cold coffee, and nuked it in the microwave. Poured as much half-and-half into the cup as would fit. It tasted terrible, but he needed the caffeine to counter his pounding head. "Do your job, friend," he said to his coffee mug.

As he got in the car and drove to meet his father, he mulled over his most recent pressing problem. Greta Crane. Five feet and six inches worth of relentless cheer except for recently, a development Greta had made clear was all Dune's fault. In the space of weeks, so many things Greta claimed to like about Dune were offered up on a virtual silver platter as liabilities. It almost felt like his father's actions had set off some kind of citywide mandate that allowed everyone in his life to grade him. His teachers, Mr. Goodwin, his friends, his mother, and now Greta Crane, who he'd somehow, inexplicably, after a series of heavily inebriated weekends, started dating.

He could hear Greta's voice asking her favorite question: "What are you thinking about?" The question was almost a tic she used to fill silences and was his least favorite question of all time because even though she asked it constantly, he never had an acceptable answer handy. He realized the point of the question: Greta wanted him to be thinking about *her*. But if he was with her, if she was sitting right in front of him not giving him a second's peace, why would he also be thinking about her? Instead of thinking about Clara. He would not think about Clara. (He couldn't stop thinking about Clara.) Or about how much he hated hated hated working at Finnegan's. Or about how he'd been offered an early acceptance at Notre Dame and instead of feeling excited, dreaded the prospect of moving away, which also made no sense because he dreaded being at home, too.

As he pulled into the diner to meet his father, he added these lunches to the list of things he resented. His father was trying, he could see that. But it was the *What are you thinking?* problem all over again because the only thing his father wanted was for everyone to be happy for him and *move on*, as if they could all snap their fingers and make life easy again. For a brief moment, Dune considered answering the question, telling everyone in exquisitely pointed terms *exactly* what he was thinking, but that would require a private reckoning, and he couldn't do it. He wasn't ready. How had his life been one thing in early December and something completely different overnight? Without Finn present, Honey hadn't lasted a full week at the lake. The house had already been closed for the winter and was freezing and Honey refused to use space heaters because they were too dangerous.

"Then why do we have them?" Fern asked.

"Don't you start!" Honey snapped and Fern and Dune looked at each other in disbelief. The situation became worse by the minute. Honey didn't know how to start a fire or turn on the water supply to the house. All the mouse droppings in the kitchen freaked her out and she declared the view of the gray, choppy water and denuded trees depressing. She spent most of her time muttering to herself about Finn. He was relieved when Honey got the call from Helen Harper about the food poisoning and they had to rush back to Cambridge Road, even though it meant an inevitable confrontation with Clara.

He knew his rage toward her was overblown, but he couldn't help placing more of the blame on her mother than his father. Mothers were supposed to be steadfast, loyal, present, and true. Fathers were fallible; it was how they were built. He believed a truly good mother, a good *person*, would have the strength and discipline to put a stop to all of it. That this equation by all rights should extend to his father was a thought he became skilled at ignoring.

Once he got to the diner, he and his father quickly ordered their usual—a BLT for Finn, a turkey on rye for Dune—and proceeded to make awkward conversation until Finn tried, again, to bring Dune over to his side. Dune didn't want his father to be his *friend*. Dune didn't want to *understand*. He didn't want to know about Finn's feelings for Nina Larkin or hear all the ways Finn believed Honey fell short. He finally stopped his father midsentence, something about Finn needing to live his life fully, and said, "Dad. I don't need to know any of this."

"What *do* you need to know?" Finn asked, leaning forward earnestly and uncharacteristically. Renewed and reborn with a different wedding ring on the same old finger.

"Mainly? I need to know how to get the garbage disposal working again. Mom's flipping out about it being on the fritz."

"I'll come over and fix it," Finn said.

"I think for the time being I should do it. Until Mom—calms down a little."

Dune couldn't read the look on Finn's face. It wasn't disappointment or relief but something more complicated. Admiration? Maybe. His father was in a big battle with his uncle Dennis. He knew there was a lot of trouble over the salmonella incident. "I hear you about a cooling-off period," Finn said. "But I'm only five minutes away. I'm not going to let all this fall on you."

"Okay," Dune said, understanding in that moment that he might have a clearer grasp on this situation than his father, a realization that made him unaccountably sad. "So. The disposal?"

The disposal wasn't that hard to unjam, and when he turned it on and it made its horrifying grinding sound again for the first time in days, Honey clapped her hands and hugged him and gave a little cheer and seemed truly happy for the first time since his father had married his girlfriend's mother. "The man of the house!" she exclaimed triumphantly before going up to bed that night. He thought of the former man of the house and what he'd be doing if he were in the living room. He walked over to the bar cabinet. Opened it up and poured himself a hefty glass of Jameson and took a big sip. It tasted awful and made him cough, but he was getting used to it. He sat in a rocking chair with the glass in his hand and patiently drank the whole thing. By the time he was finished, the pit in his stomach had mellowed a little and his mind had settled. He refilled his drink. No wonder his father imbibed every night. This stuff took the edge off his mother like nothing else.

He missed Clara, but now, into his third whiskey of the evening, he saw even more clearly that choosing to be together would be choosing to be part of the scandal. For both of them! He wasn't only thinking about himself. He stumbled up the stairs to his bedroom.

On his desk sat a decaying wrist corsage. He'd ordered it for Clara as soon as they decided to go to the New Year's formal together and had forgotten to cancel the order, so the pretty white gardenia had shown up at his door the morning of the dance that neither of them would attend. He didn't have the heart to throw it away, so there it sat. It was nothing but a decimated, formerly beautiful thing. He took the flower out of the plastic box, fully brown now, still attached to the jaunty silver wristband, opened his window, and chucked it into the yard.

Thirty-Three

Sam understood that Nina was offering him a kind of quid pro quo: she got Finn and he got freedom or something like it, but when was life ever that easy? Life certainly hadn't been simple for Finn and Nina after the salmonella incident, which Sam had also quietly enjoyed. Not the illness part—he felt terrible about the old lady who died—but the comeuppance part. The uncle had done the right thing, but Nina had sprinted to a faraway altar to marry a hard-charging business owner and ended up with an emasculated figurehead.

If Nina had managed to convince herself she was doing him a favor, releasing him to indulge in the Garret of it all, she was deluded because deep down she had to know the opposite was true. The scandal, local as it may have been, had made him the object of constant scrutiny and, worse, already placed him on the receiving end of all kinds of potential fix-ups and blind dates. He couldn't believe how quickly the masses had moved in on him. Nina had managed to release him into a previous version of himself: the reluctant bachelor once again. For now, it was easy for him to say he wasn't ready, needed to focus on his girls and work, and people would back off, but soon the pressure to start dating would return.

And then there was Garret. He had no intention of telling Garret about Nina and Finn. Not yet. But Garret found out. He'd grown up in Rochester, had worked at Xerox in Webster before being transferred to Palo Alto with the other genius recruits from around the world who were all convinced they held the future not only of Xerox but of humanity in their hands.

Every time Sam went out to Palo Alto, he found the excitement and enthusiasm at PARC contagious. In the company of the engineers, as odd as they were brilliant, it all sounded possible, probable even. So many smart people! So many bold ideas! Sam had specifically been recruited to join Xerox as it was starting to lose market exclusivity. Between expired patents and antitrust enforcement, the once-mighty copier monopoly was wounded and bleeding. It seemed obvious to Sam that the future of the company resided at PARC. He believed in the Alto computer they'd built, believed the entire Alto system was revolutionary, and Garret was the evangelist he sought out for information, understanding, selling points, because convincing the higher powers at Xerox to embrace—and invest—in the unknown was no small feat.

He and Garret had worked together on the big company conference in Boca Raton, the one that was supposed to define the company's strategy for the coming decade. They were in charge of the final presentation of the week, the highly anticipated "Futures Day" exhibit where all the top executives would finally see what the motley crew at PARC had been toiling over for the past seven years. As the PARC staff piled onto the stage of the massive hotel ballroom to begin their demonstration, a booming voice-over filled the room, telling the audience of former and current copier executives that "the problem is paper." Sam's heart sank. He hadn't approved that line, and it was sure to set everyone on edge. Still, his hopes rose during the mind-blowing demonstration of the Alto system, with its electronic keyboard, computer mouse, processor, screen, and printer. The team showed off the most advanced functions of the software: shooting office memos back and forth from California to Florida, drawing graphs and organizational charts, exhibiting a simplified way to type Japanese characters—something that had befuddled the organization for years—and so much more. The exhibit was open all day, and Sam popped in and out to watch people engage with the machines, increasingly discouraged. The senior executives reeked of disregard. Most of them stood at the back of the room, arms crossed, eyes narrowed, as their enthusiastic wives—many of them their former secretaries—learned how to use the computer mouse and excitedly worked the program. Sam knew what the men were thinking: what they'd feared for years, a tangible threat to the company's cash cow copying business, had not only arrived, it was coming from inside their own house.

"I think it's going really well," Garret said to Sam toward the end of the day. "When can we sneak out and get a drink?"

"We can't," Sam said. "I'm here with my wife."

"I'm very good with wives," Garret said as Sam thought, *Not a chance.*

By then, by the time of the conference, Garret had not only seen through Sam's carefully constructed presentation as a straight man but had successfully seduced him. Lured Sam (oh, Sam knew he was using the wrong words, he had not been a victim, he was not absolved) back to his apartment, where inexplicably thrilling things had happened. That Garret was a perfectly comfortable out gay man, someone who seemingly had zero conflicts about his identity or activism, fascinated and terrified Sam. Garret called Sam after the absurd wedding announcement appeared in the paper, tipped off by someone at Xerox, no doubt. He wanted to know if Sam was okay but almost immediately began pushing to visit. "I know it's complicated, but isn't this what the believers call a 'blessing in disguise'?"

What was Sam supposed to do now? Start dating men? Start showing up by himself at Margaret's or other gay bars downtown: Jim's or the Rathskeller? He couldn't. He wouldn't. But he also couldn't avoid Garret forever, even if they did live on separate coasts.

Now that Sam was on the receiving end of all Garret's knowledge about the gay scene in Rochester, he supposed Garret was right to call him uptight and old-fashioned. Garret told him about the private dinners around town for successful, wealthy men who were happily living dual lives, including the former mayor. The mayor! He introduced him to a deftly organized group of men and women out of the University of Rochester who had started one of the first gay newspapers in the country and continued to vocally and visibly demand basic human rights for themselves.

"I'm so damn proud of these kids," Garret said, sounding like a boastful parent. *It's a whole new world!*

Sam was not fighting for—anything. He wasn't engaged or involved or even particularly well informed because he was paranoid and terrified of losing his job. Just hanging out with Garret outside of the office was saying something. None of the sales force or higher-level executives were comfortable with Garret's brand of gay, which was unabashed. Oh, Xerox wouldn't say they'd fired Sam for being gay, they'd concoct some other reason, but the company would not tolerate whispers about their very visible marketing director. And there were his daughters to think about. They'd had enough confusion and disruption in their lives. He had no intention of exploding their world twice. He would be better than Nina in that way. He would claim the higher ground with its more satisfying view.

When he came home from work one evening in April and walked into the living room and heard Garret laughing in the kitchen with Clara, his initial reaction was outrage. How could he be here uninvited and unannounced? Sam angrily strode into the kitchen, brought up by the sight of Garret sitting at his kitchen farm table. Nina had asked repeatedly if she could have the table, which technically was hers, but he hadn't let her remove a notepad from his house. *His* house. Garret had a glass of red wine in front of him, and Bridie was sitting next to him drinking a Fresca. Clara was in her usual spot, wearing one of Nina's old aprons, standing at the stove, stirring something in an oversized cast-iron pot. The three of them were laughing as Garret drew on a piece of paper, probably some kind of computer network, and Sam watched the girls watching Garret, riveted. He cleared his throat.

"Dad!" Bridie jumped up and ran to him. "Your friend from California is here."

"I see that," Sam said, removing his heavy tweed coat, which still smelled like the one cigarette he allowed himself while driving home at the end of the day, and hanging it on a hook in the back hall.

"Garret was telling us about San Francisco," Clara said.

"I want to go," Bridie said.

"You have quite the cook there." Garret refilled his wineglass, nodding his head to indicate Clara, deftly mincing fresh rosemary.

"I sure do. I didn't know you were in town."

"Very last minute," Garret said. "Decided to come in for my mother's birthday tomorrow and I was driving by and thought I'd ring the bell and see who was home. Didn't expect to find these remarkably entertaining young women."

"How did you know this was our house?" Bridie asked, and Sam hoped he was imagining the slight edge to her voice.

"Company directory," Garret lied.

"Do you want to stay for dinner?" Clara said to Garret. "We have plenty."

"Thought you'd never ask," Garret said, winking at Sam. "I'd love to."

WHEN GARRET WALKED INTO THE house, Bridie recognized him immediately as the man in the photo that she had taken from her father's wallet and placed in the old cookie tin in her closet where she kept her pilfered items. She was happy her father had a friend visiting. Since Nina left it had only been the three of them at home, which was fine, but sometimes a little sad and lonely. Bridie snuck over to her mother's house a few times a week when Clara was otherwise occupied. She didn't talk about visiting and Clara didn't ask. Bridie supposed they'd reached some kind of detente in that way, but it was funny how having a fourth person at dinner felt better. As if they'd been sitting at a lopsided table and someone slipped a matchbook beneath the wobbly leg and everything snapped into place, even though Garret wasn't her mother.

After dinner, Garret said he had to run (Bridie noticed he didn't offer to help with the dishes) and thanked them all and mock-solemnly shook Bridie's hand and Clara's hand, saying, "Ladies. Good eve to you both," like he was a Shakespearean character or something. Sam told them he'd clean up and they should go finish their homework.

Bridie went straight to her closet and pulled out the tin and rummaged through until she found the folded newspaper photo. She knocked on Clara's door.

"What is this?" Clara asked, smoothing out the piece of newsprint on her bedspread.

"Something I found a few months ago while I was going through Dad's wallet."

"You took it?"

Bridie shrugged.

"You are such a little thief. Our crafty little pickpocket. I wouldn't be surprised if you were shoplifting all the time."

"I don't shoplift!"

"Why did you take this, sticky fingers?"

"I don't know. I liked the photo of Dad sitting in a beanbag chair. That's Garret," she said, pointing to a person on the left, leaning forward.

"Yeah, I know," Clara said, glum. She folded the piece of paper.

"What's wrong?" Bridie asked.

"Nothing."

"I thought he was nice," Bridie said.

"Yeah, he was nice. Now scram. I have homework."

Bridie left the photo on Clara's bed, and after she left, Clara took another look. Her father looked so out of place, the only one wearing a suit, his short hair slicked back with a severe side part. He was sitting awkwardly in the beanbag chair, which, according to the caption, was where all meetings at PARC were conducted. All the other people in the photo looked at ease and like they were dressed for a picnic. Or a sit-in. One woman was smoking and wearing sandals and a turtleneck. One of the men had bare feet. Everyone in the photo was smiling at the guy in front of a whiteboard full of indecipherable scribbling, except for Garret. Who was looking straight at her dad.

Thirty-Four

When they were finally through the dismal holiday season, the old year mercifully behind them, Finn and Nina started to settle into a routine, and it was possible to feel they'd soon be through the worst of it. The conversations with their respective children were every bit as awful as they'd expected and then some. The kids vacillated between hurt and angry, never at the same time, so Finn and Nina invariably dealt with a concentrated stew of both. They waited weeks to be seen together in public—they weren't allowed to attend Connie Pavone's funeral—and even though all their friends and relatives knew what had happened and where they were living, nobody called or visited. Some people wouldn't speak to them. Thomas politely suggested Nina might want to take a "sabbatical" from the paper. She knew what that meant. Some folks quietly squeezed Nina's hand when she was out and about, and she never really understood why. Were the hand squeezes signaling support, passing along their own desperation, pitying her for this gravest of sins?

All this was harder for Finn than it was for her. She'd never been interested in the social life at the country club or attended any of their organized events: the Valentine's dance, the Mother's Day brunch, the Father's Day pancake breakfast, and on and on. For years, she'd successfully begged off going to church on Sundays, saying she needed to shop, cook, and write and wasn't it nice for Sam and the girls to go to Mass and out for breakfast just the three of them? She wasn't a believer, but Finn was, and after a few failed attempts at asking him to explain to her how he squared their circumstances with his faith, she gave up. His justifications, the way he was able to twist rules into exceptions, was one of the things she hated about organized religion—its blurry borders and muscular hypocrisy for the anointed few, the people with resources, the donors.

But if the church leadership was content to give Finn a gentle slap on the wrist and slip his check into the back pocket of their black trousers, his fellow parishioners were not so kind. His first time back at the eleven fifteen a.m. Mass on the third Sunday of January was designed to avoid Honey and his kids, who generally went to the nine a.m. service. Everyone noticed him, but not a single person approached.

"Not one!" he said to Nina when he got home, looking pale, shook. "During the sign of peace, everyone acted as if I wasn't there. Like I was a leper. Worse! An apparition."

"I'm sorry," she said. "It's going to take time."

They sat at the tiny table in the kitchen of their small Craftsman bungalow, the one they'd seen as a temporary solution until they figured out the best place to buy their own home, but now that their finances had changed, they'd extended the lease for the rest of the year.

Finn stared into space, slack-jawed, looking visibly older. For the entirety of her first marriage, she had been the one responsible for lifting the mood in the house, constantly performing a little tap dance to distract from Sam's disaffected presence. When the affair with Finn began, she reveled in his exuberance, happily passed the mood baton to him, but now it seemed to be back in her hand. Instead of being disappointed, she was almost grateful and wondered why she and Sam couldn't have taken turns bolstering the other, why they hadn't fed off each other emotionally. Nina had often wondered if her and Finn's lust was capacious enough for love or grief or disappointment. Well, here it was. And she was determined to pull them through this moment. Moment was probably too optimistic a word. This phase? This transition! Yes, that was it. They were all in a period of *transition*, and transitions were hard, change was hard, it stirred up powerful emotions. But, Nina insisted to herself, on the other side of change was opportunity. Who could they all be, now that she and

Finn had thrown the cards in the air and invited everyone to redefine their lives? Everything felt possible.

"Come upstairs with me?" she said, holding a hand out to him.

What Nina couldn't get over, the feeling she wanted to hold on to as long as possible, was how everything felt sensual to her. Everything. The thrilling casual intimacy, the sight of their tangled mussed bed every morning, the musky smell of the sheets. The places they eagerly made love—the bed, the kitchen, the sofa. A solid fuck on the desk of Finn's office the day he was cleaning it out and later that afternoon a furtive but satisfying grope in refrigerator number three, which bordered on sacrilegious and because of that was incredibly hot. Some days, they were like teenagers who'd just discovered sex. She sometimes saw herself as if she were watching another, better Nina from above. Nina on her knees pleasuring Finn and sauntering across the living room, stark naked, to get a glass of wine.

She'd driven to Buffalo one morning to buy lingerie. Completely unnecessary, bordering on ridiculous. She could have quietly bought silky nightgowns and racier bras and lacy panties in any number of stores in Rochester without anyone knowing who she was, but she enjoyed performing deception now that they were safely husband and wife. They took refuge in one another. They wintered. Everyone else was inside during these short, cold days anyway.

She was surprised to find that she didn't miss writing her old column, but she did miss teaching the cooking classes. Before the elopement, she'd agreed to give a series of three classes at Saint Benedict's parish center, which had a huge kitchen. The program was centered around Easter: the first week was Easter Brunch Favorites, the second an Elegant Easter Dinner, and the final class Easter for the Family, which would feature cakes and candies that the women (it was always women) could make with their children. The slots had filled quickly, and so Nina worked diligently on the menus. If these went well, maybe she could do a quarterly series. Maybe monthly. She arrived at the kitchen early to set up eight workstations and do all her prep. She was nervous but excited. She waited. And waited. Finally, the door swung open, and Bess came barging through, "Sorry! Sorry

I'm late." Bess stopped in her tracks and took one look at the empty kitchen and shook her head. "Those bitches," she said.

NINA ASSURED HERSELF THAT BY the time the weather softened and the sun returned and the trees began to bud, at around the time the daffodils were waving their buoyant bonnets in the breeze, the town would be tired of the gossip. Tired of freezing her out. But spring was punishingly late, and although it was ludicrous to take the weather personally, Rochester made it hard not to feel that it was meteorologically against you, particularly when the winter came early and refused to leave. The first week of April, she was still wearing her winter coat, her hat and gloves, those infernal snow boots. Finn had been offering to fly them somewhere warm since mid-February, but she wasn't ready to hightail it out of town just yet. And not for any trip that would be too reminiscent of their December wedding. She was finally starting to remember the good of those days and not their churning wake.

But Nina'd had enough of Clara's cruelty. Nina had given Clara *time*, as everyone said she should. She'd let Clara dictate the terms and Clara had acted like a terrorist. Nina wasn't allowed in her old house. Bridie could go to Nina's new house but not stay for dinner because Clara was the one who made dinner now and Bridie needed to be home for the "family" meal every night. Bridie could sleep over one night a week, but not two. Nina had expected the hardest part about their elopement's aftermath would be dealing with Sam, but it was Clara who made life miserable for all of them. And poor Bridie. Nina could see Bridie pulling away from her for fear of Clara's ire. One afternoon, Clara had rung the front doorbell to call Bridie home for dinner. Nina answered the door, and her heart started pounding when she saw Clara through the window. But Clara wouldn't cross the threshold.

"I'm here for my sister," she said coolly.

"Clara," Nina said, "please come inside and sit down. You can't go for the rest of your life or even the rest of this year without talking to me. This is silly."

Clara stared at Nina, crossed her arms. "*I'm* silly."

"Clara, please."

She yelled over Nina's shoulder. "Bridie! Get out here!"

Bridie appeared in the living room behind her mother. "I think I'm going to stay here for dinner," she said, looking terrified and small, and even that set Clara off—not Bridie's disloyalty, but the meek way she seemed to be begging for permission. "Get some backbone, Bridie," Clara said, storming down the front steps and nearly slipping on the ice.

"Are you okay?" Nina hurried down the steps to help Clara.

"I'm *fine*!" Clara snapped at her.

Nina went back into the house and found a tearful Bridie. "I'm sorry, sweetheart. This will get better." But would it?

Finn and Nina started to make a few tentative forays into a social life as partners. Finn wanted to host an elaborate dinner party, but Nina did not. She claimed it was because all of her supplies were back at her old house: her specialty pantry items and copper pots and treasured cast-iron Dutch ovens and honed knives. "I'll buy new ones," he said, impatient and uncomprehending. It had taken years for her to acquire all the things she now missed. And this inexplicable development: she didn't *want* to cook. Every time she walked into their kitchen and opened the cabinets or the refrigerator to plan dinner, she became catastrophically tired. She would brew a pot of tea and sit on the sofa, which hadn't been broken in yet by husbands or roughhousing children or hours and hours of television, and open her book. The next thing she knew, Finn was gently shaking her awake in a darkening room. Finn was confused by her unwillingness to cook for the two of them.

"Let's invite people out to dinner," she suggested to him. "One couple at a time. See whom we can trust." They both understood that whether people in town approved or disapproved of their choices, Finn now had the foundation's significant budget at his disposal, an efficient balm to a lot of local outrage. The morning after one of those dinners, one that had gone well because it was with a former business contact of Finn's looking for a hefty donation, Bridie called

Nina early in the morning to report that Clara didn't feel well and was home alone. Nina understood. When she allowed herself to parse her current indifference in the kitchen, she realized that in her previous life, cooking was a way to fill a house devoid of marital love with a more tangible kind of love. A meal was an offering, an act of care and intimacy. She didn't *need* to cook for Finn, but every fiber of her being wanted to nourish her daughters.

She got to work making all of Clara's favorite nursery foods. Corn bread. Rice pudding. Toll House cookies with oats because that's how Clara liked them. She swung by Finnegan's—she still attracted sidelong glances, but she'd gotten good at ignoring them—and picked up saltines and Ritz crackers and ginger ale and orange juice. Campbell's Chicken & Stars, Progresso meatball soup, Stouffer's frozen macaroni and cheese, glazed donuts. She made a detour to Don's Original for the chocolate almond frozen custard Clara loved so much and thought how Finn should try to get the product into the freezers at Finnegan's and quickly marveled at her ability to abet the kind of predatory behavior she'd always complained about before remembering that Finn was no longer acquiring products for the store. She certainly wasn't gifting Helen Harper any of her good ideas. She stopped at a bookstore and bought *Glamour* and *Seventeen* and *Mademoiselle* and *Redbook* and a bunch of tabloid papers. She bought aspirin and Midol and Pepto Bismol to cover all the bases. A peace offering, a ticket past the front door, a gesture she hoped would thaw the air between her and Clara just a little. It had been almost four months. Four months of Clara making a point.

Nina'd only been to the house twice since she left, once the day after they returned to Rochester, the awful conversation with the girls, Bridie sobbing, Clara stone-cold, Sam glowering in the other room. The second time on Christmas morning, which felt like the worst one-act play anyone had ever been forced to perform. On her way out that afternoon, Sam handed over her "personal effects," which he'd tossed into boxes with such disregard she could feel the force of his anger every time she peered into one. Bras and panties mixed with loose jewelry and hair clips and, weirdly, a flashlight that she'd stored on the nightstand in case of winter power outages. Cosmetics all akimbo. A bunch of dress shoes but nothing practical. He'd thrown a bottle of Chanel No. 19 in with her good sweaters, and it spilled and ruined everything. It was as if a deranged animal had packed the boxes.

Car loaded with all her peace offerings for an ailing Clara, Nina drove the fifteen blocks to her old house. As always, a key to the back door sat under one of the terra cotta pots on the back step. She let herself into the kitchen.

Thirty-Five

From her bedroom, Clara heard the kitchen door open and knew it was her mother at the same moment she realized she'd been waiting for her mother. Feeling sick and sorry for herself, part of Clara just wanted to surrender, wave the white flag, and let Nina take care of her, bring her soup and toast and ginger ale. Salt water to gargle and ease her throat. But the stubborn part wanted to pretend to be asleep so she didn't have to talk to Nina.

She could hear her mother moving around downstairs, opening and shutting cupboards. So often during the last weeks, when Clara was caught up in cooking and successfully got to the finish of a dish, the exquisitely clear chicken broth she made for soup, the angel food cake that was tall and light, the Bolognese that simmered all day and was perfectly balanced, she wanted to show her mom. She wanted to point and say, *Look what I did!* to someone who would appreciate not just the effort (which Bridie and Sam did) but the achievement (which they did not unless she explained it, and that was no fun). But then she would force herself to remember her father's face the morning he read the note. How he walked around the house for days distracted and distraught, and Clara's anger flared so quickly she could feel it in her fingers and toes.

But. She was so tired. From the fever, yes, but also in her bones. A kind of tired that no amount of sleep could ameliorate. Her anger had fueled her for weeks and weeks and she didn't know how to give it up, but it was weighted. She closed her eyes and imagined walking down the stairs and approaching her mother kindly, lovingly. Nina would be so happy. She could imagine how Nina would rush to her and hug her and kiss her and say, *Oh no, you're so warm. Let's get you upstairs and back in bed.* Then Nina would make her lunch. And maybe she would sit with Clara until she fell asleep and maybe Clara would wake up and Nina would be making dinner and Clara, for the first time in ages, could relax and bask in a three-dimensional kind of love, one she could see and taste and smell. But she didn't want to fall into the quicksand of complacency so easily. She imagined her father coming home and finding Nina in the kitchen. What would that be like for him? Would it ever be okay? Could Nina and Sam be friends eventually? Maybe. But then the photo of Garret would bubble up in her head and she'd feel queasy over whatever the hell that was. Still. Maybe Clara could put down her knife, both literally and figuratively, and take a breath, take a break, take a nap. She headed downstairs.

"Look who's up," Nina said when Clara entered the kitchen, as if she'd never left. "You have a fever," she said, seeing Clara's flushed face and glassy eyes.

"I know. I took aspirin."

"Are you hungry? Do you need anything? What can I do for you?"

Clara shrugged. Avoided looking Nina in the eyes. "I don't know."

Nina felt like she was dealing with a skittish kitten and had to keep her distance, no sudden movements, she couldn't gather her firstborn into her arms and hold on for life. "I bought some things. Want to look?"

"Okay."

"Soup?" she asked, holding up the can. "Crackers? Sandwich?"

"I could eat some soup."

Nina opened the drawer where she'd always kept the can opener, but it was full of serving utensils and tongs. She stood, stumped.

"I moved it over there," Clara said, pointing to another drawer. Nina started opening all the drawers and cabinets. Everything had been rearranged. "This is—interesting," Nina said, keeping her tone light even though she was unfairly annoyed by how Clara had improved things.

"It all works better. The triangle, you know."

"I do know." Nina laughed. "How do you know about the work triangle?"

"You have all those books," Clara said, pointing to the long shelf of cookbooks. "I read a lot of them."

"When I moved into this house," Nina said, "your grandmother came and organized the kitchen for me one day. I was pregnant with you and sick all the time. For some reason I never thought about changing things. I left everything where it was. Strange, right?"

"Not as strange as the things you did decide to change."

"Well, that's true," Nina said. She filled the kettle with water and put it on the range, lit the burner. "Do you want to talk about it?" she said, turning to Clara, who wasn't looking at her but down at the floor.

"Not really."

Nina started to unload the groceries she'd bought. The food pantry remained the same, and that gave her some kind of comfort.

"Why did it have to be Mr. Finnegan?"

Clara did want to talk. This was good. "What do you mean?"

"I mean if you were unhappy and so *desperate* to leave, why couldn't you pick someone else? Someone who didn't live across the street." She gestured toward the Finnegans' house angrily. "Someone who wasn't *famous*."

Nina couldn't help it: she tried to bite back the laugh, but all she managed to do was infuriate Clara even further. "I'm so glad you think this is funny!"

"Clara, believe me, I do not find any of this funny. But Finn—Mr. Finnegan—he's not famous. Truly. He's just a businessman. Currently, a businessman who is out of his old job."

"If he's not famous, how come your wedding was in the paper?"

"I'm sorry about that. If I had known, I would have stopped it." Nina opened a can of soup and dumped the contents into a small pot and reminded herself that Clara was a teenager. A teenager who had absolutely been wronged. By her.

"Why couldn't you marry someone," Clara continued, "who wasn't my boyfriend's father?"

"What?" Clara was thrilled to see her mother's eyes widen, the pallor of her face fade a little bit. She'd hit her intended mark. "You have a boyfriend? Dune is your boyfriend?"

"Not anymore. Thanks to you. He's not my boyfriend. He's not my costar in the school play because I had to drop out of the play, so I'm not even in the play now. And he's not even my friend anymore."

Nina was dumbfounded. "I had no idea. Absolutely no idea."

"Yes, well, that was my brilliant idea. To keep it a secret until the New Year's formal. That worked out great."

Nina was stunned into silence. In one of their many brief conversations that only centered around logistics, Sam had mentioned Clara decided not to be in the play but hadn't said why. Nina was so preoccupied with everything else at that moment, she hadn't thought to ask. "Why are you not in the play? I don't understand."

Clara rolled her eyes so theatrically that Nina was simultaneously concerned and impressed. "Dune is playing Jesus, right? And I was John the Baptist, okay? They are onstage together *the entire show*. We had songs together. Duets. Dune threatened to quit if I didn't."

"Why did they let him stay and not you? It's completely unfair. Do you want me to talk to someone?"

"Nobody made me. It was my decision."

"Damn," Nina said softly. "I didn't know. I'm so sorry. That really stinks."

"My whole life stinks right now."

Nina went back to the stove. Ladled some Chicken & Stars into a bowl and put the bowl in front of Clara with a spoon and a napkin. "I know it feels that way, and I want to help. But you have to try to meet us halfway, Clara."

Us. Clara took one sip of the soup and pushed it away.

"You want something else?" Nina asked.

"I've been making chicken stock. This soup tastes like water and it's too salty."

"You've been making stock? Very impressive. Stock is time-consuming."

Clara shrugged. "I like doing it."

"Do you want me to talk to Dune? Or should Finn talk to Dune?"

Clara laughed dully. "Do I want my stepfather to tell his son he has to be my boyfriend? No thanks."

Nina sat down and fiddled with some packages of saltines. Trying to choose her words precisely. "Clara, I know this feels like the end of the world to you right now, but in just a few months you're going to be off to college. A whole new world. All new people. An exciting start—"

"Oh, I guess Dad didn't tell you that, either."

"Tell me what?"

"I deferred Cornell. I'm staying here next year. I'll take classes somewhere local."

Nina was alarmed. How had Sam not told her? When was all this decided? So that's how he was punishing her, by withholding critical information. "Can you change your mind?"

"My mind is made up. It was a family decision."

All the equanimity and understanding and hope Nina had mustered for this encounter dissipated in an instant. "I am still part of this family. You are my family."

Clara didn't look up. "Somebody needs to be present for Bridie. Senior year is important."

"I'm here, Clara. *I'm* Bridie's mother."

"When it suits."

Nina stood and went to the sink. She couldn't cry. She plunged her wrists beneath the faucet's stream of cold water, trying to calm herself. She wanted to slap Clara. She wanted to hug Clara. Clara hurting herself in the name of punishing Nina was a brilliant ploy, though. Nothing had ever made her feel worse. But she was also furious. Bridie loved Clara, but Bridie didn't *need* another parent; she had parents. Nina should have counted to ten, she should have gone to the bathroom and taken a beat, she should have kept her mouth shut, but what she did instead was turn to Clara and say: "I truly hope this is the last time you hurt yourself by exaggerating the importance of your presence."

"I'll be sure to remember that," Clara said, but Nina was ashamed to see Clara's lower lip quiver.

"I'm sorry, that came out much harsher than I meant. I mean I want you to stick to the plan you had for your future. I don't want you to miss college to make a point, Clara."

"Okay. Well, I need to sleep."

"Can I get you something else?" Nina was mad at herself now but also frustrated. Why did this continue to be so brutal?

"There's some homemade soup in the freezer. I'll take some of that. If you have the time." She took her cup of tea and clomped up the stairs.

Nina opened the freezer. It was packed with food, apparently made by Clara. She read the neatly labeled containers: beef stew, meatballs, tomato sauce, chili con carne—and that was just what Nina could see in the front rows. The refrigerator shelves were stocked with both the ordinary—milk, butter, eggs, condiments—and every now and then something completely out of the ordinary: pancetta (how had Clara known where to find pancetta?), capers (ditto), clarified butter, a raspberry jam from France. Looking into her former refrigerator was like running into an old friend who'd dyed her hair and maybe had some light cosmetic work done, familiar but different. Bridie had told Nina that Clara was cooking a lot ("She's pretty good?" Bridie had said, visibly torn between the kitchen allegiance of her mother or her sister), but this wasn't ordinary cooking. Standing in front of the refrigerator, looking around the kitchen, processing the information about Dune and the play and college, Nina now understood she hadn't fully absorbed the landscape of her problems with Clara. This wasn't resistance; this was a coup.

Part Two

1994-95

Thirty-Six

Clara was aware seconds before she was fully aware—in a way that had become darkly familiar—that she was in someone else's bed. Her head hurt, but it was a gentle twang, not an all-out battering ram, so she could be grateful for that at least. She turned her head as quietly as possible and opened one eye. Alone in the bed. She rolled over and opened the other eye. Alone in the bedroom. This was very good. She let out a soft groan as she stretched her arms and straightened her legs, sat up and looked around. Not a clue as to where she was, but it was bright and sunny outside, and the room had two nearly floor-to-ceiling windows opposite the bed. She could see the tops of trees and the rear of a row of townhouses in the distance. On the nightstand next to her were an untouched glass of water and two aspirins. Whoever had taken her home couldn't be a complete asshole based on that gesture. She popped the aspirins into her mouth and chugged the water.

She pulled back the bedcovers and gingerly sat on the side of the bed. She was wearing the tights and tank top she'd worn to work under a blousy dress yesterday. She stood and looked on the floor for her dress or shoes. Nothing. She desperately had to pee. She stood and tiptoed to the other side of the room listening for sounds of life beyond the door. All was quiet. She opened a different door to find a closet full of men's clothes. She shut it quickly, not ready to face that appraisal. She was pretty sure she'd glimpsed a few Hawaiian shirts. Not good. A third door opened onto a bathroom, and as she sat on the toilet and relieved herself, she wondered who in her world had enough money to have a bedroom with its own bathroom. She put her aching head in her hands and tried to remember the events of the previous night. After a long day food styling for a cereal print ad, everyone on the shoot had gone out for drinks at Fanelli's. A tugging at her consciousness. Philip. Philip Woolf the photographer was at the bar. Had she gone home with him? No, she wouldn't have done that. She pulled up her tights and an image surfaced of her struggling with the same tights last night in a bathroom in a dingy bar. A second location with a pool table and a mix of friends and strangers doing shots.

She splashed her face with water and put a little toothpaste on her finger and swished it around her mouth. She gently opened the medicine cabinet filled with standard-issue pharmacy stuff. Pain relievers. Shaving cream. Ah, an aging stick of Secret antiperspirant on a higher shelf behind a box of condoms. A few lipstick containers and an expensive moisturizer. She opened the lid on the pot of moisturizer, but the cream inside had yellowed on top. No one had used it in a while. What kind of person didn't have a single prescription for anything in their medicine cabinet?

She didn't see a discarded condom or wrapper in the trash can. Not a definite sign she hadn't had sex, but a promising one. She wiped off last night's makeup from beneath her eyes and tried to arrange the bangs of her chin-length bob into some kind of order. She gave her cheeks a quick pinch. She felt queasy, mostly about this early morning, post-blackout searching that had become far too frequent. She still had glue under her fingernails from the shoot. She'd used watered-down Elmer's in place of milk so the cereal wouldn't get soggy and the flakes would float properly. Lucy! Her sometimes-assistant Lucy had been at her side yesterday while the agency's creative director badgered them to find cereal flakes that weren't "flimsy." She remembered Lucy at the second bar urging her to drink a soda or have some pretzels. She remembered she and Lucy on a small stage singing along to Southside Johnny's "I Don't Want to Go Home" and that someone had handed her a toy saxophone she pretended to play as Lucy screamed along to the *reach up and touch the sky* part. She remembered dancing and dancing and then a flash of dancing a lot with one person. Not someone from the shoot. This guy had spun her around and around until—until they fell? Yes, they'd been holding on to each other's forearms like they were playground friends and somehow (her good friend Tanqueray?) she'd lost her center of gravity and had pulled him down with her.

She stood on her tiptoes and turned away from the mirror and lowered her tights enough to see the blossoming livid bruise on her left buttock. She touched it. Ouch.

From downstairs (was this a duplex?), a jangle of keys and locks being deployed, the sound of a door opening. She grabbed the robe hanging from a hook on the back of the bedroom door and wrapped it around her. *Please*, she silently prayed to an unnamed deity, the goddess of loose women maybe. She gingerly walked downstairs.

"Good morning! I got us coffee. Cappuccino for you, right?"

"Right," she said, holding the robe a little closer at her neck. "Thanks so much," she said, walking toward him and his familiar face. Philip Woolf. Shit.

Thirty-Seven

Clara moved to New York City weeks after Bridie left for college. The sister of a friend needed a roommate in her small apartment on far West Ninety-Fourth Street. Fiona's place was tiny but efficiently organized and had a certain charm even though Clara could only fit a twin bed in the room off the kitchen that at one time, before this previously grander home had been cut up into smaller apartments, had housed the family maid and, apparently, generations of mice based on the abundance of steel wool stuffed into every crevice in and around the floorboards and radiators. In addition to the kitchen and Clara's closet-sized bedroom, there was a decent living room that faced Riverside Drive and got plenty of light through three nicely spaced windows. Fiona's bedroom was big enough for a queen-sized bed and the custom shelves she'd had built to house her photography equipment, but she paid a much larger portion of the rent, so Clara felt like she'd lucked into a deal.

The only job offered to her when she arrived in town was at an Irish pub on Second Avenue in Midtown. She worked weekends, including the dreaded bottomless-mimosa Sunday brunch, which was its own circle of hell because when she wasn't ferrying endless plates of eggs Benedict and French toast and traditional Irish breakfast, she had to sprint around the room double-fisted, a carafe of orange juice in one hand and a bottle of cheap champagne in the other. By the end of brunch, everyone was too drunk to pay the check properly, much less tip. One weekend she walked into the bathroom as one of two regulars had dropped their pants to show the other how her pubic hair had been shaved into the shape of a shamrock for Saint Patrick's Day. "Wow," Clara said, stunned as the woman cheerfully displayed her pubis to the entire room. "A surprise for the boyfriend," the woman cackled.

And then, after lucking into her apartment, Clara lucked into a career.

"Can you cook?" Fiona said one morning. "My sister said you can cook."

"I can cook," Clara said, not very enthusiastically. Since landing in New York, she had not missed cooking one bit, did not miss feeding a household, but anything had to be better than roaming the floor of Molly Malloy's covered in orange pulp and J. Roget Brut.

"Do you want to help on this shoot today? My food stylist's assistant called in sick. You just need to do whatever Joy tells you to do and know your way around food. Pay's not terrible."

"I can do that," Clara said.

A bit of bad luck for the sick assistant—a case of mono that wouldn't quit—was spectacularly good luck for Clara because by the time the former assistant was ready to return, Joy only wanted to work with Clara. Clara had a knack for food styling, and she liked it. She enjoyed preparing food purely for how it might look on a plate with no regard for consumption. She liked viewing a whiteboard rendering of a roast chicken and figuring out how to make it look like a thing someone would want to eat even though her efforts—an undercooked bird painted with a browning mixture of bitters and Kitchen Bouquet, a little food coloring and dishwashing liquid—would render the thing inedible. She liked the slant, the trickery, and it appealed to her perfectionism. After a couple of years learning all she could from Joy, she decided to do a certificate course at a small culinary joint in lower Manhattan. "You don't need to go to culinary school to be a food stylist," Joy told her, "but your knife skills could use some work, and if you're in this for the long haul you want to get better at recipe development. It wouldn't be a terrible idea to work in a restaurant kitchen for a bit."

Clara loved the culinary program so much she considered doing a full-fledged degree at CIA up the river, but it was prohibitively expensive, and she refused to take any of her mother's money because it was Finn's money. Clara was still furious that Bridie had allowed Finn to pay her full tuition at Cornell. She tried not to think too often about the day she'd visited Bridie on campus, only weeks after Nina and Sam had dropped her off. Clara had wanted to take Bridie to college herself, but the parents won that round. Sam and Nina were not exactly friendly, but they had reached a certain accommodation in coparenting that Clara resented. Her high school graduation weekend had been an awkward nightmare, starting with the senior talent show the night before commencement, when Clara had chosen, against Mr. Goodman's advice, to accompany herself on the guitar she was just learning how to play while singing "Will You Still Love Me Tomorrow?" Only a few chords in, Clara lost her place and had to restart, and she could hear how shaky her normally steady voice sounded. She soldiered on through the audience's scattered coughs and uneasy silence and the sudden exit of Dune, who stood and stormed out through the swinging lobby doors as she reached the chorus.

By the following year, when Fern and Bridie graduated, the families were willing to sit in adjacent rows in the Eastman Theatre, calmly and, Clara thought, smugly. At least Dune hadn't appeared for this graduation. He was staying in South Bend for the summer.

"Probably trying to avoid me," Clara said to Bridie.

"I don't think so," Bridie said and then quickly corrected herself. "I mean, maybe!"

On the day Clara pulled up to Bridie's dorm, she couldn't help but imagine herself on campus, walking around in cutoff shorts and some boy's oversized Oxford cloth shirt, waving from the second-floor window of an ivy-covered dormitory, welcoming friends back after the summer. When Bridie showed her the old reading room off the library with its three-storied open walkways of books stretching up to the ceiling, the ornate grillwork on the railings and plush leather chairs and old-fashioned lamps that gave the entire space a warm glow, Clara felt physically ill. She could see herself sitting in one of the chairs by the front doors, reading and looking out the window and feeling like the platonic ideal of a college student. She'd regretted deferring Cornell immediately but hadn't known how to reverse course, and she still—unfairly, she guessed—blamed Sam for not dragging her off to Ithaca.

In her more honest or haunted moments, the ones that came between two and four in the morning, Clara realized she'd staked a fraudulent claim on Bridie, and she could hear her mother's admonition (curse?) as if her mother were in the room with her: *Exaggerating the value of your presence again, Clara?* She wasn't Bridie's parent. She had become something closer to an unwelcome guardian, exhaustedly watching over her sister and father, who were slowly moving away from her. Well. She could move away, too.

After the culinary course, she worked in two different neighborhood Italian restaurants for a few years, both owned by the same family, both under the radar except for locals, which gave her the opportunity to do almost everything in the kitchens, including sidestepping grabby hands and avoiding alcohol-fueled rages by an assortment of chefs and ignoring the waitstaff doing lines of cocaine in the walk-ins. Stuck in the kitchen. Again.

Whenever possible, she'd fit in a shoot with Joy, but she didn't know where she wanted to land in the food world. She struggled with the tedium of styling for print. After the hours of staging and corrections based on often contradictory feedback and the dozens and dozens of Polaroids and more adjustments, they'd photograph the "hero"—the version of the dish everyone agreed looked best. Then they'd wait for hours for the film to be developed. When the contact sheets came in, if the photographer wasn't pleased with the results, they'd reset and do it all over again, including waiting for the second round of photos and so on. Sometimes she'd get home at four in the morning, sleep for two hours, and head to the restaurant for prep. It was a grueling few years while she had one foot in two different food-based worlds. Which one to choose? The adrenaline of the kitchen or the satisfaction of sleight of hand—the two rarely coexisted. She wavered.

Until an unassuming but sneakily assertive batch of blueberry muffins changed the trajectory of Clara's career. Clara didn't even like blueberry muffins. She'd eat one if there was nothing else quick and convenient around and she was ravenous, but she'd almost rather have anything else for breakfast. An egg fried in olive oil until the edges were brown and crisp on top of a slice of toasted sourdough. Yogurt with strawberries and the granola she made herself. Oatmeal with brown sugar and heavy cream and some ripe banana slices on top. But this travel magazine wanted muffins for its June issue: The muffins should look *elevated* but also *accessible*. The recipe had to be interesting but not intimidating. The photo editor told her she wanted "homey but also a kind of downtown, kind of SoHo feel," because Dean & DeLuca's enormous space on the corner of Prince and Broadway would be prominently featured in the spread. Clara wanted to impress because this magazine was new and had an interesting aesthetic and paid well. She spent an entire weekend trying to capture the client's contradictory wishes, making batches and batches of muffins until she got a look she hoped would work.

In the photo she would forever feature on the first page of her sample portfolio, the muffins appear freshly baked. Instead of standard-issue cupcake liners, she'd used individual soufflé cups, which were pleated with a tiny rolled edge. She'd doubled the blueberries, smashing some so they bled through the soufflé paper, soft and purple. She topped the muffins with a craggy streusel and a tart lemon glaze, brightened with yellow food coloring. On shoot day, she commandeered one of Dean & DeLuca's large marble cheese boards, a white porcelain colander, a heavy silver butter knife, and a midnight-blue linen napkin. She arranged the muffins in a studied sprawl, filled the colander with blueberries, scattered a few on the slab with errant crumbs, and angled the knife with a smear of butter directly in front of a sliced muffin. She wrinkled the napkin with damp hands and tucked it beside the colander. The art director balked at the messiness of the tableau and asked her to clean it up—no crumbs, smears, or wrinkles. But the photographer, hired for his love of overhead close-ups, imperfect tableaus, and natural lighting whenever possible, took one look and said, "Who did this? It's perfect."

"Nice," Joy said to her when Clara recounted the day, feeling proud. "Philip Woolf is stingy with the compliments."

He'd flirted with her a little that day, but she hadn't seen him again until last night, and now here he was, presenting her with a cappuccino and a freshly laundered dress (in-unit laundry!) because she'd landed in a big puddle of Jägermeister on the dance floor. She was too mortified to ask about the end of the evening, but he volunteered that he'd intervened when she was about to leave with Mr. Jägermeister—"I didn't like his energy." She was grateful to him but angry with herself because some of her coworkers must have seen her go home with Philip, which broke a rule she had (okay, maybe more of a *guideline*) about not having sex with coworkers. Now, Philip was asking her a question and she tried to focus.

"The television stuff?" he said. "Do you remember talking about it last night?"

She did not. "Vaguely?"

"It's a new cable channel, called the Food Channel or something blindingly obvious like that. Brand-new. Small and scrappy. Not a big audience. I don't see how it's going to work, personally, but they're desperate for people and asked for recommendations. If you're interested, I can put you in touch with my contact. It's a bit of a mess over there, but it might be fun."

"I'm interested."

"What's your number?"

She hesitated. Ordinarily, she'd pull her usual trick, scribble the phone number incorrectly, but she was curious about the *television stuff*. She gave him her number, grabbed her bag, and left.

In the years since Clara had been living in New York City, she'd dated more men than she cared to count, all of them for relatively brief periods. A few of them still friends. Most of them left wondering what they'd done to warrant her sudden and often inexplicable disappearance in their lives. To thirty-three-year-old Clara, it was simple. Things were fun until they weren't, and then you cut your losses. What was the point of drawn-out conversations or trial breakups or couples therapy?

What was the point of talk, talk, talk? If you needed to examine your relationship with a paid professional, wasn't that the clearest sign it was over? It was to her. Could she have been a little more considerate when breaking up with people? She supposed.

The coffee at Philip's apartment had revived her, but only briefly. She felt worse and worse as the subway came closer to her stop and for one horrifying moment feared she might have to discreetly vomit into her purse. But she took a few deep breaths and, as the train screeched into her station, felt steadier. She climbed the stairs and had a moment of gratitude that she didn't have to go into work today. Maybe she'd take a nap and do laundry, which had reached an appalling condition. She stopped at the corner bodega for a Diet Coke and a bacon, egg, and cheese sandwich and when she checked her home answering machine she had two messages, one from a television producer saying he'd gotten her number from Philip and one from Bridie: "Hi, it's just me. Bridie." Clara smiled at the machine. Always the same words. Always the *just me* and always leaving her name, as if Clara wouldn't recognize her voice. "You are not going to *believe* who I sat next to last night at one of Mom's fundraising things. Call me!"

Thirty-Eight

Dune Finnegan was the last person on Bridie's mind the night they ended up sitting at the same table at a fundraiser for the Memorial Art Gallery. Bridie was at the table because her mother and Finn were board members and the evening's hosts. They'd purchased and populated several tables with friends and family. Ordinarily, at events where both families were in attendance—weddings, funerals, church functions, holidays—Bridie and Dune and Fern would politely greet one another and then retreat to separate corners. Privately, Bridie and Fern were friendly, and Bridie loved Fern's partner. Naomi was cool! But in public spaces, they could feel the eyes of everyone watching. It was irritating. They weren't the Hatfields and the McCoys or the Montagues and the Capulets; they were ordinary people and many years ago their parents had divorced and remarried. Everyone had done their best to move on. Except Clara, of course, but Clara was aiming for some kind of Guinness World Record level of resentment.

Bridie snuck into the back of the event space and tried to spot her table number, which, of course, was directly in front of the podium where her mother was now positioned. Bridie still hadn't gotten used to this version of her mother—the society grand dame. As Uncle Dennis had predicted all those years ago, Helen Harper had helped make the Finnegan family quite comfortable. Finn and Nina gave money away hand over fist, both the store's and their own, and had become forces of goodwill around town, supporting arts organizations and underfunded schools and community food banks. Bridie guessed it was nice. Altruistic. Philanthropic? She never fully grasped the semantic differences, but as a social worker did understand how the larger donors to community organizations were both a necessity and a nuisance, as many of them wanted something in exchange for their good-heartedness. Bridie didn't think her mother and Finn fell into the purely opportunistic bunch, but it was impossible not to acknowledge that they'd used their generosity to launder the long-ago scandal, and it seemed to have worked like a dream. Their wallets—and eventually the two of them—were welcomed back into the important spaces in the city. They'd quieted the critics with their good-enough marriage and generous works. Behind the podium, her mother was talking about the importance of the Memorial Art Gallery to the city and telling some story about standing in front of one the museum's paintings at a critical juncture in her life and how MAG had always been a place of comfort and joy since that day she'd escorted her daughter's class on a school field trip. This was news to Bridie. As the audience applauded her mother's closing remarks, Bridie hurried to the empty seat at her table, gave Fern and Naomi a quick wave, sat, and turned to her left to find Dune holding out a hand and introducing himself. "Hi. Dune Finnegan," he said, a little sloppily.

"Dune, it's Bridget. Bridie." She shrugged off her raincoat and draped it on the back of her chair.

"I didn't even recognize you," he said, grinning happily.

"Nice to see you, too." She offered a thin smile.

"Do you know what this is supposed to be?" he said, using his fork to poke at a piece of chicken breast covered with an unappetizing egg-yolk-colored sauce.

"No idea," Bridie said. "But it's pretty foul."

"Foul fowl."

"Ha."

"Sorry. Not a high-quality joke."

Dune and Bridie picked at their food and made desultory small talk. *Such a cold winter but not that many storms. Sure has been rainy. Good for the flowers, though. Spotted a group of snowdrops poking through the mud today, that's always a nice sign.* Plates were cleared. Dessert dropped. Wineglasses refilled and coffee and tea poured. Back at the podium, Nina introduced the gentleman who would run the live auction part of the evening. A picture of the first item, a small painting by a local artist, appeared on a large screen at the front of the room. As soon as Bridie saw the painting, she sat straight up in her seat. "Oh." She didn't realize she said it out loud.

"You okay?" Dune said.

"It's so pretty." Bridie looked at her program to see that the opening bid was $250, more than Bridie had any business spending on a painting. The work was small, maybe eleven by thirteen inches and kind of abstract but also somehow representational of a sunrise. The auctioneer was explaining that it was an interpretation of a Monet. Not the one from the MAG collection, but a similar work from the same Waterloo Bridge series. The small rendering was called *After Monet's Sun through Fog*. She wanted it.

Bridie had just moved into her own apartment after years of roommates. She thought about how much money she had in her bank account and did a quick calculation. She needed so many things for the space, but she knew exactly where she'd put that painting: on the wall directly above the carved oak mantel in her living room. She could delay other purchases she'd been saving up for, like nice pots for the kitchen, a better mattress, a chair for the front bay window, where she wished she could sit and read. $400. She could go that high. She grabbed the paddle in her fist as the auctioneer started the bidding. $250, $275, $300, up to $325 before Bridie even had a chance to raise her paddle. She lifted her arm high. "We have a very enthusiastic $350," the auctioneer said, pointing to her paddle. "Three hundred and fifty is the bid on the floor. Do I have $400? $375? Anyone willing to go to $375?"

Bridie had less than twenty seconds to savor her high bid before the room lit up again, speeding past $400 and eventually landing on $750. "I have $750 to the gentlemen in the corner. Final warning. Hammer down—sold!"

"You didn't stay in the game," Dune said to her.

"A little too rich for me."

"What about him?" Dune pointed to his father. "Peanuts for that guy. Dad!"

"No," Bridie said, putting a hand on Dune's arm, mortified. "It's fine. Someone else bought it."

"No deal is truly a done deal." Now he was slurring his words. He motioned to his father again and Finn stood and came around the table. "Right, Dad? No deal is ever done?"

"I think you've had enough," Finn said gently to Dune.

"Bridie wanted that painting. Can't we get it for her?"

Bridie shook her head at Finn. "It's fine. I'm fine." This had the makings of the kind of public scene they'd all spent years and years avoiding.

"Come on, son," Finn said. "Let's get you home."

Bridie could see her mother at the front of the room, off to the side, watching the slight commotion with a frown. She raised her eyebrows at Bridie, who shrugged in response. Finn started escorting Dune through the tables. Dune was loudly asking anyone within earshot who'd won the painting. The auctioneer stood silent until both Finn and Dune had left the room and Nina nodded for him to continue. "Please check your programs for lot number two, a Tiffany lamp that once belonged to George Eastman."

The next morning, Bridie stared at the empty space where she would have hung *After Monet's Sun through Fog*. Maybe she should have gone for it, but the price was absurd given her salary. She wondered how Dune was feeling this morning. Nina had alluded to Dune's drinking a few times over the years. Bridie vaguely recalled an incident at Notre Dame and some period of probation. She'd heard something about a detox program after graduation and before he spent several years "abroad," whatever that meant. Once when Bridie ran into Fern and Naomi at a movie, Fern referenced Dune's *European style* of drink. "That's how he puts it," Fern said, "if we're to believe that Europeans start drinking at eleven in the morning and don't stop until they pass out." She'd heard Dune was back in Rochester a few years ago and had seen him around town a bit, but they hadn't spoken. She thought she'd heard he was doing well.

She had to tell Clara about last night, even though it was probably too early to call. As usual, she got Clara's answering machine and left a message. As she was trying to decide how to spend her Saturday, make it a chore day or a fun day, the buzzer to her apartment rang. She looked out the front window and standing on the front stairs, as if her musings had conjured him, was Dune Finnegan.

Thirty-Nine

When Bridie was a senior in college, Sam left Xerox. He decided to take a downsizing buyout in the early '80s, when the company was floundering after willfully ignoring the bellwether of explosive change and doubling down on the copier market. He'd watched dumbfounded as senior management veered away from the revolutionary work at PARC even in the face of their swiftly eroding market share.

"I don't know what to tell you," Sam said to an inexplicably sanguine Garret.

"Not surprised," he said. "You know what they used to call Rochester, right?"

Sam did know: *Smugtown, USA*, after a book of the same name published in the late '50s. "I never read the book," Sam said. "Maybe I should."

"Friend, you're living it. Company town. Complacent. Safe. *Smug*. But not for long. A lack of vision isn't only going to sink Xerox. Kodak's heading in the same direction. And then what does the city become?"

The first thought that sprang to Sam's mind was *Finnegan's*. But he shook it off. The economic future of Rochester wasn't his problem. Once he packed a box with his small collection of belongings and handed in his ID to the security people at Xerox Square and waved good-bye to the building and the adjacent Midtown Plaza and drove out of his dedicated parking space in the underground parking lot for the final time, he felt elated. Released.

A few years later, with Bridie's and Clara's blessings, he sold the house on Cambridge Road. He thought Bridie might object since she still didn't have a place of her own, but she was supportive and enthusiastic. A pleasant surprise until he realized her relief stemmed from finally having an excuse to live with her mother and Finn. Or rather, no excuse not to. But even then, even after that first pang of resentment, he softened. He was finding it harder and harder to maintain outrage at his circumstances, or to continue to be aggrieved by Nina's refashioned life, which looked a whole lot like her old life. Same neighborhood. Same community. A new set of frustrations with no clear fix. According to Bridie, an unwitting but efficient source of information between the two households, Nina barely cooked anymore. Apparently, cocktail hour started very early at the new Mr. and Mrs. Finnegan's home, and one of Helen Harper's lackeys delivered prepared food on the nights Nina and Finn didn't eat out.

Sam didn't want to buy another house right away. He wasn't looking for another job. His voluntary retirement package had been generous, he still had a healthy nest egg from the money his parents had left, and if he was smart about the gains from selling the house, the truth was he wouldn't have to work again. What on earth would that feel like? When Garret invited him to come to San Francisco for as long as he wanted—weeks, months, whatever—he thought, *Why not?* and bought a one-way ticket.

"Full disclosure," Garret said, his first night there. "I'm not interested in monogamy."

Sam had never thought he was moving to San Francisco to start a relationship with Garret, monogamous or not, and although he didn't say so he was relieved. He wanted to be alone. Truly single. Those early months were heady. The gay community in the Bay Area wasn't just out of the closet—they were, in Sam's opinion, out of their ever-loving minds. He was assiduously trying to *loosen up* as Garret so often admonished him, but the hardened carapace he had so deliberately crafted for decades was not easily cracked. Garret also pestered him about coming out, especially to his daughters. The girls were adults, Garret reminded him repeatedly over the years.

Didn't he deserve to *live in his truth*? It was 1979, 1983, 1986, not the homosexual dark ages anymore! "Your daughters are curious and engaged people. You are not giving them enough credit."

Perhaps. It wasn't that Sam didn't understand Garret's logic; he just couldn't see his way through to the other side. He couldn't imagine running into his former coworkers, neighbors, friends while he was with another man. He couldn't imagine telling Bridie and Clara and having them connect his behavior to Nina's leaving. His disclosure would free Nina to tell the girls her version of the truth. Coming out would mean another parent who wasn't what they'd thought, and they would resent him, possibly forever. Or so he imagined. Until Clara came to town.

She had finally been able to quit her job at the hated Irish pub and was doing something else with food and had a small break between projects and asked if she could visit. Sam offered to put her up at a nice hotel near Union Square and they spent a few days seeing all the sights. The Golden Gate. Ghirardelli Square. The Cannery and the Wharf. Coit Tower. She told him about working with Joy and all she was learning about food styling, which he found interesting if a little perplexing.

"You don't miss the cooking part?" he asked.

She thought for a minute. "I still cook, but mostly for photographs not for people. And no, I don't miss it."

Sam hadn't seen Clara so upbeat or enthusiastic for many years. It was fun, this new poised version of his daughter, describing her own life, witnessing his with curiosity. He knew he had to finally have an honest conversation with her, but didn't know how to start.

On her last day, they drove out to a little oyster shack in Point Reyes. Clara was smitten with the place. "Look at these oyster shells," she said, laying them all out along their table after they'd slurped down the sweet meat. They were beautiful, with dramatic ridges and edges formed by the sea, all grays and whites and deep purples. The insides pearlescent and smooth. "I could style the shit out of these," Clara said. She asked the restaurant owner if she could have them, and he took them in the back to soak the shells clean and put them in bubble wrap for her. While they were waiting, Clara cleared her throat and said, "So. You don't live with Garret anymore?"

"I was only ever staying with him temporarily. My place is small and it's a sublet, but I like it."

"You're still friends?"

"Of course." Sam understood he had an opening, but he didn't know how to walk through. Clara did. "Dad," she said, "I want to know if you're being careful."

"I'm always careful. San Francisco is a big city, but—"

"Dad," Clara said softly. "I'm not talking about that. Bridie is freaking out, and to be honest, so am I a little. She hasn't known how to say any of this to you, but the clinic where she's interning right now is the city's biggest testing site for AIDS. She's started to counsel patients when they get their test results. It's intense."

"Bridie's doing that?"

"She is. Believe it or not, she claims she hasn't cried once." They both smiled and Sam ducked his head, feeling bashful. Clara continued, her voice calm but grave. "I see what's happening every day in New York. So many friends of mine in the industry are sick. Many have died. Your daughters need to know you're being careful. We love you."

He started to speak, and his impulse was to object, deny, deflect, but why? Clara took his hand, and for one debilitating moment he feared *he* was going to cry. "I promise you I'll be careful," he said.

Clara leaned over and kissed his cheek. "That's all we needed to hear."

Running the very brief conversation over in his head later that night, he was relieved but also uncomfortable. To be offered—without even asking!—the kind of consideration and understanding Clara had never been able to extend to Nina seemed unfair. But it wasn't his job to try to mend that rupture. He didn't know who could, but he knew it wasn't him. In the meantime, keeping his promise to the girls would be embarrassingly easy. He was, perhaps, way too careful about everything.

The problem, Sam realized very shortly after settling into life in San Francisco, was that he had only thought of his homosexuality as a sexual drive, and it was clear that everyone around him was building an entire identity around being out and gay. *Flamboyant* had always felt like a dirty word to Sam because it was coded, a slur, but walking down the Castro with Garret and their larger group of friends, he saw flamboyance as a reclamation, an exuberant choice. All these men, these beautiful men who didn't care how they appeared to anyone. Sam was alternately gleeful and reluctant. Was this what he was? he thought, sipping a beer and watching a man even older than he prance around the bar wearing white Lycra leggings that left nothing to the imagination, a rainbow tank top, a goatee, and roller skates?

Garret seemed to find it all amusing and landed confidently somewhere between Lycra pants and Sam's wardrobe of polo shirts, but Sam couldn't get a fix on where he fit. He couldn't even figure out what he wanted. His dalliances ("Dalliances?" Garret said, laughing. "What century are we in?") were satisfying and that was good but then he felt empty. He knew there had to be men more like him in San Francisco, but his social skills had been corrupted by furtiveness. How to tell if the two men having lunch at a restaurant looking flirty but wearing chinos and Oxford shirts were gay?

One night, a few margaritas in, Garret convinced Sam to join their "centipede team" for the annual Bay to Breakers race. The bar was loud and noisy, but from what he could gather the "team" would all wear the same costume and somehow be tethered to one another? "We don't go fast," Garret assured him, "probably like a speedy trot, but it's fun. It's a wild scene and a great party."

How much wilder could a scene get in this town?

He would remind himself of that naive thought when it became clear that their team was joining the legion of nude racers. The team costume: helmets. Any kind of helmet. Construction, football, bicycle, astronaut. The rest of the costume? Buck naked. Without telegraphing his panic and distaste, Sam claimed an astronaut helmet. At least nobody would see his face. "Socks and shoes are okay!" Garret yelled to the team on the day of the race. "All other clothing goes into this duffel," he said, walking down the line as the group disrobed. Sam carefully folded his underwear and shorts and tucked them on top of his head beneath the helmet like everyone else was doing so they'd have some clothes at the ready when they crossed the finish line.

The worst part of the race was not the crowds, the exposure, the hills, the noise, it was his balls beating against his inner thighs for two hours. The day was warm for San Francisco, and it felt like his testicles got slightly larger with every mile. Before the race started, he assumed the hardest part would be running uphill or the claustrophobic helmet or his internal mortification, but all those things receded and as he tried to ignore the throbbing pain in his nether region, he realized this was not meant to be his new life.

One night, some weeks later, without telling anyone because he knew how roundly he'd be mocked, he took himself to the Top of the Mark for a drink. He looked through the clothes in the very back of his closet, the ones he hadn't touched since leaving Rochester and took out a suit. A perfectly pressed shirt. A silk regimental striped tie and his gleaming Johnston & Murphy brogues. Pulling on dress socks, he started to feel like himself again, like he was reoccupying a familiar body, and he didn't know if it was a good thing or a pathetic thing. The doorman at the hotel greeted him with a tip of the hat and he passed through the revolving door to the quiet hush of an upscale lobby perfumed with lilies. On a Tuesday night, the bar was quiet, and he asked for a table near a window. He ordered a scotch on the rocks and sat quietly. He felt restored to himself. As much as he wanted to *let loose*, he didn't think he had it in him. He'd paid close attention to all the conversations he'd had with formerly closeted gay men like, he supposed, himself. The relief, the joy, the freedom they talked about, he didn't feel it. He wanted to, but he didn't. He felt like an outsider in the promised land and that was a new, profoundly discomfiting kind of loneliness. He could sense Garret's frustration with him and knew the larger group of friends felt the same. He understood. He was, he assumed, a big drag.

And then, Clara's admonishment. So many men were sick, dying. All the arguing in his circle about whether or not the disease was transferred through sex. Most of the men he knew disregarded the campaign of caution. Garret was convinced the rumors were planted to stop the debauchery of the burgeoning homosexual population. But Sam was nervous. And their friend Adam who was a nurse said he was becoming temporarily celibate until they had a treatment or a cure and they should all do the same. Sam didn't want to panic, but it would be just his luck to get stricken down by a disease that targeted gay men after finally deciding to declare himself as one.

He ended up walking back to the apartment because it was a beautiful night. Almost every night in San Francisco was beautiful, even the ones velveted by fog and mist. The foghorns crying lonesomely in the bay were possibly the most romantic sound he'd ever heard. Slightly buzzed and pleasantly loosened from the evening alone, he walked into his living room, picked up the phone, and booked an airline ticket home for the very next day.

Forty

"You forgot this," Dune said, holding out Bridie's raincoat the morning after the auction.

"Oh," Bridie said. "I would have picked it up from my mom. You didn't have to come over here."

"Can I buy you a cup of coffee?" He was unshaven but freshly showered. Looking a little worse for wear around the edges. "I owe you an apology."

"You don't owe me anything. I'm fine."

"I know you're fine, but I want to apologize for last night. I took a few of our beef suppliers out to dinner before the event, and boy, those guys can put it away. I don't have the tolerance anymore. I should have gone home. Can I buy you breakfast?"

Bridie had to admit she was kind of curious about present-day Dune, but didn't know if she was ready to go out on the town with Dune. She hesitated.

"Please," he said.

Over breakfast, a nice quiet place where they had a table in the back of a mostly empty room, Bridie learned that Dune was the driving force behind so many changes at Finnegan's she thought brilliant. The in-house bakery that produced better-than-decent baguettes and a good sourdough and excellent country loaves. The expansive counter with exotic (to Bridie) cheeses from Europe. The cases loaded with iridescent species of unfamiliar fish, the tiny quails nestled in a tray next to a selection of their miniature spotted eggs, the hanging cured meats and specialty sausages. He told her how he'd fallen in love with the town markets and food halls during his travels in England, France, Italy, Spain, and Denmark. He'd dreaded returning to Rochester and taking up his post at Finnegan's. "My first month, Helen had me tag along to a food industry conference in New York. Four days of walking around from booth to booth schmoozing with other grocers and retailers and food suppliers and design experts."

"Sounds interesting."

"It was interesting if you're curious about how to maximize shelf space or fit all the new flavors of Lean Cuisine in the freezer case or the genius of 'value added' meat." When Bridie looked confused, he clarified, "Lamb chops already seasoned and ready for grilling, skewers of chicken sitting in a store-made marinade. That kind of stuff. Hours and hours of conversation about how to sell convenience, but zero conversation about food. Food! If I don't care about the actual food, who will?"

Helen Harper was territorial, he explained, and suspicious of Dune and fearful about her job. "I get it," Dune said. "Her work is her life. But I like Helen. I'm happy to let her do her thing." She'd taken a lot of convincing, so he'd started small. One elaborate cheese counter at the store downtown. "We built a story around the product, starting with regions. We printed maps so customers could see exactly where in France or Ireland or Denmark the cheese came from. We know what the animals eat and how the cheese is aged and how that translates into taste. That one location sold more cheese than all the Finnegan's Grocers combined." Gradually, he said, Helen opened up to most of his ideas. "Can't get her on board with on-site butchering of entire sides of beef, but I'm working on it. It's what we used to do. The only way for true quality control."

But Dune truly lit up when he described the training program that sent their best employees all over the world to master a specialty. "Imagine," he told her, eyes wide, "one day you're working behind the meat counter in Henrietta and the next week you're down in Argentina learning about cattle." Dune told her they'd sent six store managers to a cheese cave in southern France for two months. They had a group working on a salmon farm in the Pacific Northwest.

"I'm envious," she finally said. "Maybe I should fill out an application. I've never been to Europe. Or Seattle."

"I'm talking too much. Sorry. A little nervous, I guess." He put his hands around the coffee cup like he needed warmth, but they'd been sitting there for two hours, the mug couldn't possibly have any heat to it, and Bridie noticed his fingers were trembling.

"Nervous or hungover?" she said.

"A little of both. I've been doing really well moderating with alcohol. It's hard in this business not to overdo it. A job of excess." Bridie nodded and picked at a donut sitting on a plate in the center of the table. She wasn't sure she was ready to become Dune's confidante. His friend. Even though they were just sitting and having coffee, she felt the wrath of Clara all the way from New York City.

"I haven't drunk like that in months."

"Is that what this breakfast is about? Do you need a recommendation? For a sponsor, a supportive sober community, a good AA meeting?"

Confused, he asked, "Are *you* in AA?"

"No. I'm a social worker."

"Right. Right! But no. God, no. I didn't ask you here for advice."

"I'd be happy to help."

"I'm okay." He started flicking the end of a pack of sugar, fidgeting in his seat. "I'm good at controlling the drinking ninety-nine percent of the time."

"Ah yes. That pesky one percent. I know it well. Support is really helpful. And often illuminating."

"Thanks. I'll think about it. I didn't remember you were a social worker. What do you do exactly?"

Bridie understood he was more eager to change the subject than he was curious about her work, but you couldn't push a person before they were ready. "Mostly reproductive stuff at a clinic downtown. We're affiliated with the University of Rochester. Birth control, STD prevention, unplanned pregnancy counseling. We also have a big AIDS testing program."

"One-stop shopping for private parts."

"If you need free condoms, I'm your girl!" She bent her head and tried to take a sip from her empty mug of tea. She was blushing.

"The AIDS testing doesn't make you nervous?"

"Why would it make me nervous? You don't get AIDS from being near people who *might* have AIDS." She was so tired of this conversation and realized she was snapping at Dune, but honestly. Did people not read?

"I know that. I didn't know if you had to handle blood samples or something."

"I don't. I'm not a nurse like your sister, who *does* handle blood samples. Is Fern afraid?"

"Bridie, I'm just asking questions here. No judgments. I'm glad you're *both* doing what you're doing."

"Sorry. It's just, with my dad and all, I get defensive. I know that."

"Your dad?" he said, genuinely surprised.

"My—*gay* dad?"

"Sam is gay? You're kidding me."

"I am not. How do you not know this?"

"I don't know, but I don't! You have to admit it's fucking bizarre how little we all know about one another."

"Now you know." She was irrationally pissed. The lines had been drawn years ago. Nina didn't talk to the girls about Finn's family and vice versa. It made sense at first, but Dune was right to call it strange. Talk about secrets. Talk about shame. She waved for the check.

"Wait a second. What did I say? I didn't know, but I don't care. I think it's great that your dad is gay!" He said the last sentence so loudly that several tables turned around and stared at them—half with disapproval, half amused. They couldn't help but laugh.

"Want to get out of here and go for a walk?" Dune said.

That's how it started. The occasional coffee and a long walk. Talking on the phone. Catching each other up on the past fifteen years. How much it bothered Dune that Fern still felt responsible for Honey all these years later. How Bridie worried that even though Sam had reconfigured his life he was still lonely, how it seemed as if he would never fully embrace his identity. "He brings a quote-unquote friend around every once in a while," Bridie said, "but that's it. I can't tell if he likes the solitude or if secrecy makes him feel safe."

"But you talk about him being gay? It's understood?"

"Yes. Clara and I figured it out—well, Clara figured it out before me. She went to see him back when he lived in San Francisco. We were both worried sick. If he heard you and I having this conversation, he would be mortified. I wish he were more comfortable with all of it. I wish he could find joy and companionship. Maybe he has, but he can't share it with us."

"I have to imagine that for Sam, being *kind of* out of the closet is a big deal."

"I suppose that's true. This city doesn't easily make room for anyone trying to reinvent themselves." Bridie confided in Dune how Clara still ran hot and cold with Nina, vacillating between aloof and grudgingly trying.

"Is she ever in Rochester?" Dune asked, not sounding as casual as he hoped.

"No. I've visited her in New York a handful of times. It's fun. We always have fun. But then I can't help myself. I try to get her to come home for the holidays or remind her about Dad's or Mom's or, worst of all, Finn's birthday and she snaps shut like a poked clam. Sometimes she'll have dinner with Mom and Finn when they're in New York and sometimes she's 'too overbooked.' Sometimes she's nice; sometimes she's a bitch. When was the last time you saw her?" They were rounding the reservoir at Cobb's Hill, a pretty walking spot where nobody noticed or interrupted them. A glorious summer day. The park beneath them a vivid green.

"I don't know. Maybe at the party for Fern after she graduated from nursing school?"

"She wasn't there. She only came home when Dad sold the house. Took some stuff. Spent forty-seven of the forty-eight hours she was here complaining about the weather and the restaurants and the food shopping." She looked at Dune. "No offense."

"None taken. Before my time."

"I think she has a boyfriend. She's never at her place when I call. And she thinks I don't notice that she only calls me when she knows I'm not home."

"Her loss," he said.

Bridie watched Dune's expression carefully. She'd last talked to Clara three weeks ago and had oh-so-casually mentioned that she'd gone to a Red Wings baseball game with Dune.

"Wait a second," Clara said, "are you *dating* Dune?"

"Of course not!" Bridie said, her voice cracking even though she was telling the absolute truth.

"*Of course not*," Clara mimicked. "Why do you sound like you're lying?"

"I don't because I'm not lying. I'm not dating Dune. How come you're never home? Are you dating someone?"

"Maybe." Bridie could hear the smile in Clara's voice.

"Who—"

"A photographer. But that's all you're getting because I have to run! More later."

Just as autumn prematurely poked its head out in late August, a temperature drop, a chilly breeze, the quickening red of the maple leaves, all harbingers of winter, which Bridie dreaded, Dune invited her over to his apartment for dinner. As soon as she walked through the door, she felt a charge in the air. Candles. Music. Something sublime spattering away in the oven. Over dinner, they talked about the ways that staying in Rochester was good ("Nick Tahou's garbage plate," Dune said dreamily. "That thing is disgusting," she said, "but I'll take a Zweigle's hot dog any day." "White hot?" he asked, pointing his finger at her. "Never! Red or nothing. And I couldn't live without my beloved half-moon cookies. And the lilacs. Sue me, but I love the Lilac Festival.") and all the ways that staying in Rochester felt limiting, especially given their family history. "Sometimes I see it on people's faces, you know," Dune said. "Mostly older people but not always. I was in Ireland one year and ran into the Tannenbaums. Remember them? From down the street?"

"Oh my god, yes! I think they still live in that house."

"One of those kids, I don't remember his name, introduced me to his friends and told everyone the story. Everyone. Like hey, this here is Dune Finnegan! His father eloped in the middle of the night with the neighbor when we were in high school! Like I was the evening's entertainment. In Dublin!"

"That's awful."

"It mostly felt silly. Like a story that doesn't have anything to do with me anymore but also has everything to do with me. Do you know what I mean?"

"Of course I do. Of course."

"Oh man," he said. "As usual, I'm going on and on." It was late and they stood to clear plates and as they finished loading the dishwasher and wiping down the counters, working quietly but in a comforting syncopated rhythm, they turned to each other at the same moment, smiling, like a scene from a corny rom-com, and all Bridie could think about was that old song by the Crystals: *Then he kissed me.*

And then she kissed him.

Forty-One

Clara ignored Philip's phone calls for weeks. At first it was unintentional. The producer he'd connected her with at the Food Network kept her insanely busy and grossly underpaid. She needed to supplement that job with print work, and she had zero free time. Then she ignored him out of habit; she'd listen to the messages and delete them because he sounded so—normal? Then it was deliberate. She got confirmation from another photographer that he was married. A few months after the night she went home with him, they ran into each other at a Condé Nast shoot. He was on a job for *Gourmet*, and she was finishing prep for *Bon Appétit*. "You're not easy to get hold of," he said.

"Bad news for you; good news for your wife."

He didn't say anything. Just stood there and watched her position thyme sprigs onto a seared chicken breast with tweezers. "I wouldn't have taken you back to my apartment if I had a wife," he finally said. "I wouldn't be calling you."

She stood back and looked at the plate and added a few more leaves. "I've asked around. How come people think you're married?"

"Because I was married."

"You're divorced?"

"Not quite, but soon."

"Huh," she said, looking up as if solving a complex equation, "that would make you—still married!"

"Clara"—he moved closer and lowered his voice—"you were in my apartment. Did you see any signs of a wife there?" She decided not to mention the items in the medicine cabinet. "Can I buy you a drink after this and we can talk about it? Hear me out and if you're not persuaded, I won't bring it up ever again."

Over one drink and then a few more, he explained about the woman he'd married when they were both days out of college. They'd relocated to New York from Philadelphia, and the wife hated the city. She wanted to return to Philadelphia; she missed her family and her friends. He insisted on staying in New York—his business was growing—and they tried a commuting marriage for years, until both were able to admit it wasn't working. "She has a boyfriend and they're just waiting for the paperwork to be finalized before they get engaged. She hasn't lived with me for two years. We haven't been together in any significant way for much longer than that. I completely respect your unwillingness to become involved with anyone who's married. I wouldn't, either. I'll be divorced, officially divorced, in the next month or two."

She eyed him warily. "I swear!" he said. "If you want to wait to go out on a date until I can show you a divorce decree, that's fine. I can wait. I will wait."

She didn't want to wait.

After their first date, she took him back to her tiny studio, the one she found during the years when she was working so many hours she was only home to sleep. "It doesn't look like anyone lives here," Philip said, amused. He stepped over plastic crates filled with her styling supplies to examine a wall plastered with photos torn from high-end magazines and postcards from art museums. A huge swath of the wall was devoted to classic still lifes, most but not all from the Dutch masters. On her desk, a few photographs he hadn't seen in her portfolio. "Are these yours?" he asked.

"They are. My private work, I guess you'd call it."

"Who took the photos?" Philip asked.

"David Headley."

He whistled. "Pricey."

"Yeah. He gave me a break, but I could only afford those three."

He picked up a photograph of a footed silver bowl brimming with

Italian plums in all shades of dusty purple, much of the fruit still tethered to bent branches. A single halved plum sat front and center, its interior golden flesh and woody pit drawing the eye to the surrounding leaves, many of them skeletonized from insects. A perfectly imperfect bowl of fruit. On the table beneath the plums, Clara had scattered walnut pieces among shards of broken shell. Peeking from behind the bottom of the bowl's base, the tiny head, snout, and whiskers of a mouse.

"Is this a live mouse?"

"Have you ever tried to wrangle a mouse? No, I'm friendly with someone who runs that taxidermy spot in SoHo. He lets me borrow stuff."

"Clara, these are extraordinary. People should be hiring you to do this, not plates of cheeseburgers."

"I wish," she said. "I tried last week on a shoot at the Fulton Fish Market. Went for a Chardin kind of look and the client lost it." She did an impression of the executive, wide-eyed and panicked. "'This looks like something from *The Silence of the Lambs*! We aren't trying to *repulse* people!'" They both laughed. "I guess the flayed skate on a hook was a step too far."

"We are, as they say, very much on the same page." He took his portfolio out of the large messenger bag slung across his chest and handed it to her. "The ones in the back," he said.

She flipped to the back pages, and it was like seeing her own thoughts brought to life. The photos were stunning—high-end, painterly, and expertly composed. Better than hers, though she'd have approached some things differently. "Did you use a stylist?"

"I had a little help from Annie Howe. You know her?"

"Yeah, she's great."

"Not as good as you."

"Agree to agree." She pointed to one of his photos and then to a postcard on her wall. "Pieter Claesz."

"Yes."

"Where have you been all my life?" she joked as she ran a hand over the print, a crusty loaf of bread, an empty sherry glass with a tiny fly on the rim.

"Recently? Trying to get you to answer my calls."

"Well," she said, turning to him and miming picking up a phone, "Hello!"

CLARA TOOK HER RELATIONSHIP WITH Philip slowly, steadily, seriously. Sometimes they collaborated on assignments where their affection subtly wove into the work—only to circle back and deepen their relationship. They had a rhythm, and he taught her to see the food not only from the perspective of a cook or a stylist or a diner, but as the camera would see it. Once she made that shift, she could spot and correct problems before he even looked through the lens. He was so easy to be with! Her usual style, slash and burn, working against the grain, held no appeal for her when it came to Philip. "You know," he said to her over a dinner of mussels marina that she'd made at his apartment after a long stretch of separate assignments, "when I brought up your name today with *Gourmet*, they said you were, and I'm quoting, 'talented but difficult.'"

"I guess I can be. I'm less impatient than I used to be, less temperamental. You must be a good influence on me," she said, a little flirty, a little pleased with herself. Pleased with him. "What did you say to them?"

"I said I'd never had a contentious moment with you. I said you were the most talented stylist I knew. I did not tell them you can bring me to my knees with your tongue."

"Why? You don't want me to get the job?"

He laughed and took her hand and pulled her toward the stairs to the bedroom. "Show me what you've got, and I might be able to pull you in on the Thanksgiving issue."

She resisted Philip's invitation to move in for months, wouldn't even leave clothing at his place. "Don't you see enough of me all week?" she asked.

"No," he said. Just no. That one word, stated so plainly, moved her. He wanted more of her, and she was grateful to find she wanted more of him, too. While leaving his house early one morning wearing an inappropriately heavy woolen coat because it had become spring overnight the way it sometimes did in New York City, unable to put in her contacts because she refused to keep a lousy bottle of solution at his place, eyes burning, she thought, *What is wrong with me?* The following weekend, almost exactly a year after she'd woken up in his bed, they rented a small van and moved her in. The next morning it seemed like all the wisteria on the block had bloomed at once. "Ah, look," Philip said as they walked to the local diner for breakfast, "word has leaked out that Clara Larkin is in residence."

Out of superstition or fear, Clara wasn't sure which, she kept her tiny apartment. At first, she'd stop by regularly to pick up her mail and check personal messages on the answering machine, mostly Bridie asking her to *please, please* call back. She couldn't avoid everyone forever, but she could avoid them for now. They were all used to it. Communication happened on Clara's terms, exactly as she liked. Soon, she got lazy about stopping by the old place, which was why she never got the thick ivory envelope containing an invitation and never saw the back flap of the envelope, where right below the return address, in her sister's spidery script, was one sentence: *Bridie is a Bride!*

Forty-Two

Finn discovered Fern's amphetamine drops during her senior year of high school and took her straight to the family pediatrician, who, after lecturing her about the dangers of speed, poured the remainder of the bottle down the drain and made her promise never to use them again. The following week, he wrote a letter to the editor of the *Democrat & Chronicle* objecting to sending teenagers to Weight Watchers. Just one more humiliation for Honey during the long, strange year that followed the elopement. The op-ed didn't mention Honey by name, but everyone knew what meeting he was talking about, and even though she'd had no idea that the girls were taking Dexatrim, her meetings took an attendance hit. "They run weight-loss summer camps for teenagers!" an indignant Honey said over and over to anyone within earshot. "They run huge advertisements everywhere, but *I'm* the nuisance to the community because somebody"—here she would laser focus on Fern—"did something they weren't supposed to do."

Fern reluctantly agreed with Honey. It wasn't fair that she was being cast as the villain—and Finn some kind of rescuing hero—when Jenny's mother or the doctor who'd handed out the drops like candy faced no backlash. But when Fern tearfully told Honey how Finn had found the bottle after she left it on the kitchen counter of her father's new house, Honey wasn't horrified that Fern used the drops; she was furious that Fern had been careless enough to get caught. "I mean," Honey said, handing Fern a Tab from the refrigerator, "there's no denying you look terrific."

The weight had come back on slowly but surely. "I thought it was the freshman ten, not the freshman twenty," Honey said sourly when Fern came home for the college winter break. But by then, Fern didn't care. While at nursing school she'd started volunteering at a local home for the elderly for extra credit. She discovered a thrilling authority within herself when dealing with the patients. So many of them were lonely and confused, and if some of her peers avoided spending time with older patients, Fern gravitated to them. Her stutter wasn't gone, but every time she made a move away from childhood and toward adulthood, her speech improved. Most of the residents of Maplewood Manor were hard of hearing or had mild dementia, and if they noticed her stutter they never said a thing. This made her brave.

One night, as she helped calm a distressed resident after supper, speaking to her soothingly and telling her made up stories about a baker in town called Mr. Cannoli, the nurse on duty praised her. "You're very good at this, Fern. Not everyone at your age—at any age!—has that kind of patience with older people."

By the time she graduated from nursing school, she knew she wanted to go on to a graduate program in hospice care. "But it's so depressing," Honey groaned. "My god, Fern, dying people all day. Why not work in the nursery with all the new babies. Life-affirming!"

How to explain to Honey that helping people face the end of their lives was the most life-affirming thing she could possibly think to do. It fulfilled her. It calmed her.

Fern was the only person in the two families not blindsided by Dune and Bridie's romance. After that early morning in the driveway, when she watched her father and Nina drive away, the irreparable rupture in her life seemed to grant her a kind of superpower. How, Finn and Nina's children asked themselves over and over in the weeks and months following the elopement, had they not seen what had to have been right in front of them? How were they so easily fooled?

As she got older, she developed an eerie intuition about which couples would last and which ones wouldn't. So many times on the way home from a party or a dinner with a group of friends Fern would say to Naomi, "Elizabeth and Rashid aren't doing well." Or, "Boy, Manuel is *not* into George," or, "I think Mona is seeing someone behind Richard's back," and Naomi would say, "You're nuts."

Naomi eventually stopped saying it because Fern was nearly always right. Sometimes it would take months, sometimes years, but Fern's second sense about who was happy and who was not was nearly flawless. Two couples had outlasted her predictions, and she still felt it was only a matter of time. "It's kind of remarkable," Naomi said repeatedly.

"And totally useless," Fern would always reply. What good was having a superpower that was unwelcome or downright bad news? It wasn't like anyone would be excited to hear her project or, even worse, confirm that she'd seen the dissolution of a relationship even before the parties involved admitted it to themselves. It was a useless trick.

But she was also quite good at spotting coupledom before it happened. Like at the fundraiser where Bridie and Dune ended up sitting next to each other and she'd watched their body language over the course of a few hours go from awkward to curious. If Dune hadn't embarrassed himself, she figured they were an hour away from making out in his car. Even so, she was surprised by the buffeting waves of anger and confusion when they confirmed her suspicions.

"Be happy for them," Naomi said to her the next morning, after endless rounds of conversation the previous night. "If they have feelings for each other and it works out, why not be happy?"

"Because it's déjà vu all over again."

"What?"

"Yogi Berra."

"Yogi Bear?"

"Never mind." Fern had to stop using sports references. Naomi was a violinist in the philharmonic and thought Reggie Jackson was an abstract painter.

"They'll dredge it all up again. Our parents."

"You all talk about Nina and Finn as if they weren't just another older couple, coasting into retirement. Doing their cruise ship thing. They're not that interesting!"

Fern didn't know what to say. She'd thought a lot of things about their family, families, but *not interesting*? Not in a million years.

"As an outsider, would you like to know what I see?" Naomi asked.

"Not particularly," Fern said.

Naomi barreled ahead. "I see two middle-aged people who have a decent relationship but still end up bickering over how best to drive a mile and a half to the store. I see a woman who complains about her spouse snoring and a man who thinks his wife should cook more. I see two people who seem to have a fine relationship, but who are also mortal beings you all invest with some kind of unearned superpower. Honestly? The most interesting thing they ever did was run away and get married."

Fern turned and walked into the kitchen, dumped the cold coffee from her mug into the sink—her hand was trembling from too much coffee, or too much of something. Naomi followed and Fern waited for her to apologize. But she just stood there. "I love you," Naomi finally said. "But maybe it's time to let some stuff go."

"My mother is going to lose her shit, and I'm going to have to pick up the pieces all over again. Why didn't I leave this town when I had the chance?" She turned to see Naomi's stricken face. "I'm sorry, I didn't mean it like that. I'm sorry. I just meant—"

"I give up," Naomi said, holding up her hands to stop Fern's apology. "I need to practice."

She stormed upstairs to the guest room, which was also her music studio. Fern sighed. She could hear Naomi furiously tuning the violin, shrieks where there were usually gentle moans. "Don't take it out on the instrument!" she yelled up the stairs. Silence and then a quick run of notes, the opening chords of the theme from *Love Story*. Not quite forgiveness, but an offering. Fern would take it. She could not screw this up, the best thing that had ever happened to her.

Naomi had walked into the ER one night during Fern's nursing rotation with a nasty cut on her inner arm, just above the elbow. She was in a state, she explained to Fern, she'd cut her arm clearing an old fence from her yard, which was so dumb because she was a violinist and couldn't possibly have limited use of an arm. After a quick look, Fern knew Naomi would be okay. In spite of an impressive amount of blood, the laceration was superficial. "There's no tendon or muscle damage," Fern reassured her. "You need a few stitches and it will be sore for forty-eight hours, but your arm will be fine."

As Fern cleaned the arm and assembled a suturing kit, she and Naomi chatted. Naomi had just moved to Rochester and had a lot of questions about neighborhoods and restaurants and where to shop. "You're very good at this," Naomi said as Fern gently stitched the wound closed. "I don't feel anything."

"That's the lidocaine," Fern said. "But I do try to be gentle." As she was signing the discharge papers for Naomi and explaining where to go to fill the antibiotic prescription, Naomi stared at Fern, both intent and amused. Fern squirmed a little. "Would you be interested in having coffee one of these days?" Naomi asked.

Fern understood exactly what Naomi was asking. Fern rarely dated. She didn't click with men, and she'd never seriously considered that she might click with women, but the way her heart was racing under Naomi's very direct gaze made her think again. "I'd love that," she said.

Fern tried not to indulge (she knew it was indulgent) her ongoing anger as unwitting observer of Finn and Nina's leaving that morning. She knew all the clichés—the past was past, they'd all survived, nobody was dead, nobody was dying (or, they were all dying, some more slowly than others). They were *fine*.

"You saw them *leave*?" Naomi asked when Fern told her about the infamous night at her bathroom window. "Do they know you saw them?"

"Nina knows," Fern said. "I never told anyone else."

"But that's crazy. Not even your father? Your mother? Why not? I don't understand."

And that was the problem. For all her intelligence and empathy and insight, Naomi couldn't really understand. Naomi's family was like a *Life* magazine feature about WASPs in New England: *How they live now!* She had two parents who had been together for thirty-three years. She had a brother who was an attorney in Boston. Both Naomi and her brother had gone to fancy boarding schools and fancy colleges.

After Juilliard, Naomi ended up at the Rochester Philharmonic. She talked to her father and mother every day, about silly everyday things. Nobody cried. Nobody yelled. Her parents' lefty politics left room for everyone. Her pediatrician father had opened a clinic in Roxbury when nobody in Roxbury had the money for regular health care. Her attorney mother had been a school desegregation activist, a vocal supporter of the ERA, and when Naomi was thirteen had casually said to her, "If you're interested in girls don't be afraid to tell us."

It was all confounding to Fern. The idea that a family unit could live so convivially and peacefully, supporting one another and enjoying one another's company. "It's not all as rosy as you picture it," Naomi tried to tell her. "A lot of stuff gets pushed down and none of us dig too deep in what I'm sure is an unhealthy way. But it is pleasant."

Pleasant, that was the word. Naomi's family was pleasant and peaceful and comforting, while her family always seemed to be standing on shaky ground. Fern supposed she shouldn't be surprised since all had been relatively calm for years—so, of course. Of course. Bridie and Dune. Goddamn. But maybe Naomi was right. Maybe nobody even talked, much less thought, about the Finnegans and the Larkins. And in some perverted way, she was grateful that the families had depleted their reserves of shock back in 1977. Like when she came out to her family a few years ago. What were they all supposed to say? *How dare you?* Finn was excessively supportive. Dune appropriately blasé. Bridie offered to orchestrate a meal or conversation with her father, and Fern gently and deftly dissuaded her. Even Honey, God bless her, had stifled her obvious shock and patted Fern's shoulder reassuringly. "I love you no matter what," she'd said, surprising Fern who'd been braced for disdain, refusal, objections about lesbians not shaving their legs. That Naomi was so talented and credentialed and composed, regal even, helped because she intimidated Honey. "I have something to tell *you*," Honey said shyly shortly after that afternoon. "Maybe I'm not the only one to have a—a—*special* friend."

"Mom!" Fern said, genuinely thrilled. "Do you have a boyfriend?"

"Oh, don't call him that. I'm far too old for that word."

His name was Hank. Hank! Fern didn't know why she was so thrilled by his name except that it felt like anyone named Hank would be a solid human, and Honey's Hank didn't disappoint. Stocky. Cheerful. Strong. And he doted on Honey as she feigned annoyance.

But now what? While they were all still living on Cambridge Road, Fern and Clara and Bridie had made feeble gestures toward staying friends, but whenever they got together it turned into a self-pitying game of What They Hadn't Known and then into a tortuous standoff over which parent was most at fault. Too many conversations ended in tears or shouting for them to have the will to continue. And now Bridie was going to be her sister-in-law. "Ridiculous," she said to her empty kitchen. "Totally ridiculous."

Forty-Three

In spite of her sister's teenage taunts—"Always a Bridie, never a bride!"—Bridie didn't really care about being a bride, only about finding a partner, falling in love, and falling in love with Dune had been the easiest part of her entire life. Maybe the only easy thing in her life. She and Dune *fit*. Hand in glove. Round peg, round hole. Whatever metaphor suited would suit. Bridie and Dune liked the same things; they cared about the same things—about giving back and being of use and making their little corner of the world a bit better. They both wanted a family and (maybe, probably) to stay in Rochester. She'd never felt such ease with another person.

"You're sure?" Nina asked, not even trying to hide her surprise and alarm during the weekend in February when Dune and Bridie disclosed all to their various family members in a series of back-to-back restaurant meals.

"So sure, Mom. I've never been this sure about anything in my life."

"This feels very fast, Bridie." Bridie didn't like the note of concern in Nina's voice and braced herself for what she knew would come next. "And Clara? How is Clara with all this?" Bridie had planned a response. She meant to toss off a casual lie, but it stuck in her throat.

"Bridie?"

"She knows we've been hanging out."

"Bridget."

"She doesn't return my calls. You know what's she like. I can't get her on the phone."

"Don't let Clara hear this from someone else."

"I know! I'll take care of it." But two months later she hadn't taken care of it. Instead, she'd stupidly mailed a wedding invitation and hastily written a dumb joke on the back of the envelope and had seriously considered driving to New York City to try to intercept the mail but continued to silently fret and stay frozen in place. One night, early in their romance, Dune made the mistake of being honest about Clara. "I'm scared of her," he'd said, not understanding that Bridie would grab on to that one sentence and not let go. "What do you mean?" she said, cheeks speedily flushing like a warning light for Dune: *Proceed with caution.*

"I mean, she's scary. You said it first." It was shortly after they'd told each other they were in love. Shortly after they started to talk about marriage, they hadn't even needed a proposal, it was an easy assumption.

"But if you're terrified of her that means you're still somehow attached to her. Otherwise, why would you care? Why would you care if she's mad at us or if she yells or makes a scene or disappears?"

Dune wasn't terrified of Clara's *feelings*, he elaborated to Bridie (not quite honestly) but afraid of how she might act out and intimidate Bridie. "That's my concern," he said as Bridie let her shoulders drop back into place, relieved. "I'm worried about *you.*"

She and Dune constantly told one another that it would be ludicrous for Clara to be mad. Dune hadn't *really* been Clara's boyfriend. They'd had a high school crush. They'd kissed, sure, but they'd never had sex! Gosh, they were kids, teenagers. Nobody had even known before it was over, and also? Clara had an exciting life in New York City. Why would anything going on back in Rochester impact her in any meaningful way? She would see how it was funny if you thought about it; actually, it was quite funny! What was the opposite of star-crossed lovers? Dune went to the Strasenburgh Planetarium and bought a bunch of glow-in-the-dark star decals to put on their bathroom ceiling. They were star-fated lovers, he told her. Meant to be. All the talk about how they'd done nothing wrong was true, but truth was not a rock-solid defense in matters of the heart.

If it were up to Bridie, they would have skipped all the planning and celebrating and had a small service and lunch somewhere. She hated being the center of attention; she didn't want to spend her carefully acquired money on something as ephemeral as a wedding celebration; she disliked bridal gowns and veils and the whole giving-away-a-daughter madness.

But Dune. Dune saw her celebratory reticence as, at worst, a reflection of her happiness and, at best, a parental hangover they needed to shake to survive. "Did you get hold of Clara?" he would ask Bridie every Sunday night, and every Sunday night Bridie would say, "She didn't pick up," until Dune stopped asking.

Bridie knew Clara better than anyone. The secret would bother Clara more than the fact. Maybe. Bridie realized Clara would see this as another betrayal in a long line of poor decisions involving the Larkins and the Finnegans. She would be infuriated, and she would be certain that Bridie was making a mistake. She'd be shocked and then she'd be angry. Bridie loved and missed her sister, but she also saw her with perfect clarity: Clara needed everything to be about her, and when she learned that Bridie had won something she'd wanted and lost, well—

Dune wanted the church, the reception at the club, bridesmaids and groomsmen, centerpieces, and a live band and dance floor. But all Bridie could think about when they talked about a wedding was the photos. Not having the photos but taking the photos. How would that work? How would she and Dune stand in the center with their fucked-up parental situation surrounding them? Where would Finn and Nina stand? With each other? On what side? What to do about Honey? And Clara? For the life of her, Bridie couldn't imagine the look on Clara's face if she was forced to pose in their family wedding portrait.

And she was worried about the open bar and the flowing booze of the weekend. Bridie was grateful that Dune was drinking less, but she could see, on certain occasions, that he was white-knuckling the whole endeavor, and she knew that approach rarely worked, or had staying power. She'd memorized the statistics. But he tensed up whenever she brought up meetings or counseling or quitting completely.

Whenever Bridie was faced with a wedding decision—chicken or beef; shrimp or salmon; how many at a table; what kind of music—

her brain froze. Just thinking about a seating chart gave her heart palpitations. She wanted Clara's advice. She wanted Clara's help. She wanted her mother's advice. She wanted her mother's help. But to choose one was to reject the other.

"I'll help you," Dune said over and over and over whenever he saw the frozen, overwhelmed look on her face. "Please. Let me help." She was grateful but she was also sad. And angry. And tired. Those were Bridie's phases of grief: sad, angry, tired, and she'd been cycling through them for so many years, they were almost comforting, the worn groove so familiar. Inevitably, she'd descend into her favorite old wound, the lone time Clara visited her at Cornell. Clara had donned a bemused attachment during the day. *So many people. So loud. Do all college girls have to wave and squeal at every single goddam person they see? The hugging, why all the hugging?* She and Clara laughed a lot as Bridie played tour guide on the campus she was just getting to know. Then it was time to leave, and Clara hopped into her car and cheerily waved.

When Bridie got back to her second-floor room and opened the window to holler at Clara for one last good-bye, Clara was sitting stock still in the front seat, hands on the wheel, watching a group of young men and women horsing around on the sidewalk, heading to the campus bar, arms around one another singing "Maggie May," at the top of their lungs. *Oh, it's late September and I really should be back at school!* The only word to accurately describe Clara's demeanor was *stricken*. And then, to Bridie's horror, Clara started to weep. Not just cry but bitterly weep, face in hands, shoulders trembling. Bridie stepped away from the window because the only thing that would have made that moment worse for Clara was to have been witnessed. Yes, that was a memory she stoked on certain days.

"What's wrong?" Dune said one morning, coming into the kitchen, looking sleepy and tousled and handsome and concerned.

"I need to get through to Clara," she said plainly, "and I'm not sure how."

He shoveled at least four teaspoons of sugar into his black coffee and then turned to her. "Let me help."

Forty-Four

Dune hadn't ever tried to picture Clara's life in New York City, but certain expectations had crept in. If pressed, he would have described a run-down building in a marginal neighborhood. An apartment she probably had to share with a stranger to afford. All assumptions formed by television or movies.

He certainly hadn't envisioned this tony block, the gracious trees, the relative quiet given that he was in the middle of Manhattan. He walked down West Seventy-Sixth Street, past the limestone facades and elegant brownstones. He knew Clara was a well-respected food stylist because her name often appeared on lists their advertising agency passed along when Finnegan's was launching new ads or marketing materials. It was how he'd found this address, different from the one scribbled in Bridie's address book. How much did food stylists make? He felt like he was in the wrong job, the wrong life. How had Clara Larkin, who had stormed out of her house, her town, all of their lives, one day in August of 1979, and moved to Manhattan without a college degree or any professional training, landed on this block? In this building he was standing in front of, double-checking the address, because *Clara* lived here?

He read the row of names on the buzzer to the side of a carved wooden door. She was in #3RW, whatever that meant. He hit the button and to his surprise the front door buzzed and he was inside without having to announce himself. The lobby was dark and had an ugly linoleum floor, but the staircase curving up two stories was polished mahogany. He climbed to the top, admiring the soothing creak of the stairs, the feel of the solid railing beneath his hand, disappointed by the unsightly take-out menus littering each landing. On the top floor, music was wafting out of an open door, something classical and familiar, but Dune couldn't summon the name. He knocked lightly. "Hello?" A tall, bearded man, wiping his hands on a dish towel, appeared in the doorway and stopped up short, surprised. "You are not the flower guy," he said.

"I am not," Dune said. "I'm afraid I come empty-handed."

"Can I help you?"

"I'm looking for Clara Larkin."

The man looked relieved. "Ah, okay. She's out, but she should be back any minute. You want to wait?" He extended a hand. "I'm Philip Woolf."

"Dune. I'm a friend from back home."

"Really?" Philip waved him in. Something fantastic-smelling was simmering on the stove. "This is a first. I haven't met anyone from Rochester. Does she know you're in town?"

"No. No. Definitely not. I'm, um, I'm—I know Clara's sister. Bridget? Clara hasn't been returning her calls for a few weeks. I'm in town for work so I thought I'd check in on her. Make sure everything is okay."

Philip turned the heat down on whatever it was that smelled so good Dune wanted to ask for a taste. He put a lid on the pot and pulled it off the burner. "What's that lyric from *The Sound of Music*?" Philip asked Dune.

"The hills are alive?"

Philip hummed a tune and kind of sang, kind of spoke, "'How do you catch a cloud and pin it down? A will-o'-the-wisp, something something, flibbertigibbet.' Something like that."

"Right, that one."

"How do you solve a problem like Clara? She's a tornado. A million things going on, a million phone calls unanswered. It's also possible her sister is calling Clara's old number. She keeps her old apartment but is pretty firmly ensconced in this one. Everything okay at home?"

"Oh yeah. Better than okay. I'm not here with bad news. I don't think."

"Did Bridget send you?"

"No, she doesn't know I'm here. And neither does Clara's mother."

Philip gave a nervous laugh. "Her mother can't possibly know. Right?"

"I guess?" Dune said, confused.

"No disrespect," Philip continued, "but I'm of the belief that the dead don't know what we're doing after they're gone." He shrugged. "Just my opinion. I don't believe Clara's mother is watching from beyond the grave. May her memory be a blessing and all that."

Dune went from dumb to dumbfounded, and it must have shown on his face because Philip said, "Are we sure we're talking about the same Clara Larkin?"

"I don't know," Dune said. "Maybe not. My Clara Larkin's mother is very much alive. I saw her this morning."

"*That* Clara Larkin," Philip said, pointing to a framed photo on the mantle of him with his arm around a woman, planting a kiss on her cheek. The woman smiled directly into the camera, bright-eyed, laughing, the wind whipping her long hair around her face, and Dune, who hadn't seen Clara in many years, involuntarily smiled back at the photo. "Yes. That exact one."

Forty-Five

Clara had gone to Zabar's to shop for dinner and to get some ideas for this week's television segment about summer grilling, which was bound to be a royal pain in the ass because the studio kitchen still didn't have a grill. She would have to make everything in advance and figure out how to make it look like Jimmy was grilling in the studio. She picked up a bunch of practice items: corn, peppers, sausages, and hamburger mix. Bread and tomatoes. Trudging home with multiple bags in each hand, she made a mental list of all the things she would need to bring to the studio: her favorite large white platters but also something else because the director had developed a sudden aversion to all white plates even though they were almost always the best choice for the finished product, only seen on-screen for a minute, sometimes seconds.

But Clara had learned the hard way that the absolute worst thing you could do on a television or commercial set was antagonize the director. "Dude," she'd said to one dude who was throwing a temper tantrum because he didn't like the "noodle read" on a bowl of farfalle she'd styled, "this is a jarred tomato sauce spot, not *Goodfellas*." She was replaced that afternoon, so now she treated them all like the infantile prima donnas they seemed to be and greeted every suggestion and peccadillo and complaint like it was both brilliant and reasonable, which was almost never true.

Clara still did print work, especially with Philip, but it was the television work that thrilled her. She *loved* live television and their scrappy fledgling food channel. No reshoots, no fussing with tweezers and blowtorches and spritzers of water or glycerin once the show was live. No retakes, no sitting around waiting for photos to be developed and photographers to agonize over whether the torn pieces of basil should have been placed a little bit to the right and on an angle. No advertising executives asking why the grains of rice were *irregular*. Things went wrong, sometimes spectacularly wrong, but was anyone even watching?

Clara started at the network the week they moved into a new studio space. Though it looked shiny and clean on camera, in practical terms, the set barely functioned. The sinks had running water because they were connected to the building's sprinkler system, not because they had proper plumbing. Everything emptied into a hidden bucket beneath the counter, and Clara was one of the people who had to remember to empty the slosh pail between shows. "Who built this Potemkin kitchen?" she asked at the end of her first week. "Who wanted electric stoves?"

"It's like the Taj Majal compared to the old place," one of the production assistants told her.

"How is that possible?" Clara asked.

"No rats," the woman said.

Even though Clara was pathologically organized and everything at the television studio was haphazard and last minute, she recognized the seemingly limitless opportunity of the gig. The producers needed to fill countless hours of potentially profitable television and were willing to pull in any chef in the city who was photogenic and able to keep up a mildly coherent patter while cooking.

One night, she brought two producers to her friend Jimmy La Rocco's small Northern Italian restaurant in the far West Village. She knew Jimmy was a superstar in search of a bigger stage. They gave him a trial slot and, after five flawless and entertaining demonstrations, came up with a format for what would become his show *Tre al Tavola*, three at the table. In each episode, Jimmy would cook three dishes for three invited guests, some culled from the food world, some fans, and on the occasional day when they couldn't book three guests, a few willing crew members. Twenty twenty-five-minute episodes shot in four days. Five episodes a day meant fifteen meals to prep and cook and duplicate and get just right—or right enough—for television. Clara thrived on the adrenaline.

As she turned onto her block, she thought about side dishes that didn't have to be grilled. Maybe an orzo salad. Maybe something with strawberries for dessert; they'd just appeared at the farmer's market and looked spectacular. She was smiling and humming as she walked through the front door, thinking about Philip and summer corn and peaches and plums. She heard voices as she put her key in the lock and wondered who it could be. Anyone! Philip was a pied piper, always luring people home after a shoot for food and drinks and music. At first it drove her crazy, but then she started to enjoy cooking for actual people again. She'd forgotten how satisfying it was, and she loved how their home was becoming the center of cheer and comfort. Something almost joyful. If only she could fully lean into all of it. Too often it made her testy and curt, and Philip would retreat for a bit until she softened and apologized. "Why do you do that?" he asked her once. "What is the origin of all this discomfort around comfort?" She would brush him off, but she knew they needed to talk. She had to tell him some things, confess some things, because she couldn't avoid her family forever, and he was pressing to meet them. She pushed open the door with her hip and hollered into the small entryway, "I'm home! Can you give me a hand?" Silence. She walked into the living room, arms laden with groceries. "Philip?"

"Hi." She heard Dune's voice. She froze and dropped one bag of groceries. Cherry tomatoes started rolling across the floor.

"Got enough dynamite there, Butch?" Dune said, smiling briefly. She wanted to laugh but couldn't. She turned to Philip and knew at once she'd gotten home too late. Both of them, Philip and Dune (Dune!), stood staring at her, baffled, both of them searching her face.

"Well, fuck," she said.

Forty-Six

Tre al Tavola with Jimmy La Rocco and Guests
Transcript for Episode #14, May 8, 1994—**Mother's Day Lunch**
Guests: Theresa La Rocco (Jimmy's mother), Theresa-Marie La Rocco (Jimmy's sister), and Terry La Rocco (Jimmy's aunt)

Menu:
    Bruschetta with Ricotta and Fava Beans
    Fettuccine Primavera
    Affogato

ACT II

JIMMY: *Ciao, amici!* Welcome back to *Tre al Tavola*! Before the break we were here with the three Theresas of my family—my mother, my sister, and my aunt. If you're a La Rocco there's always a Theresa in the room. But we've lost a Theresa! My sister Theresa-Marie is expecting, and she felt a little faint. She's completely fine, but we're letting her and the little zeppola in the oven rest backstage until it's time to eat. But this show isn't *DUE al Tavola*, so I've persuaded my trusty assistant and food stylist to make a rare on-camera appearance both as guest and a helping hand. Welcome, Clara!

[Cut to Clara Larkin taking a seat at the counter]

CLARA: Hi! Thanks for admitting me into the Theresa club.
JIMMY: Big shoes to fill!
CLARA: Yes, but I'm relieved to see they're all sensible pumps.
JIMMY: Ah, that's because the La Rocco women spend a lot of time on their feet in the kitchen—or as I think of it: the executive suite.

All the most important decisions happen in that room. Right, Mom? Right, Aunt Terry?

[Cut to the other two Theresas nodding and laughing]

JIMMY: Okay, let's get moving, and even though I've invited Clara to sit in the recently vacated guest seat, I'm going to ask her to move to the hot seat, back here in the kitchen, and give me a hand while we prepare this beautiful spring bruschetta.

[Cut to Clara behind the counter]

JIMMY: Clara, how do you feel about fava beans?
CLARA: I adore them, but they are definitely a high-maintenance vegetable.

[Cut to bowl of fava pods]

JIMMY: True. You have to work for those tender and delicious little parcels, but it's worth it, and, as we're about to show you, a lot of the work can be done ahead of time. We shelled all our favas earlier today and blanched the beans, which as most of you know means dropping them very briefly in boiling water and transferring into an ice bath. And here's what we ended up with.

[Cut to bowl of unpeeled favas]

CLARA: They don't look very appetizing in this state.
JIMMY: They sure don't. They look otherworldly. Like little alien beans.

[Cut to Jimmy picking up a bean with two fingers]

JIMMY: Phone home, phone home!
CLARA: Didn't our mothers always tell us it's the inside that counts?
JIMMY: And Mom's always right. So why don't you show us what's inside.

[Cut to Clara peeling blanched favas]

CLARA: I'm giving this blanched pod a gentle squeeze. Sometimes you need to tear the outer casing a bit to get to the bean. Here it is. Look at that color.

JIMMY: I can see my mom fidgeting over there. You don't like to peel the favas, do you, Ma?

THERESA: It's not how we did it back in the day.

AUNT TERRY: Everything is edible. Even the skin.

JIMMY: The Theresas have spoken! Some people leave the skin on, but I find it tough and bitter. If you have very fresh, very small beans from a garden in Italy like my mom and aunt did as kids, you can probably get away with skipping this step. I like to put in the extra work because just look at these beauties.

[Cut to pile of peeled favas on a wooden cutting board]

JIMMY: They are *gorgeous*. And you can shell and peel your favas the day before if you want and keep them covered in the fridge. Okay, so now we're going to take these slices of semolina baguette that have been lightly toasted. Spread some fresh ricotta on top—just like this, not too thick, not too thin. You can get your ricotta in a supermarket, but if you make the extra effort to get to an Italian import store for fresh ricotta you won't be sorry. Take a spoon of the favas and arrange them prettily on top. Like so. And now we're going to drizzle the bruschetta with the really good olive oil and top with a bit of grated lemon zest. Spring on a plate!

[Cut to Jimmy passing the plate of bruschetta for guests]

JIMMY: How's that taste, Mom?

THERESA: Delicious, sweetheart. Absolutely delicious. The lemon is a nice touch.

JIMMY: Ah. Nothing better than approval from Mom, who was my first—and best!—teacher. Clara, how about you? Was Mom your teacher in the kitchen?

CLARA: *Your* mom?

[Cut to Theresa laughing and shaking her head]

JIMMY: I meant *your* mom. Did she cook?

CLARA: Yes. She sure did.

JIMMY: And is Mom still with us?

CLARA: Mom is—not still with us.

JIMMY: Oh, I'm so sorry, that's—

THERESA AND AUNT TERRY (interrupting): So sorry, Clara. What a shame.

CLARA: Thank you all. But it's okay. It's been a while.

JIMMY: Can I ask how long?

CLARA: She left us one night in 1977. Very unexpected. Just like that.

JIMMY: Too young. Too young to go. And what was her name?

CLARA: Nina. Josephine, but she went by Nina.

JIMMY: I'll tell you what. This bruschetta is on my restaurant menu every spring and from now on we're calling it Bruschetta Nina! In honor of your mom and *everyone* who is missing their mom on Mother's Day.

[Camera pulls back to wide shot of the kitchen]

CLARA: How nice.

JIMMY: And I see my producer waving frantically, which means we're ready for a quick break, but don't step away, because we're about to show you how to pull together a simple but flavorful Fettuccine Primavera using the asparagus that's all over the market this week. The perfect plate to follow Bruschetta Nina! We'll be back in *un minuto!*

[Cut to commercial]

Forty-Seven

Dune had lied to Bridie about not remembering when he last saw Clara. He knew she hadn't been at Fern's graduation party. He knew down to the minute, the position of the sun in the sky, where he'd been standing when he'd last seen Clara Larkin. He was home for a week, staying with Honey because Fern had gone on a well-deserved trip to the Jersey Shore with some of her nursing school friends. "You have to come babysit," Fern said to Dune. "She's acting like I'm moving to New Jersey instead of going for five days."

Dune was living in London at the time, working at Harrods Food Halls, sourcing specialties from France, looking for all the world like he'd stepped out of a photo of Finnegan's Grocer in the 1880s in his white shirt and black apron and straw boater. Even though he was back sleeping in his childhood twin bed, he relished the quiet and space of the house on Cambridge Road and having a bathroom all to himself. At his bedsit in Wembley, a thirty-minute ride on the underground to Harrods, he shared one tiny bathroom with four other lodgers.

"Huh, look at that," Honey said, standing at the living room window the morning after he arrived. "The prodigal daughter returns."

Dune tried to sound casual. "Which one?"

"Which one do you think?" Honey said. "Not Bridie. That girl is a peach."

Heart racing, Dune walked toward the window just in time to see Clara's back recede through the front door. "I don't think *prodigal* is the word you're looking for."

"Of course it is. I know my Bible. The prodigal son."

"Prodigal because he was profligate. Wasteful. Not because he left and didn't come home for a few years."

"How do you know Clara isn't wasteful and profligate?"

"I don't," Dune said, raising his hands in surrender. "I don't know anything about Clara."

He went upstairs and tried to focus on his closet, which Honey wanted him to clear out as she was also planning on moving in a few months. How odd, he thought, that the last two left in this neighborhood would be Finn and Nina, still living in the modest Craftsman they'd rented after the elopement and finally purchased. After filling a few Hefty bags with old school papers, notebooks, cassette tapes, and outdated issues of *Sports Illustrated*, he found himself standing at the upstairs bathroom window, his old lookout spot, when Clara appeared in the upstairs window across the street. At first he thought he was seeing things, but no, she was right there, looking back at him, steadily, coolly. He raised a hand and waved. She reached up and calmly pulled the shade down. He felt like a fool, with his arm in the air, waving at no one. She hadn't even looked angry. She hadn't frowned or given him the finger, which at least would have allowed Dune a second of superiority. But no. She'd simply closed the shade. As if he didn't exist. That was the last time he'd seen her.

There were other things he didn't want to discuss with Bridie. Like how he *had* been in love with Clara and although he had very different thoughts about love now, he couldn't deny that Clara—and all they'd gone through—had left a mark. He had been so angry when his father left home. Letting in the hard truth of his father's betrayal was too difficult, so he'd shifted all the blame to Nina. She became the receptacle for his hurt and disappointment and, by extension, so did Clara. With distance, he could see how unfair he'd been to both of them and how easily he'd let his father off the hook. But what eighteen-year-old would have the maturity to handle such a complicated situation with grace? Not him. Not anyone he knew. Certainly not Clara, who had gone full scorched earth. The sustenance of her anger was a frightful thing. He wasn't lying about worrying that Clara would get into Bridie's head. Her remove made her more powerful, as she surely knew. One caustic comment about Dune from Clara to Bridie would sink a seed into her bones and take root. Although Dune would be relieved, *thrilled*, if Clara didn't show up for the wedding, Bridie would be heartbroken. So he scheduled a trip to Manhattan on flimsy work pretenses and went to find her.

Dune had never felt so awkward as he did picking up fistfuls of cherry tomatoes from the floor of Clara's apartment that day, listening to her confused boyfriend confront her about the mother-who-was-not-dead. The argument was revving up in the kitchen. It was almost funny how after all these years, Dune recognized the threatening tone in Clara's voice. He wondered if Philip had ever crossed that line. Did he know he was wading into dangerous territory? He stepped into the room that was divided by a breakfast bar and gave a little wave. "I think I should get going," he said to Clara, who was flushed and, he was surprised to see, tearful. "I'm sorry about all this—"

"It's fine," Clara said. "It's my fault. You don't have to go."

"I do," Dune said, reaching into the radiating left inner pocket of his suit jacket. "I wanted you to have this, though. Bridie wanted you to have this."

Clara took the envelope and ripped it open. Read the elegant, engraved script. "You're joking, right?"

"Not exactly a high-quality joke," Dune said.

"No, I guess not." Clara put the invite down on the counter and ran her fingers through her hair. "You people," she said, turning to Dune, "are going to be the death of me."

AFTER DUNE HANDED CLARA THE wedding invitation and exited her building, he walked around the neighborhood for a bit, trying to settle his nerves. He hoped Clara would call Bridie soon, make an overture about the wedding, but he wasn't counting on it, as it looked like she had a thorny problem of her own. It was nuts, Dune recognized, for Clara to have killed off Nina but in the annals of their family history almost understandable. He thought how much easier it would be to tell strangers that his parents were dead instead of explaining the whole convoluted truth. He could never do it, but he believed Clara could.

He found himself standing the sidewalk beneath a bright neon sign reading DUBLIN HOUSE. He shouldn't go into the pub by himself. But why not? He could be forgiven for needing a little liquid comfort. He'd done a good thing for his fiancée and had reconnected with Clara and that was weird and uncomfortable and why shouldn't he enjoy a pint or two of ale in a pub in New York City? He was spending the night at the Radisson across from Lincoln Center. Nobody but him would ever know.

Forty-Eight

Honey wanted a new dress and Fern also needed something to wear to the wedding, which is how Fern found herself sitting on a tiny stool in the dressing room trying to zip a too-small sequined number up Honey's bulging back.

"I don't get it," Honey said, trying to twist around and see the label on the back of the dress. "Is this a size eight? Because I am definitely a size eight."

Fern put on her reading glasses and looked at the label. "It says eight."

"It must be a mistake," Honey said. "Mislabeled."

"Want me to see if they have a ten? It's pretty."

Honey snorted. "I'd be *swimming* in a size ten. See if they have something similar in an eight. I like the color." Fern helped Honey step out of the dress and took it to the saleswoman. As she was going through the racks of dresses, all of them hideous, she had a memory from so long ago. One Saturday, Nina had taken her and Clara and Bridie to run some errands. Nina needed something at Sears, something in the housewares department, and she let the girls browse through the Lemon Frog shop that Sears advertised as being for "young teens." They all grabbed bunches of corduroy pants and tops with little lemon frogs embroidered on them. When Nina came to find them, both Bridie and Clara had chosen a few items. Fern was locked in a dressing room.

"Fern?" Nina said, knocking gently on the door. "Can I help you?"

Fern slowly opened the door, dressed in the clothes she came in. "Didn't you like anything?" Nina asked.

"They don't fit," Fern said. Nina could tell she was embarrassed and on the verge of tears. "I'll find you another size," she said to Fern.

"No," Fern said. "I can't. My mother only lets me buy a size seven. Sometimes a nine."

"Hold on," Nina said. She was back within minutes with a pair of dark purple slacks, size eleven. Fern put them on and although they were a tiny bit snug, they were wearable. "But they're not my size," Fern said. Nina put a finger to her lips. *Shhhhh*. Within minutes Nina had worked the paper tags off the T-shaped plastic fastener and switched them. "What about the tag on the pants?" Fern asked, excited.

"Easy," Nina said. With little effort she ripped it right out of the waistband. "Honey will never know." Fern had worn those pants until they had holes in the knees, crotch, back pockets. She loved them. She carried Honey's size eight to the salesgirl. "It's a little small," Fern whispered. "But if we change the tags—"

The saleslady nodded and smiled. She went to the rack and rifled through and grabbed another version of the dress. "Here's a ten," she said, handing the dress to Fern and turning to help another shopper. Fern swiftly undid the tags attached with tiny safety pins—so much easier!—and switched them. She checked the back of the neckline and miraculously there wasn't a label to tear out. She went back to Honey's dressing room.

"Here's another eight. Give it a try. The saleswoman said sometimes they get mislabeled."

"Aren't you going to try something on?"

"In here? No." Fern rolled her eyes. "Not exactly my style."

"What exactly is your style?"

"I don't know. I'll find something."

Honey turned to Fern, exasperated. "You live in those hospital scrubs."

"Mom, I work in a hospital."

"But why do you have to wear them off duty?"

"Because they're comfortable."

"I miss the old nurse's uniforms." Honey said. "The white dresses. The white cap. The stockings and navy capes. So smart."

"You're describing a uniform from the fifties."

"What a shame. Remember all those nursing books I bought you? The Cherry Ames books? *Cherry Ames Student Nurse. Cherry Ames Senior Nurse.* You loved those books! She wore the dress and the cape. She didn't work in hospice. I always thought you became a nurse because of those books." Honey smiled at herself in the mirror, admiring her accidental vocation influencing.

"Maybe," Fern said. She realized she'd been a little in love with Cherry Ames in all her nursing iterations. She'd spent a lot of time thinking about Cherry's tiny waist and pointy breasts. "I did have quite a crush on Cherry Ames, Dude Ranch Nurse."

"Fern. Honestly." But Honey smiled at Fern in the mirror. She'd lightened up so much since Hank. Honey slipped on the fake size eight. Fern stepped behind her and zipped the back.

"There!" Honey said, delighted. "I knew it. I don't know why, but this shop *always* mixes up sizes."

"It looks great."

Honey smoothed the skirt and looked at herself from the side. She deflated a bit. "Is this really a size eight?"

"Mom, who cares?"

"I knew it. I've done everything right, but the scale won't budge."

"Maybe because you're happy?" Fern said. "Because Hank is a great guy who doesn't care how much you weigh?"

"Even so. It will smooth out with a girdle."

"You don't need a girdle."

"I need two. I'll double up."

Fern knew Honey was thinking about Nina and what Nina would wear and how Nina would be effortlessly elegant and inevitably make Honey look like she was trying too hard. The elder Finnegans and Larkins had a working truce, a public politeness, but it had been ages since they'd all had to coexist in one room. Until next weekend. Until Bridie and Dune's wedding, when all the unwilling players would be summoned to the stage one more time.

Forty-Nine

When Dune left the apartment after his unannounced visit, Clara had a very confused and irritated Philip on her hands. She wasn't proud of that moment on *Tre al Tavola*. The second the segment was over she wanted to ask Jimmy if they could do it again or ask the director to edit out her answer, but she didn't have the courage for either, for letting them know how carelessly cruel she'd behaved. She didn't even think of Nina as dead! She had no idea why she'd blurted out that lie. Something having to do with Jimmy's mother and aunt sitting there, so proud and adoring, beaming so much love at him and each other and at her. It made her lonely. And when Jimmy asked about Nina, and she felt the hot tears gather, she heard herself say a truly unspeakable thing.

Of course (of course!) that was one of maybe four episodes that Philip had seen. He brought it up on their first date because his mother had died young—"I also lost my mother way too early," he said gravely, mortifying her into silence. She quickly changed the topic. The strangest thing about the lie was how in the weeks and months after she'd said it out loud on television, she felt some icy core of resistance inside of her start to melt. She called her mother more often. At first, she was calling to take the temperature, to see if her mother had gotten word about what she'd done, unlikely given the tiny reach of their show, but not impossible. Eventually, she called just to talk. Sometimes every week. The calls were quick. Clara set the pace. Still guarded. But something.

And then other thoughts about her and her family intruded, unannounced but not entirely unwelcome. Didn't everyone mess up? Wasn't everyone just trying to live their lives, do their best? Wasn't everyone worthy of forgiveness? That last one was hard for her. She didn't want to forgive her mother, but hadn't Clara done an unforgivable thing, too? What might happen if she put down her outrage? Just put it down and moved forward without it? And then Dune appeared at the door. And then Philip's anger and disappointment.

"After I didn't tell you the first time, I couldn't," she tried to explain. "I tried, but I couldn't bring myself to do it." She didn't know how many more ways to apologize. She was truly sorry, and he seemed to be softening a little when she made another strategic error.

"What do you mean you're not going to your sister's wedding?" he said after she casually mentioned her intention to skip the weekend.

"Oh, I don't think they really want me there," she said.

"Really? That guy came from Rochester to *hand deliver* a wedding invitation because they don't want you there?" And just like that he was furious again. Clara capitulated in the face of his outrage. She wasn't going to open up a new battlefront over Dune. They would go to Bridie's wedding. She would confess all to her mother in person, assuming Dune hadn't already ratted her out.

When they landed at the Rochester airport, the first person Clara saw was Bridie, waiting at the gate, jumping up and down and waving frantically. Clara grinned and made a beeline for her sister, Philip following close behind.

"I see you," she said, giving a wave even more exaggerated than Bridie's, using both arms as if she were helping to land a plane, laughing. She rushed to Bridie and hugged her hard. This was going to be fine. *Fine.* "I'm happy to see you, bride."

Fifty

Clara had hoped to find Nina in a quiet moment when they might have a real talk, but Nina greeted her at the rehearsal dinner by saying, "Dune tells me the rumors of my death have been greatly exaggerated, on a cooking show no less." Clara gave a feeble laugh. "I would like to explain," she said.

"Not tonight," Nina said, not seeming particularly perturbed, smiling and waving at someone Clara did not recognize across the room. "We'll talk later. After the wedding." Nina patted Clara's arm.

The rehearsal dinner was at the father of the groom's house, which, of course, was also the mother of the bride's house. A beautiful summer evening. Clara was surprised at how relatively easy everyone was with each other. Bridie and Dune and their happiness set the tone, and it seemed to throw a wash over their respective families. Bridie was glowing, just like a bride should. Dune seemed a little inebriated, but what was a celebration without lubrication, and he'd picked all the wines and was happy to share details with anyone who would listen.

Bridie had tried to explain to Clara the contours of this Frankenstein family, telling her how a welcome ease had developed during all the wedding planning. Clara hadn't quite believed it, but Bridie was right. Clara was genuinely happy to see Fern and her partner, Naomi. She didn't mind talking to Honey, who had turned from the chiseled blond wife of her youth into a slightly rounder and mellower older woman who wanted to know which Broadway musicals Clara had seen.

"None of them?" Honey said, clearly disappointed.

"Nope," Clara said. "Not my thing."

Then Honey spent the next twenty minutes rhapsodizing about *Phantom*. "You must go. The chandelier falls!"

Clara watched her mother move through the room gracefully, always the hostess. Philip was talking to Sam, who then gave a beautiful toast to Bridie. Finn gave one for Dune. It was all—nice?

"I can certainly understand why you've steered clear of those *ogres*," Philip said, tugging off his tie in their hotel room after dinner. After changing into more casual clothes, they were going to meet Bridie and Dune and some of their friends at the hotel bar. "Truly horrible people."

She felt prickly and annoyed and defensive. "I don't know what to tell you. I don't recognize those people."

"That's what happens with time, if you're lucky. People change. *We* change. Sometimes for the better." His voice was sincere but not reprimanding. She hugged him but didn't say anything. She felt a bit like a little girl who was being asked to give up her stuffed toy because she was too old. Who was she without her indignation?

By the time Dune and Bridie arrived at the hotel bar, everyone was a little tipsy, more than a little exuberant. Pitchers of beer and a few trays of shots and many spins around the dance floor later, Clara sat down at a booth to catch her breath, and the room started spinning a little. Maybe she should have some water. Instead, she went to the bar and ordered a Bloody Mary, her old tried-and-true strategy for eking a few more hours of drinking out of the night. The opening beats of the B-52s' "Love Shack" filled the room, and Clara watched Bridie in the middle of the dance floor jumping around with Philip. She looked deliriously happy. Something dark and unpleasant started to bloom in Clara, and she tried to shake it off. Maybe she just needed to urinate. She pushed her way into the ladies' room, but it wasn't the ladies' room, because standing there washing his hands and visibly weaving back and forth was Dune.

"Whoops!" she said, covering her eyes.

"You're okay. Twenty seconds earlier and this could have been very awkward," he said, hitting the button on the wall-mounted dryer.

"I was hoping we'd have a minute to talk," she said.

"You didn't have to chase me into the men's room."

"I didn't." She waved him off and stumbled a little, braced herself on the edge of a sink.

Dune ran his slightly damp hands through his hair. He'd drunk a little more than he'd intended but wasn't so far gone that he didn't realize he had to hustle Clara out of the men's room quickly. He and Bridie had had a tense moment in the car on the way to the hotel bar when Bridie'd accused Dune of dropping her hand when Clara walked in to dinner. "That's not true," he objected. (Was it true?) "If I stopped holding your hand it was because I needed to do something, open wine or help your mom or maybe my dad waved me over? I didn't even see Clara until she came over to us!" Bridie seemed to believe him.

"You okay?" he said to Clara, ushering her outside to a small room adjacent to the larger bar. Clara tried not to stare at Dune's face. It was Dune! She hadn't fully taken him in that day at the apartment with Philip standing there, and she'd avoided him when she arrived in town because of that old Rochester feeling: eyes on her every move. But this was good. Nobody else around observing.

"Philip seems like a great guy," Dune said.

"He is. He's a much nicer person than I am."

"Low bar," Dune said, only kind of joking.

"I agree."

"I'm kidding. I do want to thank you for being here," Dune said. "Bridie didn't want to do any of this without you."

"And what about you?"

"What about me?"

"Did you want me here?"

"Of course. I want what Bridie wants."

"But when you came to New York," Clara said, feeling her way through a question she now realized had been a constant undertow of her last few weeks, "was it because you wanted to find me for Bridie? Or because you wanted to find me for you?"

Dune tried to focus on the question. How many drinks had he had? "I don't think we should be having this conversation."

"But the question needs to be asked, right? It's not insane to wonder."

"It's a little bit insane," Dune said, backing a few steps away from Clara until he was against a wall.

"If you're going to marry my sister, don't you want to be sure?" She moved closer. Put her hand on his arm. Dune didn't move. "We never got to do anything but kiss," she pressed. "Don't you think about that sometimes? What might have happened? Where it might have led? What a wasted opportunity it all was?"

"Not really."

"I don't believe you."

He looked past her shoulder and said, "I haven't thought about it in a very long time."

"Ah, but you did think about it. Like I did. About what we missed."

She moved her hand down and linked her pinkie with his. Dune would never forgive himself for not pushing past her, batting her hand away, calling for Bridie, but what he'd eventually tell Bridie about that moment was the truth: he wanted to know something, to recognize kindness or vulnerability or forgiveness on Clara's face. Acceptance. He *had* desired her, and he'd regretted their ending for too many years, but he was also searching for a kind of understanding.

"Clara," he said, trying to disentangle their hands—and then he saw it, the Clara he had once loved flickered across her face: beguiling and stubborn and selfish, exactly as he remembered. And he knew then, down to his marrow, that she held no power over him and hadn't for a long time. Bridie was his home now. And his refuge. Before he could step away, Clara moved in as if to kiss him, and between his surprise and sodden reflexes, he stood there, dumbly, as her face inched closer until he heard Bridie's trembling voice.

"Dune?"

Fifty-One

Forty-eight hours after landing in Rochester for the wedding, Clara was driving a rental car back to New York City by herself, wondering how fast she would have to go to skip into a parallel universe, one where her family didn't even exist. She tried to muster umbrage, but even Clara, with her bottomless anger and laundry lists of fuckups, couldn't believe what had happened. No. She couldn't believe what she'd *done*.

Somewhere around Binghamton, her hangover started to lift and shame fully descended. She tried not to think about Philip flying back to New York without her or about how nobody would speak to her this morning—except for that punishing breakfast with her mother—all developments that a younger Clara would have used to successfully fuel her outrage. Today, they were devastating. And once she let the full force of the previous night hit her sober heart, all she could see was the look on Bridie's face, and she had to pull over and tell herself to breathe.

This morning, when they should have been getting dressed for church, while Philip was packing and not speaking to her, the phone in the hotel room rang. It was her mother. "Meet me downstairs in the hotel restaurant, please."

Nina was sitting in a booth with a pot of coffee on the table. She motioned for Clara to sit and started in before Clara could even pour a cup. "For a very long time, I have chosen to let you nurture your disappointment in and anger with me," Nina began. "And I have appreciated—more than you can possibly imagine—the recent feeling that we might be getting somewhere, you and I, somewhere accommodating. And I have tried, Clara, I have tried so hard to understand and be accountable for all the ways in which I hurt you and your sister. Your lack of forgiveness has been hard and painful. But this? What you did to Bridie—"

"But I didn't—"

Nina raised her hand. "I know. We all know because you said it a thousand times last night. You weren't *doing* anything, but who do we credit for that, Clara? You?"

Clara lowered her head in her hands. "No," she said. She was miserable and terribly sick. "I don't know what to do. I think I should leave."

"That seems to be something at which you excel," Nina said, her voice clipped.

"I learned from the master."

The waitress put the food down on their table. Nina had ordered eggs Benedict for the two of them, and the plates had been sitting under the heat lamp for a little too long, because the vivid yellow hollandaise was starting to form a slightly wrinkled skin on top. Both Clara and Nina picked up their forks at the same time and, in an identical motion, swiped the hollandaise, and broke the yolk, which was perfectly cooked. They looked up at each other. "I'm sorry," Clara said. "I'm sorry I said that. Even I don't believe it anymore."

Nina motioned for her to eat, and they dug into their breakfast and ate quietly for a few minutes. The eggs weren't helping Clara's stomach. She pushed her plate away and poured herself some water.

"What do you believe?" Nina finally asked.

"About you and Finn?"

"We can start there."

"I don't know. To be honest, my feelings around it calcified almost immediately. I thought you chose him over us, and it felt terrible. You left us, that's a fact."

"I left your father. I lived ten blocks away. I didn't leave you."

"But that's how it felt!" Clara could hear herself. She sounded younger than her seventeen-year-old self. She sounded like she was ten. Five.

"I wasn't happy with your father. I made a mistake marrying him, except of course that I'd do it again if it meant getting you and Bridie. I would do it a thousand times. But, Clara, I couldn't accept paying for that mistake for the rest of my life."

"Was it because he was gay?"

"Somewhat. Not fully, but partly. Not that this is any of your business, but the intimacy was—"

Clara winced and stopped Nina. "I get the picture."

"He had an enormous secret that closed him off emotionally. We were ill-suited. He wasn't happy. I wasn't happy. And then I fell in love with someone who loved me. If anything, I wanted you girls to know that mistakes aren't life sentences. Life is full of options, even if the world tries to tell you it's not. I wanted you to believe in choice, to trust your desires."

"I guess . . ." Clara was tired, she couldn't think straight, and she had the sinking feeling that what she'd done last night couldn't be fixed. "I guess I wish it hadn't been so easy for you to go."

Nina put her hands out, palms up, and beckoned to Clara. Clara took her mother's hands, crying now, and they both held on tight. "It wasn't easy, my love. None of it was easy."

"LET THINGS SETTLE FOR A bit," her mother said as she helped Clara load her luggage into the back of the rental car, the vile turquoise that only seemed to exist at Hertz. "And then you're going to come back to fix this."

Back in New York after the endless ride home, she went directly to her old place and sat forlornly in the kitchen of the apartment she'd never thought would be her apartment again, looking out the window onto an airshaft covered in pigeon shit.

For so many years, she'd believed rage was the fire that ignited her. She realized, as a person who was no longer a teenager, that what she'd felt during all the years since the morning of the note, wasn't anger or resentment or fury or plain sadness, but something else. Grief. The thing that had propelled so many bad decisions in her life, that had brought her to this sad spot in this sad room with its sad view, was grief. She hadn't known what to call it back then, but she recognized it now that she'd endangered so much in her life. And because she wasn't a selfish child anymore, just a sloppy adult, the grief flared with renewed vigor, made itself comfortable and felt horrific.

Fifty-Two

Bridie had refused to look at the weather report all week. Not that it mattered whether the day was sunny or cloudy, whether it rained or snowed, which wasn't likely in early November but certainly possible. But when she woke that morning, the sun was brightening a cloudless sky. A perfect day for a wedding. Her previous wedding dress was still on a padded hanger in a voluminous white garment bag at the back of her closet, but she wasn't going to wear it. She'd thought about it for weeks. It wasn't the dress she wanted. That dress was for a different wedding and a different girl. Someone less sure of herself, afraid of her own shadow. Someone who had let herself be talked into an ivory gown with puffed sleeves and a too-long veil, a vestige of that obnoxious board game.

One afternoon, she'd found a vintage suit at a secondhand store downtown that fit her like a dream. The material was a soft wool flannel in a deep forest green. The peplumed jacket had tiny gold-rimmed pearl buttons running up to the rounded collar. The skirt fell to her midcalf. She bought a pair of Mary Jane pumps with a block heel and a silver strap across the top of the foot. Nina had given her a seeded-pearl brooch that looked like a spray of flowers to wear on the jacket collar and because it was November, she was going to carry a nosegay of orange and yellow tea roses.

She played with her hair, tried to pull it back into a chignon but couldn't figure out how to get it to stay in place, so she finally brushed it smooth and let it lie around her face and shoulders. She was late, so she ran up the steps to the courthouse and when she entered the waiting room, she saw Dune before he saw her. She watched him fiddle with his shirt cuffs, brush something off his pants, run a hand over his clean-shaven face. When he turned and saw her, she felt the weight, the comfort, of all the Bridies and all the Dunes. Dune on a bicycle weaving erratically down the street after taking off his training wheels and then slamming into a tree when he forgot to brake. He still had a thin white scar on his chin from that day, shiny and whisker-free. She saw him throwing a football in the street and delivering papers before the sun was up and waving to her from their respective bathroom windows and then the emptiness of the always-curtained window after their parents married. She saw him take the chair next to her that night at the fundraiser and the surprise on his face when he realized who she was. She saw him at her front door one Sunday morning weeks ago, looking gaunt and sad and carrying the little painting from the auction that he'd tracked down for her: *After Monet's Sun through Fog.* "I can't accept this," she'd said. "Please, Bridie," Dune said, referring, she knew, not to the painting but to all of it. To them. "Please," he said again, and handed her something else: his ninety-day chip from AA, and she felt the first glimmer of hope she'd had in months.

Dune took a step toward the door and saw a flash of nine-year-old Bridie with denim shorts and skinned knees and torn sneakers, begging to play with her sister. He saw her walking to school in her too-short navy school uniform and coming out of the house one spring evening in a light pink prom dress, on the arm of someone who didn't appreciate her.

He thought about a moment so many years ago—was he fourteen? Fifteen?—when they'd agreed to play hide-and-seek with the younger kids on the block. She went to her favorite hiding place, under the arbor in the Tannenbaums' backyard, the one the girls called the wedding bush because when it was in full bloom, they could shake the branches, and tiny white petals would fall all over their hair and shoulders like a veil. When she swept away the blossoming branches one day, Dune was already sitting there hiding. "Shh," he whispered and motioned for her to sit next to him. They sat quietly and tried not to laugh and as the minutes went by and their breath started to synchronize, they could smell each other. Bridie smelled like the cedar chest where her sweater usually lived and strawberry shampoo. Dune smelled like Irish Spring and grass and the chocolate bar he'd just eaten. They both realized their legs were touching, and when Dune looked at Bridie and she didn't make a move to inch away he clocked the nakedness of her expression, how her guileless smile opened her face like a flower turning to the sun. He felt his heart start to pound. "Are you okay?" she whispered, and he wanted to ask her a question, any question, but at that exact moment someone yelled, "Olly olly oxen free!" and she jumped up and said, "We won!" They both thought about the night they first kissed. How easy it was. How terrifying and true.

She moved across the threshold of the door toward him and all their parents sitting in a row, chatting and smiling. Finn with his arm around Nina. Honey holding Hank's hand. Her dad, fiddling with his watch, slightly apart from the others. Bridie felt a twinge of regret that Clara had honored Bridie's request to stay away, just for this one day, because Clara could have been a companion for Sam; he wouldn't have had to sit alone. But then Sam leaned over and whispered something to Nina and Finn and they all laughed quietly. Why had she thought it would be so hard to have her parents here? It was good. It was lovely. Dune put out a hand.

"I'm sorry I'm late," she said. "I hope you weren't worried."

"Never," he said. "Never worried. Always grateful."

And she stepped into his arms and felt peace. He kissed the top of her head.

"Next!" the county clerk yelled to a room that only contained their party. Ten minutes later the judge was saying to the beaming couple, "I now pronounce you." I pronounce you. They were pronounced.

Fifty-Three

When Nina thought the time was right, Clara got on a plane and flew to Rochester. Clara knew, or hoped, that she and her mother were going to be okay when Nina demanded that Clara come home. For so long Nina had treaded oh-so-carefully with Clara, but in that moment Nina sounded like a mother, like *her* mother, for the first time in forever.

As she was driving the rental car to Bridie's apartment, she took a long-forbidden route. It seemed so silly now. How before she left town for good, she would drive in a circuitous manner to avoid passing by any of the Finnegan's Grocers around town. As if the looming edifices would sense her avoidance and feel slighted. Her mother should have stated it more gently on that long-ago morning, but Clara had, in spite of the inelegant warning, spent a lot of time overestimating the importance of her presence. And her history. At a dinner party recently, she'd told the story of the elopement and after answering the usual questions with her canned responses, honed for effect, a woman she didn't know said, "Wasn't that what *everyone* was doing in the seventies?" And the conversation moved on to a new downtown restaurant.

She found herself pulling into the parking lot of the store where her family had always shopped. It looked completely different. She knew the stores had repeatedly been expanded and remodeled. *Finnegan's!* in its evergreen script with the tiny shamrock dotting the letter *i* still looked exactly the same. She might as well bite the bullet. She'd laughed when she'd read an article about Dune Finnegan and his embrace of the European food hall experience, but he'd done a good job. She had her quibbles. The prepackaged meat and fish were not to her liking. Too many cheese platters all offering the same things, and nobody needed a pile of syrupy walnuts next to a tired bunch of grapes. Why was there an entire section devoted to back-to-school supplies? Hardware? Video rentals? This is where the European food hall met Finn Finnegan's love of the very American one-stop shop. You would not be able to buy a folding lawn chair with beer holders in the arms at Harrods, she was pretty sure of that.

She went to the bakery section and chose a plastic clamshell (hated those, too) filled with half-moon cookies, Bridie's favorite. She got back in her car and opened the plastic package and bit into one cookie, which was—she would argue this to the death—a far superior version of the New York City black and white. Softer cake. Frosting instead of fondant. People in New York City didn't understand what they were missing. She took another bite. It was a commercially produced product, not as good as the ones at the little bakery they frequented as kids, but good enough. She ate the whole thing. And then another. These cookies were her Proustian snack.

WHEN BRIDIE SAW CLARA STANDING on the other side of the screen door they'd neglected to switch out against the chill of the coming winter, she stood stock-still. They looked at each other warily. Clara raised the container with the remaining cookies and waved it a little. Bridie put a hand on her hip and shook her head, but Clara could tell she was biting back a smile. Finally, Bridie stepped forward and opened the door. It was a start.

Part Three

1998

Fifty-Four

In spite of Honey's best efforts, Bridie's baby shower did not take place at the house she still owned at the lake or at the country club or even at Nina's house, which would not have been Honey's first choice but one she would have accepted in the name of custom and tradition. Bridie had her own ideas these days that Honey believed constituted a warfare on all the rituals of family, starting with their courthouse wedding and ludicrous lunch at Don's Original. "I don't understand," she said to Dune one afternoon when he brought her a bunch of groceries and reheatable dinners from the store. "Why is she so against the usual way of doing things?"

"I don't think that's it," Dune said. He was used to his mother railing against Bridie and tried to dismiss it but understood that with a baby coming he might have to start pushing back a little harder, for Bridie's sake. "She—*we*—want to make our own traditions."

Honey sighed. Even she could see futility in her protests, but a baby shower in a restaurant? "What on earth do I wear to"—she looked down at the invitation—"a *canal house*?"

"Whatever you want, Mom. This is brunch at a nice restaurant. You'll like it."

Honey did like the place, though she tried not to. The shower was held in a private room in the back of a structure that had been built alongside the Erie Canal. Nina had decorated the room flawlessly, of course. No paper storks or pink-and-blue balloons or oversized plastic pacifiers. She'd filled vases with bunches of spring flowers, tulips and daffodils and hyacinth. Little yellow rubber ducks at each plate held place cards. Honey came prepared to argue about her seat. She imagined Bridie sticking her in the back somewhere even though she was one of the expectant grandmothers. But when she made her way to the tables, she heard Fern call out to her. "Mom! We're up here." Fern was standing at the front of the room waving at her. Nina and Bridie had sat her at the head table, along with Fern and Naomi and Clara. She was taken aback by how happy this made her. Well, maybe enough time had gone by. And then there was the baby. A baby fixed so many old resentments, she supposed, if you let it. Look at Clara and Bridie. It didn't seem like the sisters were back to normal exactly, but it seemed like they were both trying. Clara took her position next to Bridie as the gifts were unwrapped, writing down names and items and being—*second fiddle*, was what came to Honey's mind—in a way so uncharacteristic for Clara that it seemed like the continuation of an apology.

Honey and Nina had even shared a moment during the silly games that some of Bridie's friends had insisted on, rolling their eyes in mutual stupefaction when everyone was handed a few pieces of pink Bubble Yum and asked to "sculpt a baby" for Bridie to judge.

"I'm making a fetus," Fern said, working two pieces of gum into one and biting her lip in concentration.

"Don't you dare!" Honey said.

Fern laughed. "Mom, you are no longer the boss of me." Fern won the prize with a sculpture so lifelike—"Look at the umbilical cord!" Bridie marveled—that the tiny bubble-gum fetus got passed around to admire.

Toward the end of the day, shortly after Finn and Dune arrived to load all the gifts into the back of the SUV purchased as the new family car, Nina pulled Fern aside. "Can I talk to you for a moment? Privately."

"I know this is probably silly," Nina said as they went out onto the lawn overlooking the placid canal, dodging goose scat, "but I thought I should ask your advice about something."

"Of course," Fern said.

"I hate to be one of those people. 'Nurse, can I tell you about my back pain?'"

"Nina, please," Fern said. "You aren't 'one of those people.' We're family."

Nina nodded her head, visibly moved. "We are, aren't we? And getting bigger with every passing minute."

Fern was slightly taken aback by seeing Nina emotional. She supposed this was what happened with grandmothering. "What's up?"

"I've been ridiculously tired lately. Unusually, maybe worryingly tired." Nina did look tired, Fern thought, seeing beyond the casual acquaintance she had with Nina's face and viewing her more like a patient. Dark circles. Unhealthy pallor beneath what Fern now realized was a lot of makeup, more than Nina usually wore. Nina pulled back the sleeve of her dress. "And then this started happening." She offered her arm to Fern. It was spotted with tiny red dots.

"We call this petechiae," Fern said. "What else?" Fern asked. "Any bruising?"

"Yes," Nina said.

"May I?" Fern gestured to Nina's neck. She didn't like the way these symptoms were adding up. She gently put her hands on Nina's throat and felt the lymph nodes, enlarged and tender. "This is sore?" she said. Nina nodded and said, "What do you think?"

"I think," Fern said, putting on her neutral nurse's voice, "this could be a lot of things, and we need to start with some basic blood work."

"Could this be anemia?" Nina said.

"It could."

"Could it be cancer?"

"It could be *lots of things*," Fern said, all business. "Let's get the bloodwork done."

By the time Bridie's baby was born, a little girl she named Josephine after Nina, they had the diagnosis: acute myeloid leukemia. Fern wasn't surprised, but she was saddened. At almost sixty-eight, Nina's chances of remission were not great. A long remission? Even worse. When she read the results, she asked Nina's doctor if she could be present when he delivered the news to Nina and Finn. When her father entered the office and saw Fern sitting there nodding bravely, he started to weep.

"So much melodrama!" Nina said that night. They were sitting in the kitchen eating bowls of goulash that Helen Harper had sent over from the store. Nina added a dollop of sour cream and chopped dill to everyone's bowl. "If this means chemotherapy, I'm in for whatever they bring. I'm ready. None of you people are getting rid of me so soon."

The medical team certainly brought it: a grueling few months of chemo that flattened Nina but never put her into complete remission. "What's next?" Finn asked Fern. She wasn't used to seeing her father at a loss. He looked terribly old very quickly. "What about a stem cell transplant?"

"They probably wouldn't have considered a transplant at her age," Fern said, "but without remission, it's not an option at all."

"What are you talking about!" Bridie said days later, standing and bouncing baby Josephine in her carrier, trying to keep her quiet. "Why no more treatment? I don't get it. Fern, talk to her." Fern looked at Nina imploringly. Bridie needed to hear this from Nina. "I thought you said a lot of new treatments were coming along," Bridie continued, "targeted treatments with longer survival rates."

"I did," Fern said. "But without remission? Our hands are tied."

"Bridget"—Nina patted the chair next to her for Bridie to sit—"the treatments they have aren't working. And, love, I am tired." Bridie wouldn't sit. She furiously wiped away tears so they wouldn't fall on top of Josephine's head, looked at Finn, and said, "Why are *you* so quiet? Do something!" Finn walked over to Bridie holding Josephine and took them both in his arms. "We've done what we can," he said as she sobbed into his shoulder.

"Fern," Nina said a little while later, after Bridie had gone home and they were standing in the kitchen making tea. "I want to stay home as long as possible. Is that realistic?"

"You know you have a hospice nurse in the family, right?"

"But you have your own work," Nina said. "And I don't know if this presents a conflict for you. I thought you could recommend someone."

Fern's expression was a mix of confusion and hurt, a look that brought Nina right back to that December morning so long ago, when Fern was a little girl in her pajamas, standing in the driveway, frightened. "I can recommend someone if you want," Fern said, "but I would like to be that person, unless—"

Nina interrupted her. "I would love nothing more than to have you be the person."

Fifty-Five

Nina'd had a rough night, so Dune sent Bridie home to get some sleep and spend the morning with baby Jo. As frequently happened, Nina seemed to settle and sleep just as the sky started to lighten. He went down to the kitchen and Finn was sitting at the table in a robe and slippers, hair askew, gray whiskers prominent in the morning light. He looked haggard. Not a word Dune would ever think to apply to his father. Dune knew he wasn't imagining that Finn was shrinking. Nina's loss would be most visceral, the hardest for Finn, but for most of Dune's life, his father had been a sturdy tree, an elm or a maple, towering over everyone, sharing his canopy, providing strength.

"Dad?" Finn looked up with a start, smoothed his hair, smiled. Some of him was back. "Did you get some sleep?"

"A little."

"Take tonight off, too. You should try to sleep more."

Finn smiled and slowly stood, seeming to work to get his feet under him before he started walking. He put a hand on Dune's shoulder. "Go home. I'll take tonight. There will be plenty of time to sleep."

Dune knew Clara was standing by, ready for the call to come home. He was still skittish around Clara, even though Bridie wasn't. After Josephine was born, Bridie had struggled mightily. She'd had a difficult pregnancy, an unduly long labor ending in a C-section. Josephine was only two weeks old when Bridie developed a bad case of mastitis in her left breast and they'd had to work to get Jo to take a bottle, all while Bridie was feverish and heartsick. Finally, when the infection started to clear and the pandemonium of the early weeks began to fall into a loose pattern, the depression had descended. Dune had, reluctantly, called Clara. He didn't know what else to do.

Honey thought Bridie was being indulgent. "She needs a good. Long. Walk!" Nina and Finn were far away on a cruise, not expected home anytime soon. Fern was working nights; he couldn't ask her to come over during the day to help with a newborn.

Clara had swept into town like Mary Poppins with a bag full of tricks. She'd cleaned and cooked and coaxed Bridie into the bath every night. She was helpless with Josephine at first, but that was okay. She became Bridie's nurse, her caretaker and confidante. When he heard them laughing one morning when he was trying to burp Josephine, the baby splayed across his lap in what seemed like a ludicrous position for a newborn but also worked, he startled. He realized he hadn't heard laughter in the house since they'd come home from the hospital with the baby. He tiptoed into the bedroom and saw Bridie, fully dressed, trying to pull on a pair of boots. "I got fat in my feet!" she was saying through tears of laughter.

"That's not fat. You're bloated, you fool."

"Are you two going somewhere?" Dune asked.

"Oh yeah," Bridie said. "A movie and lunch." Dune stood dumbfounded. "I'm joking. We're going to the doctor."

"Good," Dune said. "Good. You and Clara?"

"No," Bridie said softly. "You and me. If you have time."

"Give me this nugget," Clara said, taking Jo and looking both bemused and terrified. "We'll be fine, won't we?" She lifted Jo's tiny hand and waved it in Bridie and Dune's direction. "Just don't dawdle!"

"Are you sure?" Bridie said. "If you're not comfortable—"

"I am great." Clara gave Dune a look, a look that said, *Get her out of here.*

The SSRIs didn't work overnight, but they worked within a few weeks, and as Clara packed for the airport, Bridie sat nearby nursing Jo. "I've been thinking," she said.

"You keep thinking, Butch. It's what you're good at."

"Dune always says that to me!"

"He does?" Clara turned away so Bridie wouldn't see the look on her face. She was surprised to feel hurt.

"So dumb," Bridie said.

"Yeah, it's pretty dumb. What were you thinking about?"

"I was thinking"—Bridie paused in a way that made Clara suspect what was coming—"I was just thinking, wouldn't it be nice if you moved back here? Back home?"

Clara turned and looked at Bridie. Raised a brow.

"I mean it. Look at your niece. She adores you."

"And I love her. But Bridie?"

"Yes?"

"Not a fucking chance."

Bridie smiled and looked down at Jo. "We knew that's what she would say. Right?"

Fifty-Six

What a strange business, thought Finn, *waiting for a person to die.* Waiting for the person you loved most in the world to die. He'd always thought of himself as a problem solver, but this *passage*, as Fern liked to call it (he hated the word), these final steps of Nina's, were an unsolvable problem, an unstoppable force. All he could do was sit and try to make his presence a comfort and not a burden. "What are you going to do without me?" she'd said one afternoon months ago. She tried to pass it off as a joke, a lighthearted remark, but he could hear the deep thrum of sorrow beneath.

"Oh, I'm not," he said. "I'm going with you. I didn't say?"

"Sorry, I've only got one ticket."

They were out on a walk that afternoon through their neighborhood. Most of the trees had lost their leaves. A few, the maples, the ginkgoes, were still in full color. They held hands as they blithely kicked the fallen leaves on the path. She stopped and said, "I want to tell you something."

He wasn't prepared. "Not yet," he said.

"Finn." She turned to face him and made him look at her. "I have had the most spectacular life." And then he did the thing he'd sworn he wouldn't do: he collapsed into her arms—the brilliance of her smile, the lambent light of it, destroyed him. He sobbed and she shushed, and they stood that way as the sun went down. "Come," she finally said. "It's getting dark. Figuratively and literally." She wiped the tears and snot off his face and kissed him full on the lips. "I wouldn't change a thing," she said. "We released each other, made ourselves more than we were before we were together. What else can anyone ask than to be made *more*?"

Fifty-Seven

Nina was drifting in and out of sleep. The baby was crying. Was it her turn to get up? Of course it was, it was always her turn. Sam never got up with the kids. He had to work in the morning. She could hear the baby but couldn't find her body. It didn't make any sense. She was in her body. Her body hurt, but she couldn't get any of the parts to move. She started pounding Sam's side of the bed with her fist to wake him up.

"What is it, Nina? What do you need?" Fern adjusted the pillows behind Nina's shrunken frame. Tucked in the blankets. "Try to sleep."

"No no no no," Nina was becoming agitated. "Clara's crying. She's hungry. She needs to be fed."

"Okay." Fern patted and stroked Nina's arm. "I'll get the baby and the bottle. Go back to sleep." Nina quieted. From the corner, Bridie whispered, "Should I not be here with the baby? Is it upsetting her?"

"No," Fern said. Bridie's face crumpled and she lowered her head to Josephine's. "I shouldn't be sad when I'm feeding the baby," she said, looking up at Fern, distraught. "I'm transferring negative emotions."

"You're not," Fern said. "You are doing two incredibly hard things at once and nothing you're doing is wrong." She handed Bridie a box of Kleenex. "I think we need to call Clara."

AS SOON AS CLARA GOT the call, she packed as quickly as possible. She knew the call was inevitable but had refused to get a bag together based on a healthy dose of superstition and a little dab of hope. Last month, right before Christmas, Nina had seemed to be at the end of the line, but then she rallied and had a few good weeks and even though the doctors didn't change their prognosis, who was to say she wouldn't beat back this episode, too? Now Clara was sorry she hadn't prepared better. She made a few calls and put all her work on hold or reassigned what she could to colleagues. She had become a producer at the Food Network and had an assistant and a proper office and a spanking new two-bedroom apartment.

She also had a dog. A rescue mutt that Philip had encouraged her to adopt while they were in the death throes of coupledom but still pretending they might survive. "A dog is not going to make me want kids," she told him, dubiously eyeing a spirited beagle mix. "Does this one have a name?" she asked the volunteer at the shelter.

"He does! His name is Fettuccine Alfredo. We call him Alfie."

"Kismet," Philip said.

When Clara finally broke it off for good, when she realized she'd prefer to be at her place with Alfie instead of at Philip's place with him, when she admitted to herself that she would always feel like a failed human under his gaze, he offered to be an occasional dog sitter. It was nice. That they still saw each other and were friendly and could work together. He came and got the dog while she was packing. "I'm sorry," he said, and gave her a quick hug. He had a girlfriend now. A nice woman with two kids who doted on Alfie.

She sent Philip off with the dog and a bag of toys and pet food. She pulled her one conservative black dress off of its hanger. Was this morbid? Was she summoning death by packing it? She picked up the phone to call Bridie and realized she couldn't ask Bridie. Clara put the dress in her suitcase. Took it out. Then she imagined what it might be like if Nina did die and her first task had to be finding a proper funeral dress at Sibley's. Or wearing something of Bridie's, which was equally unthinkable. An uncharitable thought but true.

She dialed Fern's number. "Hey, it's me," she said. "I don't know how else to say this, but am I packing a black dress? Is that too—"

Fern cut her off. "Pack the dress."

She put the dress back in her bag but kind of haphazardly rolled it, as if it were an afterthought, a thing she probably would never wear on the trip. As she got into a taxi, her cell phone rang. Bridie. "Hi," she said. "I'm on my way to the airport."

"Good." Bridie sounded awful.

"What's wrong?" Clara panicked. If Nina died before she got there—

"What's *wrong*?" Bridie snapped.

"You sound like you're crying. Is Mom?"

"Mom is sleeping." Clara exhaled in relief. "But she heard Jo crying and thought it was you. You as a baby."

"Oh," Clara said softly. "Hang in."

"I can't do this without you."

"I'm on my way."

THEY ALL TOOK TURNS SITTING with Nina and when it wasn't Clara's shift she cooked. She made tomato soup and grilled cheese sandwiches on repeat. She made a beef bourguignon over three days and everyone who walked through the door said, "What is that amazing smell?" She baked cookies and brownies and an Alsatian tart and made lemon curd and chocolate pudding. She cooked with love, not fear or regret. She put forgiveness into every bowl, love on every plate.

One afternoon Clara and Bridie were looking through Nina's nightstand for a clean nightgown, something warm and sturdy. Nina's nightgowns were all lightweight, flimsy things. Were they sexy? Clara shook the thought away. As she was reaching toward the back of a drawer, hoping to feel flannel or cotton amongst all the silk, she felt a box. She pulled it out. She knew she shouldn't open it, but at this point who really cared?

"I hope it's not a photo of Garret," Bridie said.

"That would be something."

"Is it a vibrator?" Bridie said, voice lowered.

"Are you serious?"

Bridie shrugged. "I don't know. What else do people keep hidden in shoeboxes in their bedside table? I don't think it's her stamp collection."

"I guess I know where your vibrator is." Bridie rolled her eyes and Clara opened the lid. "Huh," she said.

Nina had fallen asleep, so they tiptoed out of the room and brought the box downstairs. Everything inside was from the infamous elopement. A stack of photos, matchbooks, postcards. A tiny piece of pink soap that faintly smelled like roses and looked like a scallop shell.

"Look at this one," Clara said, sliding a snapshot across the table. "I remember that dress."

"Me too," Bridie said looking at their forty-five-year-old mother standing in a hotel room with a balcony behind her. "She looks scared," Bridie said. Clara nodded. "I never thought of her as being scared during—all that." Clara and Bridie looked at the other photos. Nina in the shallow end of a pool with some brunette bombshell, both holding drinks and waving at the camera. Nina wading in the ocean. Nina sitting at an outdoor restaurant with a huge seafood cocktail in front of her, miming shock at the size of the platter. One on the steps of a government building with a small group of other people, mostly men, surrounding an unsmiling Nina wearing a black dress.

"Finn must have taken all the pictures," Clara said. "He's not in any of them."

"He's in the one by their bed," Bridie said.

"Right."

"I never asked her about this trip. Did you?"

"Never. I wonder why she hid all this."

Bridie snorted. "Really?"

"Everything's not my fault, you know."

"I didn't say it was. Did anybody, including me or Dune or Fern, ever ask about it?"

"I guess not."

Clara stood to put the teakettle on. Grabbed a couple of mugs off the shelf. "Should we prop the photos up in her room where she can see them?"

"That would be nice," Bridie said.

When Bridie walked into the kitchen later, Clara was taking a cake out of the oven. *Another one?* Bridie almost said but didn't. The counters were overflowing with food that Clara had made or was in the process of making or was planning to make. More food than any of them could ever consume.

"Look what else I found," Clara said, gesturing toward the counter and the faded copy of *The Joy of Sex*.

"Oh my god," Bridie said, flipping through the pages. "This is even stranger than I remember."

"And a lot hairier," Clara said.

Bridie laughed. "This book *terrified* me."

"Whatever happened to Bess Pfeiffer?" Clara said. "Is she still on Cambridge Road?"

"No. Not for years. She sends postcards to Mom from Taos. I think she runs meditation retreats or sound baths or both."

"Sounds right," Clara said.

"She was the only person who stuck by Mom after everything. The only person who was kind to her for so many months."

Clara nodded. "I always liked Bess. We should let her know what's happening."

"I'll look for her number," Bridie said.

"Is it my turn to go upstairs?"

"Fern is there now. Then you." Bridie looked around at the sink full of mixing bowls and the counters covered with cutting boards and rolling pins and little bowls of who knew what, spices, herbs, egg whites. The wooden spoons in the sink, the flurry of tongs in a ceramic holder. Most of these things had entered the house in the past few months. Every time Clara came home, she bought more supplies for Nina's kitchen. "How many tongs does a kitchen need?" Nina had asked on her last visit, the last time Nina had the strength to eat at the table downstairs.

"An ungodly amount. As many as possible," Clara said. She'd put three cobalt-blue ceramic bowls down on the table, one each for her, Bridie, and Nina. A soft cloud of polenta covered in sautéed mushrooms, crispy bits of pancetta, two perfectly soft-boiled eggs, and a sprinkling of minced parsley.

"Almost too pretty to eat," Nina said as they all picked up a spoon and took a moment to admire the meal before they dug in. They barely talked as they ate, occasionally smiling at each other, the occasional "This is so good."

Clara was heating up some chicken broth, dropping in spoonfuls of pastina because it was easier for Nina to eat than noodles. "Do you want to bring this up to her?" she asked Bridie.

"Sure."

"What's wrong?"

"Clara, you have to stop asking me what's wrong."

"Right, sorry. Why are you frowning at me? I'll clean everything up."

"I didn't realize I was frowning. I was remembering that our house looked like this after Mom left with Finn. Like a hurricane had come through but only touched the kitchen."

Clara shrugged. "I don't know what else to do. I cook."

NINA WAS ALERT FOR THE first time in days. Fern recognized this part; the surge, they called it. The surge could be hard for families because it looked as if the patient was improving, but they were just getting ready to die. "Can I get you anything, Nina?" Fern asked. "I think Clara has some soup ready."

"Fern," Nina said, sitting up taller. "Come here." Fern sat on the edge of the bed. "I owe you an apology," Nina said, and Fern didn't have to ask what she was talking about.

"You don't."

"I looked out the window," Nina kept talking, "and there you were." She turned to Fern, her voice weak but her eyes blazing. "I was so surprised I thought I was imagining you. I almost waved back. Did you know that? I was going to wave back to you and then I thought, *What are you doing?* Not just about the wave."

Fern smiled at her. "It doesn't matter anymore."

Nina put her palm on the side of Fern's face. "It does. I'm sorry you had to watch us leave."

BOTH BRIDIE AND CLARA HAD fallen asleep on the sofa that had been brought into Nina and Finn's bedroom over the past weeks. Finn was sitting in his usual chair, a small lamp throwing a little light on his book. Nina was restless and Fern was trying to make her comfortable. Bridie stood suddenly. "What's wrong?!" she said.

"Nothing," Fern said.

"It sounds like she can't breathe."

"She's okay; it's normal."

Clara sat up. "What's going on?"

"I think we're almost there," Fern said. Clara and Bridie stood and moved to one side of Nina's bed. On the opposite side, Finn took Nina's hand. "Keep talking to her," Fern said. "She can hear everything you're saying."

"What should we say?" Bridie whispered.

"Whatever you want. Anything. Sometimes it helps to let people know they can go. That you'll be fine."

"Do you think we're keeping her here? Sitting in the room like this?"

"No, I don't think that."

The sisters sat on one side of the bed, hands on their mother's leg, her arm. "We will miss you so much, Mom," Bridie said, trying to keep her voice steady. She was done crying; she wanted to meet this moment with grace. "We love you."

Clara leaned over, close to her mother's ear, and whispered, "We love you, Mom, and we're going to be fine." She said it over and over until Nina opened her eyes and looked at them with perfect attention. "Mom?" Bridie said, excited, grateful. "Mom," Clara said, inching closer to Nina. "Can you hear me? I want you to know something."

Nina needed her suitcase. The green one with the ivory trim, the one with the tiny stain in the corner she could never get out. She would need the suitcase, and she would need her lightest clothes. A few linen dresses. A swimsuit. She looked out the window and saw the snow swirling and worried their flight might be delayed, worried it might not be delayed.

"Mom," Clara said as Nina turned and looked her straight in the eyes, "it's okay for you to leave."

Nina felt the reassuring warmth of her hand in Finn's, so gentle and soft. She marveled at the kindness of it all. The almost liquid competency of Bridie covering her with an extra blanket, Clara's hand on her arm, nothing left unsaid in this room. They were all going to be okay.

And then she was in the front seat of the station wagon and Finn was brushing snow off his hair, smiling at her and reaching out his hand and she smiled back and thought, *I love you*, and he said, *Here we go*, and she thought, *Yes!* It was time to go. "Thank you," she said.

Thank you.

Acknowledgments

A heartfelt thank-you to "the team": Helen Atsma, Sonya Cheuse, Meghan Deans, Miriam Parker, and Rachel Sargent. Eternal thanks to the legion of people at Ecco/HarperCollins for supporting my work over the last decade with care, joy, and humbling enthusiasm. Thanks to Allison Saltzman for envisioning the perfect cover for the third time. To Henry Dunow for knowing exactly what I need to hear and when. To Joy Wiedner for generously speaking to me about her years in food styling. To Catherine Sheehy for critical research, Julie Schweitert Collazo for fact checking, and Janet Rosenberg for the keen copyedit. All errors are mine and some are intentional, like moving the Xerox "Futures Day" meeting up a month for my own convenience. To my dad, Roger, for filling in a lot of blanks about Xerox in the 1970s and 1980s and for his wise reflections about Rochester in general. To the excellent staff at the Central Library of Rochester for their research assistance and extreme patience every time I sent the microfiche spool spinning in the wrong direction.

I am especially grateful to my early readers—Jade Chang, Andrea Sarvady, Katherine Schulten, and Rufi Thorpe—for asking smart questions, helping me figure out thorny plot issues, and, in general, making this book stronger. To the glorious Ragdale Foundation for giving me a room straight out of a storybook, at a critical moment, allowing me to finish this book. And to my cohort of Ragdale seedgatherers for the excellent company during those weeks.

To my sons and husband for being excellent cheerleaders, enthusiastic supporters, deeply funny and interesting human beings, and the best company I could imagine.